Madam May: A Tale of Madams, Morphine, Moonshine, and Murder

Janet Hogan Chapman, Ed.D.

2nd Edition

Copyright © 2018 Janet Hogan Chapman

All rights reserved.

ISBN: 1724682830
ISBN-13: 978-1724682833

If you enjoy reading *Madam May, A Tale of Madams, Morphine, Moonshine, and Murder*, you will love knowing about her later journey in life through the following books, also by Janet Hogan Chapman.

AFTER MADAM MAY
What Came Next?
and
DOROTHY MAY
Can She Find a Forever Family?

DISCLAIMER

Although this novel is based on true events as told by various family members, gleaned from newspaper articles, and documented in public records, it has been fictionalized to bring the past to life and exhume secrets from the grave. Nearly all the characters were real people, but due to limited information and the passage of time, it is impossible to claim these portrayals are accurate representations. The order in which real events occurred has been modified to enhance the storyline.

Most names have been changed, but some are used as they were recorded in newspaper documents and public records. This historical fiction is not intended to slander, or otherwise cast disparagement on any characters or their descendants. To the contrary, my desire was to show the hardships, strengths, and determination of generations now long gone. Efforts were made to contact known descendants, some successful and some not. I have also tried to maintain historical integrity. Any errors are unintended and I accept full responsibility for such.

Janet Hogan Chapman, Ed.D.

DEDICATION

Dedicated to all the strong women who came before. May their secrets remain buried, or not.

CONTENTS

Acknowledgments	I
Chapters 1- 44	6 – 231
About the Author	232
Book Club Discussion Guide	233
Newspaper Articles	234

ACKNOWLEDGMENTS

There are many who played a part in helping me create Madam May. Family members, especially my sister Sandra Hogan Orr, shared memories that were invaluable in writing about our paternal grandmother. My Conyers writing group read, re-read, and critiqued the entire manuscript throughout the process. Thank you! Maryanne Blackwell and Nancy Haley proofread and copyedited. Gloria Hahn Tinsley also provided feedback. Invariably, errors may persist and I take full responsibility for any that may have been missed. I would also like to thank author Jocelyn Jackson for her encouraging remarks early in the writing process. The cover illustration is an actual newspaper illustration of my grandmother from The Atlanta Constitution of January 23, 1907, page five. Due to the date of publication, no copyright infringement is indicated. Finally, thank you Willie May Wheeler Collis Stamper Hogan Cobb, without whom I would not exist.

Janet Hogan Chapman, Ed.D

1
JANET
2010

    Willie May Wheeler Collis Stamper Hogan Cobb was strange. A woman who thought people on the television, especially Arthur Godfrey and Milton Berle, were talking directly to her. She just knew they were looking into her home and trying to spy on her too. She feared for her safety from real or imagined threats and kept a loaded pistol by her bed. She built a concrete block wall around her property for protection. She pinned money inside her housedress and never put money in a bank. She did not trust anyone except her only son, Jimmy, my daddy.

    My sister told a story about a time when, as a little girl, she spent the night at Granny's house.

    According to Sandra, who is eleven years older than me, it was hot, humid, and dark sitting on the front porch of Granny's house, as people in the south did in those days. The cicadas kept up a racket of buzzing that summer evening. She was the only child there, and the grownup talk turned to ghost stories. They didn't think twice as they retold the story of The Golden Leg.

> *There once was a wealthy man who lost his leg in a tragic accident. Since money was of no concern, he a leg fashioned of solid gold made to take its place. All the town admired the golden leg and knew it had cost a fortune. Alas, the man grew old and eventually died of old age. His will stipulated his golden leg be buried along with his body, so that no one would profit from it. And so it was done.*
>
> *Of course, being so well known, even grave robbers knew of the buried treasure. One industrious fellow wasted no time in digging up the grave and retrieving the golden leg. He sold the precious metal and was living high on the hog off the profit.*
>
> *A few months later, on a dark winter night, the robber settled down in his luxurious bed and went to sleep. He was awakened by a loud thump on the stairs of his mansion. He passed it off and tried to go back to sleep, but it came again. And this time, there was voice.*
>
> *"I'm on the first step, and I want my golden leg!"*
>
> *The robber thought he might be dreaming, and drifted back to sleep. Again, he was awakened by a louder thump.*
>
> *"I'm on the second step, and I want my golden leg!"*
>
> *Before the robber could get up to investigate, the voice came again, closer and louder.*
>
> *"I'm on the third step and I want my golden leg!"*
>
> *By now, the robber was getting scared. He cowered in his bed as the voice and thumps grew even louder and closer.*
>
> *"I'm on the fourth step and I want my golden leg!"*
> *"I'm on the fifth step and I want my golden leg!"*
> *"I'm on the sixth step and I want my golden leg!"*
>
> *By the time the voice had reached the ninth and last step, the robber was beside himself with fear.*
>
> *"I'm on the ninth step and I want my golden leg!"*
> *"I'm on the tenth step and I want my golden leg!"*

The robber could stand it no longer. He leapt from his bed and threw open his bedroom door to confront the ghost.

BOO! Gotcha!

Sandra yelped and nearly jumped out of her skin. The grown-ups laughed!

"Oh, poor little thing," Granny said. "Did that spooky old golden leg story scare you?" And then she laughed right along with all the others, making fun of her granddaughter's petrified expression.

Eventually, the evening wore on, the other adults left, and Granny and Sandra got ready for bed. It was just her and Granny in the house. Sandra had a little bed in the back room, the same room where Granny slept and spent most of her time sitting in her rocking chair staring out the picture window.

Of course, Sandra was too scared to sleep but lay still and pretended. Granny moved around the house before finally settling into her own bed. When she heard Granny's snores, she knew she was sound asleep. Sandra thought she would creep into the hall and turn on the bathroom light so it wouldn't be so dark.

She made her way across the room and slipped into the hallway. The bathroom door was slightly open. There was a window in the bathroom and light was streaming in from a street lamp. Just as she reached for the light switch, she saw it. There it was! The golden leg lay right across the toilet seat! Poor little Sandra screamed in terror and ran back to the bedroom.

She ran smack dab into Granny, whose long black hair, normally worn in a bun at the back of her head, was straggling down around her face. Granny wore a flowing white nightgown and was cackling in a sinister way, just like an evil spirit.

"I got you! I got you good, little girl! Did that golden leg scare you?" She laughed and laughed as Sandra burst into tears.

"Oh, go on, you little crybaby. It weren't nothing but

an old wrapped up log. I was just trying to scare you a little bit. You hush crying and get on to bed now. I'll leave the hall light on for you."

Sandra ran to her bed and hid under the covers, even though it was stifling hot. She sobbed and sobbed, wanting to go home. Granny shuffled around, still chuckling and mumbling under her breath. Somehow, Sandra survived the night, and it was the last time she ever spent the night at Granny's.

As for me, I only have a few memories of Granny. I remember her coming to our house in West End one day in her two-toned black and white 1956 Ford sedan. I always thought it looked like a police car. And, as you'll find out later, that very well could be why she got that color combination. That day, she had several galvanized steel buckets on the floorboard.

"Jimmy! Come on out here." Granny hollered from our swept-dirt front yard. "I need you to help me fill up these buckets."

Of course, being about six years old, I was on the front porch lickety-split. My Daddy, Jimmy, came out right behind me. It was unusual for Granny to show up at our house. In fact, it was unusual for Granny to leave her own house.

"Mama? What do you need water for? You got water at your house."

"Yep, but my water ain't no good. Somebody's trying to poison me. I ain't drinking no water from my pipes."

Daddy knew there was no sense trying to reason with Granny. He mumbled "crazy old woman" under his breath as she filled the buckets with water from the hose. He carried the heavy buckets of water to the car and sat 'em in the floorboard. There was no worry they'd spill since Granny didn't drive any more than about ten miles an hour. This is my earliest memory of strange Granny May.

Years later, as a grown-up, I learned from various family members that Granny was more than just a little strange. Before her last husband, EJ Cobb died, she had relegated him to the sleeping porch. He was barely allowed in the main part of the house. They would get in knock-down-drag-out fights. Usually, it was either his drinking or her paranoid imagination that got things started. One of those times, she really meant business and stabbed him in the arm with a butcher knife. She wouldn't let him go to the doctor, but stitched and bandaged him up and doctored him herself.

When Mr. Cobb died, supposedly of a brain tumor, he was "laid out" in the front room of the house. No funeral parlor. I remember mama saying they had cut open the back of his head, taken out his brains, and stuffed it with cotton. She said you could see little wisps of cotton on the sides of his head. That scared me too and it was years before I would ever go in that front room of Granny's house. Imagine telling a child such a thing! I guess it was just different in those days.

Most of my memories of Granny are from much later, after we moved from West End to a new house built on the lot right next door to her. She'd given Mama and Daddy the lot and money to build a house. I never spent much time there, except to go over and play her player piano, which I dearly loved. She was pretty much of a recluse. I can still see her sitting there in her rocking chair, her hair shoe-polished black and pulled back into that bun, staring out that picture window on the side of her house that faced our back door.

She watched our comings and goings. Occasionally she'd knock on the window and shake her fist at me if she saw me climbing on the wall she'd had built around her property. She would call Daddy to fix things or ask him to bring her some cigarettes, soup, crackers, or coffee from the store. Then one Christmas Eve, while we were all away at my Aunt's house, it happened. None of us were home when she fell. Going into our house in the freezing cold, late that night, we saw there were no lights on at Granny's. Waiting for Daddy to get our back door open, we heard the faint voice calling,

"Help! Jimmy? Help!"

We were hustled inside and Daddy ran next door. He found her lying on the floor, having knocked over her slop bucket and fallen. She didn't live much longer after that. Weeks in the hospital, a futile attempt to live at home with a nurse's aide, then a few days in a nursing home, and she was gone. As far as I and my siblings knew at that time, Willie May Wheeler Hogan Cobb died on August 14th, 1963 at the age of 84, and took her secrets to the grave.

Yes, it took about fifty years for those secrets to work their way out of the ground, but work their way they did. When I began researching my genealogy, the skeletons in the closet began to rattle and demanded to be let out. All I knew about Granny was her maiden name, Wheeler, and that she was from Newton County, Georgia. I searched and searched for a marriage record of Willie May Wheeler and Jesse Hogan, my grandfather, to no avail.

Eventual advances in online genealogy research led me to a tiny blurb of a newspaper article from The Atlanta Constitution, March 23, 1906, that stated:

> John Collis first married Miss Willie Wheeler of Newton County, and about two years ago he was divorced. Last fall he married Miss Ludie Anderson and went to keeping house at 69 Tennelle Street. The first wife was living in the country but recently moved to Atlanta and has been living at 18 Bush Street.

Aha! This led me to search for a Wheeler-Collis marriage in Newton County and voila, there it was. Willie May Wheeler married John Collis in Newton County Georgia on September 10, 1898. This opened a whole new line of research that led to shadowy and shocking revelations about the Granny I thought I knew. That first bit of information turned out to be the tip of an iceberg. Did my Daddy or Mother know these tales but never tell? What did Mama mean when she told my sister "I could tell you stories that would make your hair stand on end?"

That remains a mystery, as both my Mama and Daddy have been gone now for many years. So many unsolved mysteries! Two husbands prior to my own grandfather. Morphine addiction. Arrest records. Death from alcohol poisoning. A half-sister I never knew. An adopted aunt, Dorothy, parentage unknown, who came to live with Granny under mysterious circumstances. FBI agents. Who would have thought that over a hundred years later, Willie May's secrets would be recovered from the grave? Could her past explain how she became a reclusive, paranoid, mean old lady? As I came to find out, it very well could have. Granny was indeed a strange woman, and not just in her old age. I would come to find out she had always been that way. Strange, but strong.

2
MAY
1898

My bare feet made little dust cloud puffs on the red clay path. Life in the little community of Stansells, Georgia was nothing but heat, dirt, and work in the summer; cold, soot, and confinement in the winter. I did not intend to spend the rest of my life in this hell-hole like my mama had done. I'd do whatever it took to get away. My eye caught the wagon as it made its way slowly up the washboard road. Those weeds could just keep a-growin'. I eyed a fellow I didn't recognize climbing down from the wagon bed.

Close enough now to get a better look, I gave the unknown man the once-over. He was introduced as John Collis and had hitched a ride down from Burnt Mountain with Uncle Wash and his family, who were comin' to visit a spell. This Mr. Collis appeared to be in his mid-twenties, a strapping young fella, easy on the eyes. Collis made himself welcome by bringing in the belongings and such. I was standing off to the side, trying to size him up when Daddy said, "Willie May! Girl! Make yourself useful and help Mr. Collis with those bags."

I sauntered over to the wagon. Mr. Collis flashed a wide smile and winked as he handed over one of the lighter bags. I took my time toting it inside, and by the time I started back out, he had everything else unloaded. Mama said dinner would be on in a couple of hours, so Daddy, Uncle Wash, and Mr. Collis went out back. Daddy kept a jug hidden under the porch in a hole in the ground where the scant coolness made the white lightning a bit more palatable.

Mama put me and my sister, Dora, to work at the stove, then got Uncle Wash's wife settled. Aunt Mannie looked about to bust waitin' on another baby to come. Her and Uncle Wash's passel of young'uns had already scattered outside. Mama and Dora prattled on about poor Aunt Mannie's fragile condition, and didn't Uncle Wash know he was slowly killin' her having her birth one baby after another? I mostly just listened, swearing to myself I would never let any man put me in that position. I intended to be independent and have money. I just didn't know yet exactly how I was going to get there.

Our conversation turned to the stranger, Mr. Collis. Mama wondered how Mr. Collis happened to have taken up with Uncle Wash. It wasn't so unusual for young men to get into trouble and leave home. Maybe the Collis fella was running from the law or a pregnant girl's daddy. Who could tell? My mind began to churn out all kinds of reasons he could be on the run. As I was pondering, an observation began to dawn on me. If men could just up and run away, why couldn't I? If Collis had run away, maybe he could give me some advice. He seemed friendly enough. After all, he had smiled and winked at me earlier. I wasn't above taking advantage of a man in a tight spot if it got me out of Stansells, Georgia.

It seemed like only a few minutes had passed, but dinner was about ready. The men came inside and we served them up plates from the hot cooking pots. I made it a point to cater to Mr. Collis, serving him the choice portions of the ham hock, beans, and cornbread, along with what I considered shy but suggestive smiles.

The men ate and talked, lamenting about this and that. Hot weather, no rain, little food, even less cash. Mr. Collis kept quiet for a bit then cleared his throat. "If you want to get ahead, you got to get to the city. That's where the money is these days. I've got myself a business arrangement, and when I get to Atlanta I'm goin' to be high on the hog." Daddy and Uncle Wash guffawed at this announcement, but I was all ears.

"I'd rather just stay here and eat that hog," Daddy said as he forked the boiled fat rind out of the beans and into his mouth. "No city life for me."

Uncle Wash laughed and said, "Well, that's fine long as you've got a hog to eat, but maybe young John here is on to something."

Mr. Collis' statement ignited a fire in my soul. *Holy Sweet Jesus! Has God sent this man to deliver me from this hell-hole?* I paid careful attention as the men went on talking and I served up the food. I wanted to show Mr. Collis I was interested and went so far as to inconspicuously brush my small breast against his shoulder. I made what should have seemed to be an innocent movement, but Mr. Collis turned a knowing eye on me. I returned his look and moved back to the stove. I might not be married yet, but I had already been around with the country boys. My brother Ollie's friend, Eb, had been the first. Lester, Merk, Ruben, and Jules followed in quick succession. After that, I lost count. I knew the ways to get a man to do whatever you wanted. Could Mr. Collis be my ticket out of this life I despised? Could I work my magic on him?

I had to work in the field that afternoon. Supper was cold cornbread and buttermilk, kept cool in the spring. The men stayed to themselves as the women did the chores and looked after the young'uns. I took advantage of their being preoccupied to sneak a swallow of Mama's Resteasy Tonic. She bought it from the peddler who came around every so often. I had discovered the syrupy patent medicine tonic did indeed help one to "rest easy."

Darkness fell and a faint coolness took over the fields and woods, then the ramshackle house. The men had retired to the back porch again. I was exhausted from the day and filthy dirty, but I had also figured a way to approach Mr. Collis with my appeal for help. I made it a point to stand near the open window so as to be sure the men heard me tell mama, "I declare I feel right pekid. So hot and dirty! I'm goin' down to the spring, get out of these clothes and cool off; maybe I'll feel better." Mama and Dora paid me no mind and just uh-hummed me. I gathered a clean nightdress and rags. I carried them over my arms and went out the back door so anyone could plainly see that I was intending to take a bath. Passing the men on the porch, I pretended to pay them no mind.

"Hot evening, ain't it Miss Willie May?" John's voice came out of the dimness. "Your daddy and uncle here were just talking about how hot and dry it is for early July."

Daddy said, "Sure 'nuff hot. But we'll be wishin' for this heat come February."

"Well, by February it'll make no matter to me," said John. "I'll be livin' in comfort in Atlanta. You mark my words."

Uncle Wash added his two cents' worth, "Well, that don't make it any cooler now. Miss Willie May, you go on and get yerself cooled down. We don't need another gal fallin' out like Mannie. Course, she's got more cause than you to feel poorly." He chuckled to himself but was greeted with stony silence by the other men.

"I'll be better directly," I mumbled as I headed down the path. It was just a short trail from the clearing around the house to the little stand of trees and brush where the cool water flowed from a spring, birthing a creek that ran for miles. Just as I hoped, it wasn't long before there were masculine footsteps behind me. The steps stopped as I reached the spring, their owner just out of sight. I pretended not to hear a thing and acted like I was totally alone. Slowly removing my top clothing, I stretched my small but strong wiry frame. Wetting the rags in the cool water and moving them over my body felt like heaven after the stifling heat of the day. I began with my face, working downward. I decided to turn up the intensity a notch, so Mr. Collis would have no doubts about my intentions. Removing my skirt and underwear too, I deliberately turned so that anyone on the path would have a clear view. I preened and stretched a bit before turning and finishing up the bath. Last, of all, I loosened my hair and let it fall. *If there's one thing I can be proud of, it's my hair. But it sure is hot!* Bending and exposing my full backside, I wet and stroked the long black coils, finally straightening up and wrapping them in a clean rag. I used more rags to dry off and pulled on the clean nightshirt. *If that didn't get his attention, then it can't be got.*

Gathering up the damp and soiled things, I heard the crack of a twig breaking nearby. I stood absolutely still for a moment, but not another sound was heard. As soon as I began to mosey back up the path towards the house, a hand fell softly on my shoulder. I turned, and the features of Mr. Collis materialized like an apparition.

"Well, Miss Willie May, that was quite a show," Mr. Collis said softly.

"I can do as well as I can show, Mr. Collis," I suggested in a hushed voice.

"I'll just bet you can, Miss Willie May, I'll just bet you can." He stared into my eyes and I just as boldly stared back.

"And anyway, I'd rather be called May, not Willie May or Miss."

"Then May it shall be," he whispered.

"Did you like what you saw?" I whispered back.

"Oh, yes indeed, May, yes indeed."

"Well, in that case, I have a proposal, Mr. Collis," getting so close our bodies were all but touching.

"I thought it was the men who was 'sposed to do the proposin' in these parts," he said.

I smiled. "That's not the kind of proposal I mean, Mr. Collis."

"Well then, May, let's hear it," he said as he leaned in and kissed me right on the lips.

I returned the kiss and turned aside to whisper in his ear. I explained what I needed and let him know I'd do whatever it took to make it happen, no matter the consequences. And so it was that just a few weeks later, on September 10th, 1898, I was married to Mr. John Collis by the Justice of the Peace of Newton County, Georgia.

3
MAY

I remember well my first day in Atlanta…

The engine hissed and belched as it pulled into the depot around 10:15 in the morning. The depot was the largest building I had ever laid eyes on. Even though this long building was only three stories high it was the tallest building I had ever seen. There was certainly nothing like it back in Stansells, or Covington, or even all of Newton County!

"Wait here just a few minutes," John said after we climbed down from the train to the platform. "I need to go in and check on our living arrangements."

I had been so intent on getting to the city I hadn't given any thought to the details. Where would we live? As I waited, the train moved on and revealed another astounding sight. Right in front of me, there stood the not quite ten-year-old State Capitol Building. Sitting on the right side of the train, and with my view obscured by the train itself, this was my first image of the city. I realized I must truly look the country bumpkin with my mouth hanging open, eyes widening at the sight. The huge white building with the rounded dome gleamed white in the morning light. I had heard about the capitol building, but could never have imagined such a sight. It was like I pictured temples in heaven, lacking the streets of gold.

Although there was gossip that said some high-falutin' government men wanted to gild the capitol's dome with gold from the North Georgia mountains. Despite my distaste for that little Baptist Church back in Stansells, it was nearly my only exposure to realms beyond rural Georgia. The Bible stories and pictures showed temples, cities, and golden idols. Between church and the publications at the general mercantile store, that was all I knew of life in cities. The shiny vision of the capitol building now surpassed the depot as the largest I'd ever seen. This was a pattern that repeated itself nearly every few steps I took that day in the city.

Now that I had a wider view, my eyes roved over the surrounding area. There were banks, hotels, saloons, grain wholesalers, law offices, and a whiskey distillery. Commercial buildings extended as far as I could see and distant factory smokestacks loomed up like burned trees, smoke still emerging from the charred trunks. People were everywhere. Jarring me out of my fascination, John shook my elbow.

"I've found us just the place," he said, steering me toward the end of the platform. At the end of the building, we crossed over the tracks and approached the infamous Peachtree Street. Even out in the country, we had heard of Peachtree Street, the supposed heart of Atlanta. I had assumed that meant beautiful homes and shops and a wide tree-lined thoroughfare. Instead, I saw dirt, dust, construction, and horse and mule droppings. The foul smell nearly made me retch. Even though I was used to animal smells in the country, the air here somehow seemed heavy and putrid. It assaulted my nostrils as the cacophony of sound invaded my ears. Electric streetcar tracks crisscrossed the muddy streets like giant fingernails had been pulled across the wet clay.

I moved my eyes from the street, raising them upwards. In front of me looked like something out of a fantasy: the seven floors and fanciful exterior of the Kimball House Hotel. In front of the grand entrance, exquisitely dressed women were being handed down from fancy carriages by liveried footmen. Fine-suited gentlemen strolled with equally beautifully attired ladies. I vowed to myself right there and then that one day I would be dressed just as fine as these visions of success. The gorgeous colors of the flowing dress trains and feathered hats reminded me of one of those pictures I'd seen at the Baptist Church of God's creation of the fowl of the air. The women, in their tight fitted bodices and trailing skirts, moved with grace as if they could take flight at any moment.

We turned north on Peachtree Street and I made note of the directions so later I could explore on my own. I had roamed woods and fields in the country and had a good sense of direction, but the city was different. Just ahead, two newer and even taller buildings came into view. John was prattling.

"That's the Equitable and Flatiron buildings. Folks here call 'em skyscrapers."

I could understand why. Once again, my reference point for the tallest building I'd ever seen changed. We walked on to Gilmer Street, heading east. I made note of the grocery, dry goods, and pharmacy shops, craving some of Mama's Resteasy Tonic to calm my nerves.

The skyscrapers gave way to a few low-rise buildings, then to houses neatly laid out in blocks. In the distance, along the eastern tracks we'd come in on, belching smokestacks stained the morning with blackening soot. The homes started out as grand two-stories made of brick with porches and fancy woodwork, the gleaming windows framed on the inside by lace curtains. I imagined myself in one of those upstairs rooms, gazing out at passers-by through the filigree, and waving hello with my little finger crooked delicately in the air.

I kept waiting for John to stop and say, "This is it! Our first home!" Instead, he plodded determinedly down the street, never so much as pausing. I did not want to appear too anxious, but I did venture to comment, "Why, what pretty houses! There sure ain't anything like this back in Stansells." The brick houses gave way to slightly less grand white clapboard homes, but they were still beautiful to my eyes.

"Isn't. There isn't anything like this back in Stansells," John corrected and kept walking. It took me a moment to understand his comment, and then I realized he was referring to my speech. At first, I was insulted, but then understood I had to start sounding like the lady I intended to become. I would make a careful note from now on of how others talked and follow their lead.

The houses became smaller, less well kept, and eventually downright dingy. Near the end of Gilmer stood the dingiest of the lot. My impressions had swung on an arc from amazement to disappointment, to disgust, but at least it wasn't Stansells, and surely our new abode would be only temporary.

The street dead-ended into a factory with smokestacks that coated everything in blackened grime. John stopped in front of a little house, the last one on the street before the factory. I hung back, looking around dismally as he walked up to the stoop and rapped briskly on the door frame. A small but stout woman, clad in faded black, with gray hair and a haggard look, opened the door.

"We've come about the room?" John intoned hopefully. A simple, silent nod was the woman's only reply.

"Is it still available?" Another silent nod.

"Could we have a look?" Yet another nod and the woman opened the door wider and stepped aside. I came up the short path to join John and we went inside. The woman closed the door and motioned us to follow as she walked toward the back of the house. I took my cue from John and followed silently. It didn't look like I would get any help with speech from this taciturn crone.

I tried to look around without appearing too rude, noting the spare front room. I was intrigued by the soft glow of an electric lamp casting shadows on the plain walls. How lovely! Nobody in Newton County had electricity yet. We followed through a dining room, sparse but clean, nothing fancy, but still more refined than the homemade furniture back in the country. Next was a small kitchen that included a wood stove and a white enameled storage cupboard. It suddenly dawned on me. It was an icebox! What my poor old mama wouldn't give for such an appliance.

The woman turned right into a small space with three doors. There was a slight difference in the floor level as it slanted downward. I was accustomed to this; Mama and Daddy's house, like most out in the country, rested on short stacks of rocks and the floors sagged and slanted all over in haphazard directions. I figured this part of the house had been added as an afterthought. The woman opened one of the three doors, revealing something I'd never seen: Lo and behold! An indoor bathroom! *Surely I have died and gone to heaven!* Although small and plain, just to be indoors was a luxury I had not imagined. *No more cold baths at the spring for me.* There was a toilet and deep claw-foot tub. There were gas lamps on either side of a mirror over a pedestal sink. A little gas heater, cold in the summer heat, was off in a corner. I only had one worry – could I learn to work these contraptions?

A second door revealed a plain but exceptionally clean bedroom. This was to be my first home in the city. An iron bed with a quilt cover, a wardrobe with a mirrored front, a side table, another electric lamp, a comfortable looking armchair and a faded rug furnished the bedroom. I tried to play the role of the modest bride and avoided looking at the bed, but I did run my hands over the back of the armchair. I may as well have been in a fancy hotel. I had never seen such an inviting, cozy room.

"Oh! How charming! Is this the room that's available?" I spoke for the first time, smiling demurely at the woman, who remained silent. John exchanged glances with the woman, then turned to me. I lifted my eyebrows and gave a nearly imperceptible nod. Finally, John spoke.

"I understand room and board is $6 a week?" Another silent nod.

"We'll take it," he said.

"Well, now, that doesn't set the deal. I'll have to decide if I'll take you." The woman finally broke her silence, speaking in a gravelly voice. Gruff but assertive. *Sounds like a woman who knows her mind. Maybe we do have something in common.*

She continued. "The rules are no smoking, drinking, or morphine. No music, carousing, or late hours. Breakfast at eight, lunch at noon, tea at four, and supper at six-thirty. If you're late, your plate will be removed. Leave the bathroom clean, do your own laundry, and do not entertain guests. Any infractions will result in immediate removal."

Her steady stare was her question of our acceptance. Again, John and I exchanged glances and gave the woman two silent affirmative nods.

"Fine," she replied. "Too late for lunch today, but you can have tea and supper."

John turned on his charm. He seemed determined to win

this woman over. "Thank you kindly, that will be perfectly acceptable. Please let us know if we may be of any assistance to you in any way."

The woman gave us a hard look and said, "Just follow the rules." She walked out of the room, leaving us, leastways me, perplexed. She turned and went through the catty-wonkered vestibule. I watched her open the one remaining closed door, enter whatever was beyond, and firmly close it behind her.

Finally, alone, I glared at John. Although this was the fanciest house I'd ever been in, I had anticipated something much grander. I was pleased but did not want John to think this was going to keep me satisfied. He read the thunderclouds on my face.

"Oh little May," he spoke carefully, taking me in his arms. "It's only for a few days. We'll be moving up the street before you know it."

I purposefully did not soften to his embrace. I was getting madder by the minute. I did not like being patronized or referred to as "little May."

"You better make sure of that," I declared, and turned away to unpack our few belongings.

"I absolutely will," John said to my back, "and to that, I must be out and about making sure it does. I will see you again at supper." With that, he turned and walked briskly back through the house and out the front door. Dumbfounded that he would leave me alone so soon, I hurried to watch through the front window. He did not turn back toward town but instead turned right toward the factory.

4
MAY

I was curious why John went towards the factory instead of towards town, but first things first. I had to find some tonic; my nerves were jangling like a sack of nails. No sounds came from the other room, so I figured the old woman did not want to be disturbed. I took my time to look around the parlor, dining room, and kitchen. I poked into cupboards and opened drawers, only to find no bottles of Resteasy tonic or any other remedies hid away. There was nothing to fancy up the rooms or give any hint about the taciturn woman. I didn't even know her name! What kind of a person lets strangers into her home and doesn't even introduce herself? I might be from the country, but I did have a few manners. Mama had made sure me and my sisters knew how we should act, even if we didn't always do it.

Back in the boarding room, I unpacked our things. There were so few it only took about two minutes. I was beginning to feel a bit hungry and John had made it clear he wouldn't be back until supper. I had about five dollars I had scrounged up over the past few weeks hidden away in my underclothes, unbeknownst to John. I figured he didn't need to know everything. I peeled away one of the dollar bills and placed it in my home-made reticule that had been a wedding gift from Dora, who had patched it together from some scraps. I would take a stroll, find a little something to eat and try to procure some tonic too.

I felt quite the lady as I made use of the indoor bathroom. Pulling the chain on the elevated water tank, the noise of the flush of water startled me and I jumped back. S*o this is how the city folk do it!* I pulled the chain again just to watch the water drain down and rush back in. I giggled to myself as the water swished and gurgled. *Why, if this isn't almost fun!* Looking in the mirror, I adjusted my clothing, hair, and hat. *Not exactly the fancy outfits of the Peachtree Street ladies, it would have to do for now.* I pinched my cheeks and headed out the front door.

I was torn between going the same direction as John, just to see what he might be up to, or toward the more enticing draw of the big buildings, shops, and Kimball House. My curiosity about the city and my need for tonic won out, so I took a side street that put me through to another main street where a dirty wood board sign read Decatur Street. I'd noticed the little town of Decatur when the train stopped there earlier in the morning. Walking towards town I passed a barber, a dry goods store, a pharmacy, a business office the ilk of which I could not determine, and finally a small market. I entered the market and browsed. There was no Resteasy tonic to be found.

My hunger was getting the better of me though, so I purchased a small loaf of bread and an apple, and had the grocer cut a portion of the black rinded cheese. I noticed him giving me his full attention, looking me up and down as if he were appraising a side of beef. I wondered if he eyed all his women customers this way. *Was he curious? Was he wondering about my obviously home-made utilitarian clothing?* His penetrating stare seemed more than curious, it felt down-right suspicious. "Anything else I can help you with, ma'am?"

"No, thank you, this will be all. But oh, by the way, would you happen to know of a reasonable dressmaker in this area?"

Ignoring my question, the grocer answered with a question. "New in town?"

"Why yes, my husband, Mr. John Collis, and I have just taken a room at the end of Gilmer Street, near the factory."

The grocer paused and edged slightly backward. "Oh! I didn't know Mrs. Cox was letting out that room."

Taking note of the landlady's name, I replied, "Oh really? And why should it be so surprising?" *And how did he know it was Mrs. Cox's house anyway?*

"Well, since you're new in town and all, you wouldn't know. The last fellow that boarded there had some trouble with the law and spent a few days in the tower. When he got out, he went back but was found dead in the bed the next morning. Natural causes was the official word."

"And was there an unofficial word?" I asked, forthright with my question. *Let him think I am too bold for a lady if he wants, it would only serve my purposes better. He certainly didn't hold back in questioning me. I didn't care what he thought. If he did think there was more to me than met the eye, so be it. I had the same thought about him.*

"Considering he wasn't the first fellow to be found dead there, one could speculate. But then again, Mrs. Cox can be a mysterious old bat. She's never been the same since the loss of her husband and baby years ago. Some say the morphine has taken ahold of her mind, and who knows what goes on in that house."

"I see. Well, thank you kindly, Mr...."

"Baker," interjected the grocer, "Robert A. Baker, or Bob to my friends."

"I can assure you, Mr. Baker, there is nothing going on in that house, untoward or otherwise, but now that my husband and I are there that could change. Thank you and good day, sir." I gave Mr. Baker a bright smile. Before I turned to leave, I glimpsed his astonished expression.

As I left the store I was deep in thought. *So Mrs. Cox was known to have a past, possibly some shady business, and what could have happened to the previous boarder? For that matter, what happened to her husband and child? Did this have something to do with why the woman was so close-mouthed and secretive?* I was becoming more and more curious about this Mrs. Cox. The more I learned about her, the more convinced I became that I would have to work hard at being friendly. She just might be a key figure or maybe even a future partner in my plans. I was so deep in thought it did not even dawn on me that the question about a dressmaker was never answered.

Next stop, the pharmacy. *Surely they will have something comparable to Mama's Resteasy tonic.* Even if they didn't have tonic, I had seen an advertisement for Coca-Cola in their window and was anxious to try the concoction. Word of it had reached Stansells, but not the product itself, although one could get it in Covington. Anything rumored to refresh and revive was something I had to try. There was just enough change from the bill I had paid Mr. Baker for the food to get a Coca-Cola.

The pharmacist looked at me inquisitively as he pulled a dark bottle out of a metal chest filled with ice. He turned to the back wall and slipped the bottle under the lip of a device mounted there. I heard a distinct "pop" and a sizzling noise. The man turned back to me and placed the bottle on the counter. I would not have to wait to see what the cola inside the bottle looked like, it was spilling out over the top! My eyes must have given away my amazement.

"First Coca-Cola?" the man asked.

Not wanting to appear a hayseed, I replied, "Oh no, I just never cease to be amazed by it."

I lifted the bottle to my lips and took a big swig, just as I'd seen daddy do, and as I had done myself on occasion when no one was looking, with the jug on the back porch. I was quickly overtaken with a fit of some combination of sneezing, coughing, and snorting. My mouth and nose were tingling just like I'd taken a nip of Daddy's jug. After recovering from the first swallow, coughing, and spluttering, I took another, better prepared to handle the effect this time. I wasn't sure if it was the ice cold or the cola that was so refreshing, but I had to admit I was won over.

I realized the pharmacist had an amused expression. He must have concluded it really was my first Coca-Cola after all. I decided to play along and make light of my reaction.

"Does the same thing to me every time." I winked and smiled. He responded with a doubtful look.

Now that I had regained my composure, I was ready to get back to my quest for the tonic.

"Sir, would you happen to carry Resteasy Tonic? My dear Mama back in Stansells is about out and the peddler doesn't come around as often as he used to. She really depends on that tonic to get through bad times!"

"Well ma'am, I don't have any at present but should be getting something comparable next week. You could try the pharmacy in the Kimball House if you need it today, er, that is if your mama needs it right away. Might be a bit pricey though."

To pry out a little more information about my surroundings I revived the same ruse I'd employed with Mr. Baker.

"Thank you, Mr...."

"Willis. James Willis, ma'am."

"Mr. Willis then. Would Mrs. Willis perhaps have apprised you of a reasonable but quality dressmaker?"

"Oh, there's no Mrs. Willis," he sheepishly replied. "But there is a Miss Willis, my sister. As a matter of fact, she's employed by a dressmaker at a shop in the Kimball." He glanced down at my homespun dress and continued. "If the shop prices are too high for you, she might be willing to take some work on the side for less. Just ask for Hattie, and tell the proprietress that James Willis sent you." Then, he quickly slipped in the question, "New in town, are you?"

Well, folks around here are certainly observant. And nosy. I had hoped for a bit of anonymity in the city.

"Yes, my husband and I, just recently married, have taken a room with Mrs. Cox on Gilmer Street," I replied while lowering my eyes demurely. Again, I was met with a surprised look.

"Hmmm, that's interesting," replied Mr. Willis.

"Indeed? How so?" I retorted. I could not remain demure if I wanted to get more information.

"Oh, nothing, nothing. I actually conduct quite a bit of trade with Mrs. Cox. I'm just surprised she hasn't mentioned new boarders."

"Well, we only arrived this morning."

"Then that explains it." He clucked, wished me a good day, and turned aside, clearly dismissing me.

Somewhat miffed, I returned a clipped "Good day yourself, Mr. Willis," then added, "I hope to conduct quite a bit of trade with you, too." I turned and walked briskly out the door.

I could see the tops of the tall buildings and headed in that direction to find the Kimball House. I wasn't having too hard of a time finding my way about so far. I just kept heading towards the so-called skyscrapers, holding onto to my small bundle of food and my bottle of Coca-Cola.

Crossing the street first, I came alongside the depot where we had arrived that morning. Benches lined the platform. I noticed some folks pulling bits of this and that out of paper wrappings and eating right out in the open. *Well, I suppose' that's acceptable then*, I thought and sat myself down to do the same. It was a good spot for watching all the comings and goings. There were ladies and gentlemen, as well as more common men and women bustling about. There were even a few Negroes, but they kept their distance from the white folks. I sat and picked at the bread and cheese. Never did have much of an appetite, leastways for food anyway. The pleasantly sweet fizziness of the cola, still near freezing-cold from the metal ice chest, cooled my throat as it tingled its way down to my stomach. No doubt, the small amount of "coke" known to be one of the secret ingredients would give me a little boost too.

Ruminating on what I'd learned so far about Mrs. Cox, I casually cast my eye on the fashions as people walked by. Not long now and I would be dressed like the ladies about town. Then, several yards down the platform, I caught sight of a familiar waistcoat, and there was my husband! He stood talking with a group of men: one who looked to be rather common, another who was obviously quite the gentleman, another who was dark and swarthy, and one a Negro who wasn't adding much to the conversation, but whose stance definitely included him in the group. John's back was towards me, so I did not fear being discovered, but I was keen to know what was being discussed. The men's faces looked intense, but their voices were low. It appeared through his gestures the gentleman was conveying some type of orders, and the others were nodding in agreement or understanding. Abruptly, the group broke up and the men went in different directions. John never turned, keeping his back to me, and started walking toward town. The gentleman entered the depot, and the other men walked in my direction. I was not surprised that having concluded their group discussion, the Negro walked several paces behind the other two. I supposed some things weren't so different in the city.

I hurriedly packed up my victuals and entered the station,

hoping to catch sight of the gentleman, but there was no sign of him. Who were these men? How did John know them? Were they some of his business associates? They seemed an unlikely combination of fellas. When I returned to the platform, the two men and the Negro were nowhere in sight, and I could barely make out the back of John's waistcoat as he crossed the street.

    I followed John at a discreet distance. First, he went into the post office. When he came out he was refolding a letter and placed it in his pocket. Who would be sending him a letter? Who even knew he was in the city? Was it business or personal? I would have to contrive a way to get a look at that letter. John moved on. He was not casually sauntering along as if out for a stroll. He walked briskly and determinedly, as a man of purpose. He stopped and bought a bouquet of flowers. *Oh, my!* I had never received bought flowers, or any other kind of flowers, from a man. John turned into Willis's Drugs but reappeared in just a minute. I thought he'd be heading back to the house but I was mistaken. He continued his hurried walk toward the taller buildings and was soon approaching the entrance of the grand Kimball House. Not hesitating at all, he strode right on inside as if a current guest, accustomed to the grandeur. I was not about to lose him now. I paused momentarily, then entered the opulent building on my own.

    It was hard not to be awestruck. I had never seen such a beautiful place. I'd heard the original Kimball House was destroyed by a fire but was rebuilt. The chandeliers hanging throughout the massive lobby had been outfitted with electricity, as well as the original gaslights that ringed the walls. Such brilliance inside a building – like the sun shining inside! Plush rugs underfoot hushed the footsteps of throngs of people. Elegant wallpapers covered the walls and the woodwork shone with a high polish. Taking it all in, I realized I must look a sight. Definitely not attired as someone who was a guest or had business at the Kimball. Just in time, I saw John enter an elevator.

    This was problematic and it piqued my interest. I didn't entirely trust such a contraption, although I'd heard of such lifts but had never seen one in operation. I had to admit it was more appealing than walking several flights of stairs. Even more concerning though, was John. Why was he here? Why was he entering the lift? I figured the upper floors were guest rooms, and he was no guest.

    Perhaps John was meeting more business partners. If the gentleman at the depot was any indicator, he was dealing with some rather well-off folks. It would not be surprising if they were lodging here at the Kimball. I decided to keep my eye out for John's return from upstairs while I looked for the dress shop where Mr. Willis told me his sister worked. I turned from the lifts and began to stroll the lobby.

5
JOHN

I knew May was none too pleased with our accommodations at Maude's, but if things worked out we wouldn't be there long. She could cool her heels a bit and be patient. I had mainly agreed to her plan just so I could have some female companionship while I was in the city. And I'd be out of town a great deal anyway. Leaving the house I turned right towards the factory. I had some weighty business to attend to.

What I'd left behind back up near Burnt Mountain weighed heavy on my heart, too. Times were hard there with winter coming on, but dang it, if I was going to make anything of myself I had to go where the business was, and that was in town. The folks back home, including Amanda, would have to be patient too. All the same, I was looking forward to spending some time with her occasionally when she could make it into town. She never had to know about May, and May would never have to know about her. Amanda had never known of any of the other lady friends I had scattered around the state, and I intended to keep it that way.

By the time I reached the mill, I had relieved myself of all guilt. I was about to be in my element, wheeling and dealing. I had done business in the past with the day foreman at the factory, Jim

Nation, and he was first on my list for this new enterprise. The clerk in the front office said Jim was on the floor, but I was welcome to go on back and find him. Going through the door to the operations area, heat blasted my face and the acrid odor of burning coal felt like it was scraping the inside of my nose and throat raw. The heat was necessary to set the just-mined coal that came in on train cars and prepare it for further processing. God almighty, it was hot as Hades in there. I'd had my fill of working in such conditions and did not ever intend to do it again. But I had made some valuable contacts during my brief employment with the factory.

Jim was just where I expected, on the catwalk above the vat floor. I was sure from the shrewd look and squinting eyes he recognized me. We had not parted on the best of terms. Jim just kept on chewing a cigar in the side of his mouth, like he was waiting for me to begin the conversation.

"Well, I see you're still cracking the whip over these poor fellas," I said in a none-too-friendly manner.

"That's what some men need to make 'em work," retorted Mr. Nation with an emphasis on the *some*. "Not that you would know anything about that, now would you?"

"May be," I said, "but there's easier ways to make a living than this. Think you'd be interested in a little business proposition?"

"Depends on how good a business proposition it is if you get my drift," he said, rubbing his fingers together to let me know that how much cash was involved would be the key to him wanting in on the deal.

"I'd say we might be talking about up to $20 a week, plus a little product on the side for your trouble," I explained.

"Hmmm....just what product are we talking about?"

"A product very much in demand, and likely to become more scarce as time goes on. I'd rather not give away the official name just yet, but we can corner the market on the stuff if we get in on it now."

Mr. Jim Nation still looked skeptical. "What do I have to do?"

"Just take the delivery here, like a factory order, then let my distributors make their pickups. You can pick up your cash from Mrs. Cox, just like we did before."

"I'm willing to give it a go, but only if you guarantee me $20 a week for at least a year. I ain't taking no chances on going to jail for just pocket change."

"Oh, I don't think that'll be a problem." I gave him a few more details and we shook hands.

Well, that went smoothly enough. Now, if all else goes well the dough should be rolling in this time next week. I headed back towards town and the depot. Most of my old business acquaintances passed time around there, and I figured I'd round up a few of them. When I walked back by Mrs. Cox's there was no sign of May from the outside. *Probably primping in front of that bathroom mirror with the lights on either side.* I didn't give May another thought as I headed on down the street. When I reached the depot, sure enough, there were some of my old cronies.

"How'do, Mr. Parks!" I tipped my hat to the portly man.

Parks nodded and gave a slow "I'm fair to middling, John, how do you do?"

I took in his rather doubtful look before I answered. "I'm just fine and dandy, Mr. Parks. Got a new gig on some product and already made the delivery arrangements. Think you can be my supplier? Of course, I'd need a little advance with this being our first delivery."

Standing just slightly behind Mr. Parks was a Negro man. Hard to tell what age these darkies were, but I figured him to be around 35 to 40 years old. Parks looked askance at the Negro and addressed him. "Boy, do you think you can make it up there and back down here by tomorrow, say 3 pm?" A couple of other men standing with Parks remained silent.

"Yessir," was the Negro's sullen response. He did not look into Mr. Park's eyes, but he did look directly at me. He knew I did not hold with going against a man because of his color. Only thing concerned me was a man's ability to serve whatever purpose I needed at the moment.

Parks seemed to ruminate for a minute. "All right then, Mr. Collis, here's your advance for a week of costs. Now mind you, I expect my $200 dollars by this time next week," he said with a hard look as he handed over two $100 bills.

"Oh, you'll definitely have it. Shall we meet back up here?"

"That'll do," was his only reply as he turned and went inside the depot. The other men and the "boy" went on down the way. "Boy" glanced back, gave me a sly smirk, a wide grin, and an affirmative nod before I continued on my own way in the opposite direction.

I was whistling as I left the depot. I decided to stop in at the post office, and it was a good thing I did. I had left word up at Burnt Mountain that I could be reached by sending a post to the Atlanta post office. Hopefully, there wouldn't be anything, but no such luck today. Just as I'd dreaded, there was a letter. My dread turned to a more sensual excitement as I saw the familiar handwriting and scent. Amanda was in town, at the Kimball Hotel! From the letter, she didn't sound too happy either. I knew I could change that within just a few minutes of seeing her. I stopped at a flower stall and picked out a bouquet. *This should soften her up a little.*

Next stop, the pharmacy. I needed a tin of tobacco to fortify me for the afternoon that was quickly approaching. Entering the store, I went directly to the back and approached the man behind the counter. With a big smile and outstretched hand, I said out loud, "Hello there, Big Jim! You probably didn't think you'd be seeing me this soon, now did you?" Big Jim stuck out his hand and we exchanged a firm shake.

"Oh, I figured you wouldn't be far behind that new young wife of yours. She was here a few hours ago. Purty little thing she is but looks a mite like a spitfire," Big Jim said with a wink and a grin.

It was my turn to be surprised. "May's been here?"

"Oh yes. Looking for her some Resteasy Tonic and asking about where she could find a good dressmaker. Didn't seem to have a clue about Mrs. Cox or your business in town, but I don't expect it will take her long to figure it out. Got a bright mind on her, that one does," was Big Jim's astute reply.

"Well, I'll be...." I chuckled. "Miss May and I just might have a lot more in common than I thought. How about a tin of that tobacco up there?"

Big Jim handed over the tin and I paid with a fresh bill. "We can catch up later, Jim, I've got some other business to attend to right now."

"I'm sure you do, John. Never known you not to have several irons in the fire." I just laughed, Jim shook his head from side to side, and we concluded our business. I hurried back toward Peachtree Street, hoping to see Amanda at the Kimball and still get back to Maude's in time for tea.

6
MAY

There were quite a few shops housed around the lobby. I had never seen the likes of such. All we had in Stansells was a small store that sold everything from staples to hardware to piece goods. Here there were specialized shops, separate ones for shoes, hats, fancy foods, and perfumes. There was a barber, a confectioner's, and a pharmacy, just as Mr. Willis had promised. The dress shop was just across the lobby. Entering the small shop, I fingered the fabrics. Such beautiful colors and textures! Much more elegant than anything I'd ever seen. There was even a strong smell of rich dyes used to produce the deep colors. Such sophisticated refinement brought out even more how much of a country bumpkin I must look. As I perused the finely drawn illustrations and patterns a young woman approached. Her expressionless face and flat voice gave away her doubts that someone attired like me would actually be shopping at a dressmaker's. The plain but sad-looking woman spoke without inflection.

"May I help you?"

"Yes, I definitely want a dress made. Are you the seamstress? I was told to ask for Hattie."

The young woman's face changed from doubtful to surprised as her eyebrows shot up. "Why, yes, I am Hattie."

"Well then, Hattie, I'm pleased to make your acquaintance. Your brother said you sometimes do custom work on your own?"

Hattie looked a little suspicious, "Do you know my brother?"

"Well, not exactly; we only met this morning. I was in his pharmacy. I inquired if he knew of a dressmaker, seeing as how I'm new in town, and he recommended your services."

A shrill voice emanated from behind a curtain where I assumed the workroom was located. "Miss Willis, is that a customer?"

Hattie Willis lowered her voice and said, "We really shouldn't discuss this here. May I meet you at the pharmacy later this afternoon? Say about four o'clock?" To the voice behind the curtain, she called, "No, Mrs. Black, just someone asking for directions."

"Well then, get on back here to work. We've got piles to finish."

"Coming ma'am, I'll just point this lady in the right direction."

I deliberately pointed at and silently ran my hand over a gorgeous blue wool fabric, indicating my choice to Hattie. Hattie gave a nod and silently pointed out an illustration on the wall. I nodded in return, giving my approval. Then, I raised four fingers to indicate I would be at the pharmacy at four o'clock.

The shrill voice called sharply. "Hattie!"

"Coming ma'am!" Hattie nodded back, and I departed the shop.

To take advantage of the time before four o'clock I made my way over to the pharmacy, browsing other shops on the way. A feathered hat from the milliner would be just perfect for the new dress, and new leather day boots would complete the ensemble nicely, I thought as I admired the fine goods in the shop windows. But I'd best have the dress made first. Heady scents wafted from the perfumers where cut crystal colored bottles lined the shelves. Making a mental note to myself, I thought I would definitely have to come back and make a day of shopping here. The sweet shop caught my eye and gave me an idea. Maybe a little treat would loosen up Mrs. Cox's tongue. I entered the shop and browsed, secretly pocketing pieces of some of the wrapped candies heaped in bowls. When the clerk asked if she could be of help, I smiled sweetly and said I was just browsing. The candy in the folds of my skirt would be just enough to present Mrs. Cox.

Finally arriving at the pharmacy, I was surprised to see it was quite different from Mr. Willis's. Items were displayed tastefully in artful arrangements and the shelves were not overcrowded with merchandise. Interesting. One would think in such a place there would be high demand for pharmaceutical products. As I perused the wares a young man stepped forward and asked if he could help with anything in particular. He had the same doubtful look as Hattie when he looked over my clothing. The sooner I got that new dress the better!

I spoke with authority and thought to allay any questions he might have about my affording products from this shop. "Yes, indeed. I just recently arrived in town and I'm afraid I do look a sight in these dowdy traveling clothes, but my former pharmacist suggested you might have some Resteasy Tonic, or something similar?"

"Yes ma'am, I think I have something that might interest you. It's much better than Resteasy, and is sure to give you a peaceful spell. Let me just get it from the back."

He returned momentarily with a dark bottle labeled "DeepSleep Sweet Dreams Tonic." Entranced with the name of the product, I suddenly realized I had no more money. Just the sight of the bottle and the promise of the label made me quite anxious for a swallow right then and there. My body willed my arms to reach out for it, but I had to maintain my composure for the time being if I was going to act out another successful ploy.

"Oh! Thank you kindly, sir. That sounds like just what I need."

"Well ma'am, it is quite popular with many of the ladies here in town, but it doesn't come cheap. It's a rather refined product." I noticed the clerk sweep his eyes over my attire yet again.

"Oh, that shouldn't be a problem. You see, my husband and I only just arrived in town this morning. Why we haven't even had a chance to change out of these horrid country traveling clothes. He's checking us in as we speak. We'll be setting up accounts with several of the Kimball shops. And I am so impressed with your merchandise, Mr...."

"Curry," he interjected.

"May I go ahead and open the account so I can take the bottle with me, Mr. Curry?" I gave him my sweetest and most determined smile, but Mr. Curry looked hesitant.

"It is a bit unusual for the wife to open accounts. I might need to check with the owner to see if this is acceptable." Mr. Curry seemed well aware of how desperate some women could be to get their hands on such a potent tonic. He pulled the bottle back closer to his body. I leaned in close to him, placed my hand on his arm, and spoke to him in a conspirator's tone.

"I can assure you it will be worth your while, as my husband and I will be trading quite a bit in patent medicines and other pharmaceutical items. It will be a very profitable account. We will be sure to spread the word that such a potent product is available right here in his little shop. Surely the owner will be pleased with your business foresight."

The young Mr. Curry hesitated, but only for a moment. Then he nodded and took out paper and pen to record the needed information. I had never opened an account anywhere in my life, so I was anxiously fabricating my facts.

"Name for the account?"

"Willie Wheeler," I replied. I don't know why it came to me so suddenly, but the words just seemed to flow smoothly, like warmed molasses. The clerk looked up as if to say is that all, so I added, "And you may find me or my husband John in room 300 here at the Kimball."

The clerk looked somewhat abashed. He knew if we were on the third floor here at the Kimball, he need not worry about us making good for the account. I had pulled the number from thin air, but Mr. Curry seemed especially pleased to note the room number.

"Certainly, Mrs. Wheeler," he stammered. "Is there

anything else I can help you with?"

Again, just as my words had gushed, I decided to take full advantage of the situation.

"Well now, let me see." I looked around a bit and chose several cosmetic items including lavender for Mrs. Cox and pomade for John. I made sure to choose the most expensive brand.

"This should do it for now, and of course, the tonic."

Mr. Curry dutifully noted the items on the ledger. I watched as he entered the balance brought forth as $15.00. I was taken aback but hid my shock at such a sum. I'd never spent that much money in my entire life. That DeepSleep Sweet Dreams Tonic had better outdo Mama's Resteasy! I needed to get used to making such purchases since this was only the first of many more to come. Mr. Curry wrapped the items into a parcel and thanked me profusely.

"We look forward to serving you again, Mrs. Wheeler."

I imagine you do, Mr. Curry. I imagine you do.

There was about an hour before I was due to meet Hattie Willis at her brother's pharmacy and there was no sign of John returning to the lobby. I went out the east entrance of the hotel and thought I'd take in a few more sights. Sidestepping horse droppings and cautiously crossing railroad tracks, I made my way towards the Capital Building. All the while, I was craving just a sip of the DeepSleep Sweet Dreams Tonic. I did not dare to take out the bottle and swallow a dose right here on the street. What could I do?

Then I saw my chance. Just in front of the Capital building were two churches.

I first came upon the Catholic Shrine of the Immaculate Conception. This was like no other church building I'd ever seen. Back in Newton County, all we had were the small wooden frame structures of a Baptist church, a Methodist church, and one or two other churches with which I was not at all familiar. I had never seen anything like this imposing building. The tall stone spires and carvings appeared almost sinister to me, and I had heard Catholics practiced strange rites and infant baptisms. As much as I needed that swallow of tonic, I could not bring myself to enter such a place.

I skirted the Catholic building and came to the church

directly across the street from the Capital building. The red brick building with the single steeple was not nearly as imposing. The placard read "Central Presbyterian Church." I wasn't sure what Presbyterians were, but I did not feel the same sense of trepidation I had at the Catholic's. I opened the heavy door and peered inside. It was not completely dark, but dim light entered from the narrow stained-glass windows and glowed from a few candles on the altar. It was a large building; surely I could slip unnoticed into the church, sit near the back, and surreptitiously have a sip of tonic while appearing to be in prayer. I went in, choosing a pew near the back. There were a few other souls on their knees with heads bowed, but they were sparse and far towards the front. Perfect! In that posture, no one would see what I was about to do. I had to open my parcel with as little noise as possible, but the paper crackled and crunched. In the soaring room, it sounded like breaking glass. A head turned my direction, but only momentarily. Finally freeing the dark tonic bottle from the wrapping, I pulled out the cork stopper. After managing this with my head down I took my first sip of the oily syrup. The taste was surprisingly sweet and pleasant. I took another sip, a little larger than the first, and carefully stoppered the bottle. I remained in my reverent position a minute or two more before rising to leave the church.

Instinctively, I grasped the pew in front of me and swayed precariously. I was not prepared for the sensation that overtook my body. Standing as still for a few moments, until I thought no one would take notice, I finally thought I could move on and began to edge my way down the pew, holding on for fear of falling and causing a stir. At the end of the pew, I turned slowly and moved out into the aisle. I was so intent on getting out into light and air that I did not notice a woman already in the aisle. I was tilting to the side, holding onto pew ends as I made my way slowly towards the vestibule. Just as I pushed open a door to the welcome outdoor light, the woman from the aisle came from behind and clasped my arm.

"Mrs. Collis? Mrs. Collis? Are you ill?" It was the mysterious Mrs. Cox! I tried to still her unfocused image in my vision, but she seemed to be waving about. Then I realized it must be me who was weaving this way and that way, not her.

"Oh yes, I'm fine, just a little tired," I said as I held onto the stair rail.

Mrs. Cox looked skeptical. As the fresh air washed over me I was regaining my balance. Now, if my eyes would just settle down and focus!

Taking a deep breath of fresh air, I assured Mrs. Cox. "I'll be fine. The travel and heat must have overcome me. Just a few more errands to run and I'll be home for tea." I straightened, took another deep breath, and managed to paste on a small smile.

"Well then, I'll see you at four for tea if you're sure you're all right." Mrs. Cox, her brow wrinkled in a scowl, continued to look worried. I just nodded and made my way in the opposite direction of Mrs. Cox and did not look back. It dawned on me a few minutes later that my appointment with Hattie was at four, so there would be no tea for me. I supposed the tonic was going to have to get me through until supper.

7
MAY

    I was still in a dreamlike state from the tonic and it was nearing four o'clock, but I didn't mind missing tea at Mrs. Cox's. Let the old woman wonder what I was up to instead of the other way round. Reaching Willis's Pharmacy, I heard a feminine voice near the back.

    "Do you think she can pay?" Hattie was asking her brother.

    "Oh, I expect she'll pay quite well," was his response.

    I stood stock still hoping to hear more.

    "You said you know her husband?" Hattie was asking.

    "John's an old business acquaintance. In fact, we'll be doing business together again real soon. Along with Mrs. Cox, Mr. Thompson, Mr. Nation, and that boy, John Frank Lawrence, we've got a lucrative set-up. But don't you worry your pretty head about it, Hattie." I pictured her brother giving her an affectionate pat on the head. "You don't need to be mixed up in any of that. Don't you have second thoughts about May Collis; you'll get your money."

    Their shoes on the wooden plank floors clopped like horses' feet as they came towards the front of the store. I shifted my stance so it would appear like I'd just walked in and addressed

Hattie directly.

"Hello, Miss Hattie. I see you're very prompt."

"Oh, I'm always prompt. I believe in respectability and keeping one's word. It's rather like the attention to detail in dressmaking, Mrs. Collis."

"I see." I noticed Hattie had called my name, but I had deliberately not introduced myself at the dress shop. Obviously, I had missed part of the previous conversation between Hattie and her brother, and there had been some discussion about John and me. I briefly mused that Atlanta might not be so different from Stansells in that regard. Everybody seemed to know everything about everyone else and their business. It would do me well to be careful in my own dealings apart from John. Why it sounded as if Jim Willis knew more about John's business dealings than I did. I would find out more, just give me time. I needed to know what John was up to if I intended to look out for my own interests.

"Yes, that would be desirable I suppose. I want something in the absolutely latest fashion for day wear. A dress that will do for the change of seasons is my first priority. I liked that wool I indicated at the shop. Next, I'll be wanting a nicer evening outfit, more day wear, and a coat."

I lowered my voice, leaned into Hattie and shielded my face with my upraised hand in a conspiratorial manner just enough for appearance's sake. "Eventually I will be needing several more items that will accommodate a woman in a delicate condition." I shifted my eyes down to my mid-section to be sure Hattie got my inference. I backed away and asked, "How much would you expect all of that to run me?"

Miss Hattie was not to be taken in so quickly. Her brows knit in concentration.

"The first daydress in the wool will run about $30.00. I can't really say about the others without knowing more specifics of the design and fabrics. But I can work you up some samples and we can discuss it." Hattie spoke sweetly but firmly.

"How soon can you have the first dress ready?" I spoke just as sweetly and firmly, in what I hoped was a manner of a well-to-do woman addressing someone in the service industry. I did not want Hattie to think she could bamboozle me. Just because I was new in the big city did not mean I was ignorant.

"I'll need to get your measurements and I could have the first dress to you by Wednesday of next week. At that time I can bring some fabric samples for the others and work up the costs. Will that be acceptable?" I suspected the slight deference Hattie showed was contrived in an attempt to gain my favor.

"I was hoping for a new dress sooner than that. Couldn't you have it by Monday?"

I figured Hattie had built in an extra day or two in her proposal so she could appear to be giving in more to my demand. She replied sweetly, but with a sly look, "Why, Mrs. Collis, I think I could manage that, especially for a valued business partner of my brother's."

I was not shocked by this acknowledgment of conspiracy. In fact, I rather liked that Miss Hattie was no mealy-mouthed seamstress, but a clever business girl. Her reply did pique my suspicion about how much she and her brother knew about my marital arrangement.

I chose to ignore the implication of complicity and responded simply, "Why, that will be just fine and dandy, Miss Hattie. Shall we proceed?"

Hattie held up a tape measure and started to the back of the store. "Then let's get started," she said briskly. The measuring session went quickly. We exchanged only minimal comments. I observed as she wrote complete notes in a fine script on a piece of her brother's office stationery. She was definitely an educated, independent woman. Not every woman could read or write, especially folks like me from outside the city, but I was a quick study and had been fortunate to learn from my brother, although I kept my knowledge to myself thinking it might be to my advantage someday.

Presently she was finished with the measurements and took her leave to get back to the shop. I speculated she would have to volunteer to work late and close up the shop so she could measure and cut the fabric for my dress after hours. The proprietress, Miss Black, would not miss the fabric cut off the large bolt and would be totally unsuspecting of Hattie's after-work shenanigans. Yes indeed, I admired this girl's spunk and business acumen.

After Hattie left I readjusted my frugal clothing. I glanced toward the front of the store and saw other customers had entered.

Mr. Willis seemed engaged with them so I took advantage of the opportunity to look around the back room. Maybe I could discover a clue to his secretive business arrangements with John and Mrs. Cox. A few stacks of boxes, a work table with pharmacist's utensils, shelves with vials, bottles, crocks, and jugs, some unmarked crates; and off in the corner what appeared to be a little office area.

I quietly stepped over and tried to look at some of the documents on the desk without disturbing them. Not much there that I could make any sense of. Then a small slip of paper caught my eye – "Shipment for Mrs. Cox next Wednesday. See John."

Shipment? What kind of shipment? I would have to be on the lookout. There was definitely more to the working relationship between Mrs. Cox, Mr. Willis, and John than met the eye. I looked around but could find no other references to a shipment or anything else mentioning John or Mrs. Cox. Suddenly, the bell on the door jingled indicating the customers were leaving. Enough snooping for now. I emerged from the back room and gave Mr. Willis a big smile.

"My, my, this certainly is a busy place. You seem to have a constant stream of customers. That must mean you are an especially successful purveyor. You must offer quite a variety of products and services." I was hoping to flatter Mr. Willis into revealing a little more about his transaction, but he did not take the hint.

"Well, I do all right. There's a lot involved in the pharmaceutical business many folks don't know about. We can be a pretty resourceful contact for a variety of both familiar and lesser-known products." Willis turned and busied himself straightening items on the shelves. Apparently, that was all I was going to get out of him. But what an interesting response! To what lesser-known products could he be referring? I would definitely have to be more observant if I was to learn more.

"Oh, I'm sure you're right about that, Mr. Willis. Why, a knowledgeable proprietor like you must have all kinds of contacts and resources for less common products. That's good to know. I will surely keep that in mind. One never knows what need might arise."

Still no response from Willis. I took this to mean the

conversation was indeed over. I changed tactics and said brightly, "Thank you so much for advising me about your sister. I think I shall be very pleased with our arrangement. And, I look forward to doing business with you, Mr. Willis."

Mr. Willis turned at this remark, nodded, and pronounced, "Indeed, Mrs. Collis. I look forward to doing business with both you and Mr. Collis. I'm sure our working relationship will be most profitable."

"I certainly hope so, Mr. Willis, and I'm sure it will be. Good day!"

8
JOHN

I sat across the dining room table from Maude. The little sandwiches and cookies had allayed my hunger for the time being. I wasn't surprised May had not made it home in time for tea. Knowing her to be perfectly capable of managing on her own, her absence did not worry me. In fact, it gave me time to discuss a few things with Maude, who wasn't showing any of her former reticence. She actually laughed and halfway flirted with me. Maude and I went back a ways. She'd helped me out of that nasty business with the previous boarder, we'd been business partners before, and so far, this new set-up was coming off without a hitch. I was sure she looked forward to the additional income playing the middleman would bring her way. She was ready to modernize the whole place with electricity!

Maude was telling me about her encounter with May in the church. "I damn near thought she was going to fall flat on her face, and then what would I have done?"

"Aww, you would have handled it just fine, Maudie. Anyways, she was probably just setting up for her performance. That's part of her plan, to put on that she's lost the baby she's supposed to be carrying. Then she'll be free to go about her business in the city now that I've gotten her here."

Maude's eyebrows shot up. "Baby? What's this about a baby? Surely May's not…"

I stopped Maude mid-sentence and went on to explain. "No, May's not in a delicate condition. She's strong as an ox. She's just pretending to be for a few days. That was part of her plan for us marrying and getting her out of Stansells. Soon, we'll be notifying her family that she's lost the baby. Those country bumpkins will never know the difference. Yes, indeed, May's far too smart to let a real baby slow down her ambitions."

Maude sat back and let out a sigh of relief. "I sure hope you know what you're letting yourself in for with this one, John. Sounds like you may have met your match where schemes are concerned."

I chuckled a little at Maude's observation, but I did have to admit she might have a point. "You may be right about that, Maude, you may be right. It's a little soon to say, but she might be a good partner for us. She has the deviousness such a business requires, although I do worry a bit about her soldier's disease. She's a mite young to be so dependent on her tonics."

Maude looked thoughtful. "Well, you never can tell about some folks. I could have sworn her breath had a strong smell at the church. And I know she'd been through my cupboards and didn't find a thing. That means she got access to some tonic somewhere else just this afternoon."

I told Maude about May asking for Resteasy Tonic at Big Jim's. "She didn't get it from him, but he sent her to the Kimball. I 'spect that's where she got hold of some."

"Mighty pricey over there, if she did," Maude said with arched eyebrows. "How would she manage to pay for it? We should be cautious. I don't trust that woman."

I wiped my mouth with the napkin and sat back a bit. "If I know May, where there's a will there's a way. I'm sure she devised a way to get whatever she wanted. As for the other, I don't trust her completely either, Maudie, and with good reason, considering her willingness to marry a man she barely knows and move away from home to a city she's never even been in before. Still, it shows a good bit of gumption on her part, and that's what it takes to get ahead these days."

"You may be right about that, John, but we need still need to be careful. Neither one of us knows May well enough to trust her yet. If she was that conniving with you, no telling what else she is capable of. We'll have to be on our toes to make sure she doesn't end up causing more trouble than she's worth. At least for the time being."

"True enough, Maude, true enough. But that's enough about May for now. Let's get down to business. I met with Nation this morning and he agreed to accept delivery of the moonshine from Park's men. Then he'll bring a few pints by here and ferry some to a few other houses. Should be here this time tomorrow. So you can spread the word we're back in that business."

Maude grinned and said, "You sure didn't waste any time, did you? Haven't even been here a day yet and you've already got it set up. That's some pretty fast work."

"Well, Maudie, that's the easy one. The other scheme, getting the high-potency tonics, might take a little time to get going. And I had a surprise visit from Amanda. She did send a letter ahead, but she was already in town. In fact, we spent a pleasant couple of hours together this afternoon."

"How did Amanda say those darlin' tots of yours are doing?"

"Well, she's not liking it too much that I'm going to be away so long. Says the children miss me! Ain't that something? Sounded like she could have cared less about me being there for her if you know what I mean. But she sure did seem to enjoy our time together."

"Is that so? You better be careful with so many schemes up your sleeve, John. You just might get burned. Especially with May. If she's as high-spirited as you say, she'd be madder than a wet hen if she finds out you're two-timing her. No telling what she would do for revenge."

"Oh, you're right about that, Maude. I will need to be quite discreet. Even though this marriage with May is a set-up for convenience and business, I don't think either she or Amanda would take too kindly to the idea of another wife."

"I do imagine May can be quite resourceful, John. She's sharp as a knife, she is. And out to get what she wants. That can be a dangerous combination in a woman who has nothing to lose. We women know how to recognize these things in another woman."

I patted Maude on the arm. "Right again, dear Maudie. With May, where there's a will there's a way. Now, don't you worry though, you know I'll look out for you."

"It's not me I'm worried about, John. I've been around a long time. It's you who better be looking over your shoulder. Seems like women can be worse than men when it comes to getting revenge. I wish I'd been more resourceful myself back in the day. I let that scoundrel husband of mine get away with…"

Maude stopped suddenly and shook her head. I was intrigued. I'd always heard about a husband and child in her distant past but she'd never opened up to me about them, or the circumstances surrounding their disappearance. Well, I'd just have to let it go for now.

I laughed and said, "You're probably right, Maudie, old girl. You'll likely be around long after me. You've managed fine so far, and that's no small feat for a woman on her own in Atlanta. Why, you'll most likely outlive me, May, and Amanda to boot!"

"I don't know about that, John, but I do know I can tell a determined woman when I see one, and May is hell-bent on achieving wealth and power. I just hope we don't fall along the wayside as she's doing it. You've had some close calls in your relatively short life so far, and even though you're as much of a rascal as you are, I'd hate to see you get hurt or worse. Just be careful."

"Oh, I'll be careful all right, Maude. I'll be careful. May and I are not so different. We both have the same desires and goals. I think we'll make a good partnership."

"Maybe so, John, maybe so. But there's more to life than money and power, and I ought to know. I've had both, and look where it's gotten me. An old woman, alone in this world."

I could see the wistful, faraway look return to Maude's eyes. Fond as I was of the old woman, I didn't have the time or patience for such melodrama. I leaned over and planted a kiss on her wrinkly, powdered cheek.

"Maudie dear, you'll be fine. If all goes as well as I think it should, you won't have a care or a want in the world. You just mark my words."

As I pushed back from the table, we both heard the front

door open. Time to change the mood and play my part as the concerned husband.

 About that moment May came through the front door. I instantly changed my jovial look to one of concern, and Maude quickly wiped away her bemused smile and took on her bland, reticent persona. I noticed May herself appeared perfectly fine when she first opened the door, but then took on a tired, wilting facade.

 I immediately went to her, took her in my arms, and crooned, "My darling May, you look like you've been drug through the wringer. You must be famished!"

 I noticed Maude purposefully removing dishes with a stern glance in our direction. Even if May had been famished, which she was not, it wouldn't have swayed her house rules.

 May melted against me. "Oh, I'm just a little tired, John. You know that's not unusual for a girl in my condition," making sure to look towards Mrs. Cox, who pretended to not be paying any attention. "I think I'll go lie down a while. I suppose I can wait until dinner to eat something." Again, May directed a look at Mrs. Cox, who went on through the door to the kitchen without a backward glance.

 I led May back to our bedroom where she brightened up considerably. "That mean old witch!" she said to me as soon as we were behind closed doors. "She just might upset my plan. I'll have to stay in all day tomorrow and the next day, pretending to be tired out. Then we'll have to hope she goes out and we can put on that I've lost the baby."

 I snuggled May up close as she lay back on the bed. "Oh, I wouldn't worry too much about old Maude Cox. She won't get in our way. In fact, she may turn out to be a help in our cause. And as for you having to stay in the bed for two days, well, I can be sure to make your time here worthwhile!"

 She gave me a scornful look but then softened and giggled. "You can start making my time worthwhile right now, Mr. Collis."

 Afterward, we lay sweating in the afternoon heat. It was late September but still sweltering hot. May asked how my business went and I assured her all was in order.

 "I spoke with several key players and already have an advance. It's going just fine and dandy so far." But I did not want to give away more than that just yet, so I turned the tables.

"And just how did you spend your first afternoon in the city?"

May answered, "Oh, just getting familiar with what's close by and getting my bearings in the neighborhood." She started to turn away from me dismissively.

I put my hands on either side of her face and looked her directly in the eye. "Why yes, I understand you've made the rounds, struck up some acquaintances, and even took a little respite in the church, the better to take your tonic. And I can't wait to see you in that new blue dress!"

May opened her mouth to exclaim, but I didn't give her a chance to get out a single word. I kissed her again and we were soon engaged in another round of newlywed bliss.

9
MAY

After another round of lovemaking, I thought about John's comment acknowledging he knew at least part of where I'd been that afternoon. It took me somewhat by surprise that John knew so much about where I'd gone and what I'd been doing. Atlanta was growing smaller by the hour. I had some surprising questions for him too.

"And your business, Mr. Collis, is it going to operate out of the coal factory, the depot, or the Kimball Hotel?"

Now it was John's turn to be taken by surprise. "You do get around, don't you, you little vixen!"

I warned him, "John, don't keep secrets from me. As you well know, I have my ways. You won't be so infatuated with me when I turn angry and vengeful. Watch your step!"

"Oh, my little darling, I wouldn't dare try to fool you. You're way too cunning for me. Just keep in mind that for now, I am your source of income."

Did I detect a note of sarcasm? Perhaps, but John had always seemed fairly mild-mannered to me. I measured my reply.

"Hmmm. You may be right for now. I won't forget that.

How could I? But that's not to say it will always be that way." For now, we'd just have an unspoken pact that each would not interfere with the other's business. Besides, it seemed each of our escapades just might be to the other's advantage. I sighed and settled in for a nap, feeling quite satisfied with the day's events so far.

At supper, I tried to appear a little freshened up but not too lively.

"I wanted to thank you, Mrs. Cox, for coming to my aide in the church today. I had gone in looking for a spot of coolness from the afternoon heat. I suppose I just didn't realize I was overdoing it for my first day in the city. I'm not used to having to take precautions with myself, but I suppose I must, now that I'm in such a delicate condition." I demurely glanced at John and lowered my eyes as John placed a hand protectively over mine.

Mrs. Cox's coldness seemed to melt away. "Yes, my dear, you will have to be careful. You wouldn't want anything unforeseen to happen. You just take it easy and let old Maude Cox take care of you."

"Why, thank you, Mrs. Cox," said John. "That's mighty kindly of you to offer. I'm going to be pretty occupied with my business over the next few days. It'll be a comfort to know May has you to look out for her."

"Anything I can do to help, Mr. Collis. I can be fairly resourceful in getting things accomplished around town. I've been here a while and know most business folks. You just call on me whenever you need to, you or Mrs. Collis."

It was my turn to play the charade. "Why Mrs. Cox, that's just about the kindest offer I've ever heard. Taking care of me and helping with John's business too. Seems like we're going to make quite a team!" We enjoyed the rest of suppertime with John sharing amusing stories.

That night in our room, John and I determined that before things went any further we needed to end at least one part of our trumped-up circumstances. Since I had already appeared faint that afternoon, it seemed only natural to follow through with that part of the plan. We decided to proceed with the first opportunity.

The next morning at breakfast I purposely moved slowly and tried to appear as tired looking as I could. Maude suggested I stay in and take it easy since yesterday had proved so draining.

"I do have to go out for a while," she said, "and I probably won't be back before lunch. Maybe not until after tea time. But I will leave you something prepared in the icebox."

John and I exchanged glances. He jumped right in. "Oh, we'll be fine, Mrs. Cox. I planned to take today to help May get settled in, so I'll be right by her side. Don't you worry about a thing, although you are so kind to offer your assistance. I'll take good care of my girl, and you can take care of whatever business you need to attend to."

"Yes, Mrs. Cox, we'll be just fine. Please don't change any of your plans on account of us." I smiled and looked directly at John. "We don't mind being left on our own, do we, John?" I was hoping my bold comment might cause Mrs. Cox to believe we just wanted some newlywed alone time.

Maude was not to be taken in. "Just be sure not to overdo. A woman in your condition has to take precautions." She looked pointedly at John, then at me. We both nodded and I forced a slight blush.

As soon as Maude was out of the house, John and I began to discuss options for carrying out our plan. We decided it would be best not to pretend the event would take place there at Mrs. Cox's. There would be so many explanations. Better to let the supposed evidence of the miscarriage be in a place unlikely to be found or frequented by Maude. John said he knew just the spot.

We went out together and headed downtown. At Marietta and Broad Streets we boarded the Nine-Mile Trolley. This electrified streetcar made a loop around town and went out to Piedmont Park, where just a few years earlier the famed Cotton States Exposition had been held. As we went along, the open-air trolley offered somewhat of a cool breeze, especially when we went through the more wooded areas. I marveled at the new residences being built along the way. I'd never seen so many houses in one place, and each one was prettier and more splendid than the one before.

When we arrived at the stop for the park John said, "I think this will fit the bill. Let's head up this way to the exhibition hall and the rest stations."

I observed several buildings and a great expanse of lawn, as well as a small lake. We strolled along the paths with other sightseers. It was obvious the park had become a big attraction.

"So, what do we do now?" I asked.

"Well, we enjoy a stroll, buy some light refreshment, then get back on the trolley and enjoy the rest of the circle. At least that's what we'll really do. Of course, it will be a different story than what we tell Maude."

"All right. Give me the details again. I want to make sure our stories are the same."

John proceeded. "We'll explain to Maude that we had thought the fresh air of the park would be rejuvenating for you, but it turned out the strolling was just too much, and shortly after we arrived at the park you went into the ladies' comfort station. When you didn't appear after a reasonable time, I engaged a woman park attendant to check on your well-being. She entered the building, then came back out to tell me you were being attended to by several ladies and appeared to have been bleeding heavily. I'll say I was distraught, but the woman assured me she would go back and oversee your care, this was not that much of an uncommon occurrence, and she had handled such circumstances before."

I looked at John seriously. How did he know so much about such a situation? He seemed to have come up with this plan rather easily. "Then what? Am I just supposed to have lost a baby and then trot along home as if nothing had happened?"

"Oh no, May. Remember I said what we really do is one thing, but what we tell Maude is another. We'll say the ladies at the park took care of you, even providing some fresh clothing, and that we decided to discard your old traveling clothes, being as how they were soiled and outdated anyway. We could even go further and say they procured a doctor to check you over and make sure you were well enough to get back home."

"I suppose that sounds reasonable. How do you know we won't run into Maude with all this gallivanting about?"

"Believe me, May, Maude's business won't take her anywhere near the park or the developing neighborhoods in this part of town. It's not exactly the kind of area where her business takes place. We won't have to worry about that."

Again I thought, *how did John know so much about Maude's business and where she might conduct it?* There seemed to be more to this story than he was telling. I chose to remain quiet on the matter but tucked it away for future reference.

"If you say so," I responded. "But how do we handle the part about getting back home?"

"I was thinking we could say that after you were tended to and checked by the doctor, the ladies brought you out to me. The doctor advised that you had been very early in your term and most likely lost all the blood and, er, remains, at once, and that you should be fine after a day or so of rest. Then I hired a carriage to get us back home. We'll arrange to arrive at home well before Maude's return so we can have you comfortably tucked into bed."

"Hmm, sounds convincing, I suppose. So, let's get me that new outfit and something to eat!"

John laughed. "That's my girl! We'll get some refreshment here. There's a ready-to-wear shop not far from the end of the trolley loop. We'll stop there to get you a new skirt and shirtwaist. We'll throw away those old rags you've worn for two days."

We did exactly as John had said. We strolled the park, bought lemon ices and tea cakes that we ate on the lawn, and re-boarded the trolley. The route took us by homes even more magnificent than the ones before. New construction seemed to spring up everywhere, but the trees were preserved and provided verdant shade and beauty to the homes' surrounding lots. The completed homes had lawns and gardens, perfectly tended. We exited the trolley at a few other stops, taking time to look about the new neighborhoods. Again, I vowed to live in such a home one day.

As we got closer to the end of the loop, near the northern end of Peachtree Street, there were more commercial areas. We went into a small shop, nothing too fancy, but it would do. The newer style of ready to wear clothing had not yet reached the country, but I had seen the pictures in the catalogs at the general store in Covington. John assured me the cost was no matter. I chose a white shirtwaist with just a small amount of trim on the mutton sleeves. A full-length gray skirt and a rose-colored belt completed the ensemble. My old boots, hat, and reticule would have to do for now, but I hadn't forgotten I wanted to return to those shops at the Kimball.

"What do you think, John? Of course, I'll need new boots and a hat, and maybe even gloves. I saw some that would do perfectly yesterday when I was at the Kimball."

"That's quite pretty, Miss May!" John said upon my exit from the dressing area. I glowered at the use of "Miss May," but I hugged him openly. "Thank you, my darling!"

Suddenly, John's face turned pale.

"May, did you just say you were at the Kimball yesterday?"

"Why yes, dear," I said brightly. "I strolled around the lobby for an hour or so."

More color drained from his face. I continued, "Why? Is that not proper for a lady in the city?" Let John wonder if I had seen him there. Better to keep him on his toes and not know where I might turn up. He did not need to know my whereabouts every minute of the day.

John seemed to regain his composure a bit. "Oh, no, May. That's fine. I just didn't know you'd been there yet. I wanted to show you around there myself. But we can do that another time."

The store clerk averted her eyes briefly, then came towards us holding my old clothes at arm's length. "I believe you forgot these, ma'am."

"Oh no," I declared. "I'll never wear those old things again. Do what you want with them; I don't care!" As we went out the front door of the shop, a carriage awaited. In the new clothing, I truly felt like a lady as John handed me up, paid the driver, and we headed back to Maude's.

10
JOHN

    May and I enjoyed our outing. It was rather fun playing pretend! When we got back to the house, Maude still had not returned. May and I retreated to our room.

    "Now darlin', you're going to have to play this out, so be prepared to spend two or three days in bed. Not that I might not spend some time in here with you!"

    May did not look too happy about this part of our charade. "If you plan to do that, then you better learn how to be more of a gentleman," May said. "You make enough noise to tell the whole neighborhood what you're doing. Just keep that in mind!"

    I chuckled at May's observation, especially since I could say the same to her! "Oh don't worry about that, I'll manage," I said. We spent a pleasant hour in bed and May was enjoying a nap when I heard Maude return. I quietly dressed and went out to the dining room. It seemed our little tea-time chats were ideal for discussing business alone, without May, whether it was personal or trade-wise. Maude had the tea set on the table shortly.

    "So how did your rounds go?" I asked. But Maude was not

to be distracted from May's absence.

"That can wait," she said. "How did your rounds go? And where's May?"

"Well Maude, that's something we need to have a little chat about. Seems May won't be joining us in the dining room for two or three days." With a wink, I went on to add, "Doctor's orders. She's to stay in bed and rest."

Maude looked at me suspiciously. "Oh come on now, John. Doctor's orders? You don't have to try and fool me. It's a good thing too. I saw that overdone playacting yesterday."

"Aw Maudie, just go along with me on this. May doesn't know that you know the baby was just a made up circumstance. May didn't think it was such a good idea to let you in on our little secret. She doesn't know I told you about it. I knew all along you'd be too hard to fool. As for playacting, you put on quite a performance yourself at supper yesterday, cooing about taking care of 'our May'."

"You're damned right, John. I know enough about you and everybody else to know when something's up. If you expect my cooperation, I need to know what's going on. Now, let's hear the whole story."

I explained the whole situation to Maude. How May had seduced me back at the spring in Stansells, how we conjured up the baby pretense in order to get her married and out of that Godforsaken place, how we planned to lose the baby once we were in Atlanta, and finally, how we would build up our resources together and then go our separate ways.

I added, though, "I have to admit, I'm becoming fond of that scrappy girl. I dare say she will stop at nothing to get what she wants. And what she wants is to be independent and successful. Never seen a woman so set on making her own way. A little surprising since most women I know just want a husband and babies."

Maude's response was measured and thoughtful. "Well John, I hope you know what you're up against. That girl is feisty. I've seen plenty of girls come and go, but May's the most determined wench I've come across in years. She's in this for the long haul. The more I hear the more I like her determination. Some women think that way for a while, and then there comes a time when they realize all that so-called success doesn't substitute for the warmth of holding a baby in your arms. I know that from experience. You just better look out for yourself and be careful. I agree with you – I don't think she'll stop at anything to get what she wants."

I looked solemnly at Maude. She had mentioned almost the same thing just yesterday, and there were those stories about her losing a husband and a baby years ago. Folks around town seemed to think that had made her the peculiar person she was. I never knew any details, and Maude rarely mentioned it, so it was surprising she brought it up twice in just a few days, but it was obviously not something she wanted to discuss. I quickly changed my expression and laughed at Maude's serious response.

"Oh, I'm not too worried. I think she's actually become attached to me too. That should make things easier. I'll just have to be careful not to let Amanda find out. Good thing neither one knows what the other looks like. That was a close call when May was at the Kimball yesterday afternoon the same time as I was there with Amanda! What we need to do for now is go along with the "doctor's orders" and let things settle down a bit. In the meantime, I plan to be stashing away the bucks as they come in. Course, I'll give May enough to keep her happy. And I may have to keep play-acting by moving up our living quarters. I'm sure you can help with that."

"You're right about that, John," Maude said. "I think you might be surprised at the properties I've gotten ahold of since we last worked together. That last fellow never knew what came over him, and he had quite a tidy sum. Anyway, I'll play along. Just don't say I didn't warn you!"

The next few days and weeks were uneventful. I made sure my deliveries of the finest moonshine in North Georgia were on time and handled efficiently. I cut in everybody that was due payment from the profits. No one was the wiser that I paid myself, Maude, and May a little extra premium. On the other hand, the tonic scheme took a little longer to get off the ground. I was no scientist, but I was hearing some of the stories going around about the questionable ingredients of most tonics and patent medicines. England had already passed a pharmacy act, and there were rumors the United States Feds were looking into such an act. Even the popular Coca-Cola was coming under fire since it contained cocaine.

As I thought about some of the implications for the tonic scheme, I had to take into consideration that most of the tonics had pure morphine combined with alcohol in syrup. It was common knowledge many an injured Confederate veteran had the soldier's disease, and doctors thought it was a result of taking morphine for pain. It stood to reason the tonics might eventually become regulated. Hell, there was already a temperance movement calling for the ban of liquor! Although this made it more difficult to get the tonic trade going, there would always be some willing to pay the price and take the risks involved in making it available. In that sense, it was a surefire profit maker. Most of us opportunistic businessmen knew that prohibiting something just made it that much more desirable. The tonic trade wasn't booming yet, but it was growing steadily.

I mused on May's own fondness for her tonics. I knew May would take a swig of her pa's moonshine jug now and then, but what she really craved was her ma's tonic. I figured I'd get the safest but most powerful tonics available. Knowing May's determination, she would find a tonic one way or the other. I might as well make a little profit off her purchases. And there were plenty of soldiers and women about who already depended on tonic to get them through the day. Why, practically every woman I knew back home kept a steady supply.

11
JOHN

The three of us, myself, Maude, and May kept up our pretenses. The weeks stretched into months. May seemed generally satisfied, going about her days accumulating housewares and the latest styles in fashion. The following spring we were ready to leave Maude's for our own rental property. Eventually, we settled on Blackgum Street, and this time, it wasn't just a room. We leased the whole house! May was thrilled to upgrade the furniture and feel like she was in her own home. We had gone along and not made any mention of eventually splitting up. I stayed away for days at a time, often seeing Amanda as well as a few other lady friends. I was careful, though, to not let on to Maude or May. Maude probably knew anyway, but I suspected May would not take kindly to being two-timed or even three-timed. And I observed that Maude and May were becoming closer as time went on. I wasn't absolutely sure I could trust Maude not to reveal my true circumstances, so I was keeping some secrets even from her. I figured as long as I kept May in money, I'd be okay.

The Blackgum Street cottage was definitely a step up and

May was pleased. Although we weren't owners yet, May was happy we were on our own and had some privacy. It didn't seem to bother May when I was away for days at a time. In fact, sometimes it seemed like a bother when I was there.

"So John, how long are you going to be away this time?" May asked nearly every time I was leaving out.

I'd answer rather nonchalantly. "Oh, just a few days. Why, are you going to miss me, dearest?" I didn't fully trust May and would rather keep her guessing.

"Oh, no particular reason, *dearest,*" would be her usual retort. "I just like to have an idea so I can have our cozy little home in order for your return. You know how much I'm enjoying fixing up the place."

"Yes indeed, darling. I know how you enjoy spending my money on fancy furniture. If I'm not careful I might walk in one of these days and think I'm in that fine Kimball House."

May did indeed enjoy spending my money. Of course, it was nice being on our own in the new house. Although modest, it was more than what May had ever had back in Stansells and more than just a room to board in. The four-room cottage was on a quiet street, away from the industrial factories but close enough to walk to Peachtree Street. The house itself was fairly new, as were so many in Atlanta. White clapboard, a covered front porch, and big windows gave it a cheery look.

May had set about furnishing our new abode in the latest fashion. The parlor was papered in a green print, and a flowered rug covered most of the dark hardwood floor. The windows had dark curtains, and gas sconces on the walls provided plenty of light after dark. Matching horsehair covered divans and chairs provided comfortable seating, and a parlor table and side tables completed the look.

The kitchen had painted white woodwork cabinetry, a gas stove, and even an ice box. We used an enamel-topped table with chairs for our private meals, using a few inexpensive pieces of crockery and enamelware, but May insisted on more formal furnishings for the actual dining room. She purchased a heavy dark wood table and six matching chairs, as well as a sideboard. We had not accumulated many dishes or frivolities, but she did invest in a set of blue china we used only on special occasions, a set of cut glass crystal glassware, and a set of silver plated flatware. You would have thought we were going to entertaining the Queen of England herself with what May insisted on having.

May was content to let the less public areas of the house be a little plainer. Our bedroom had a metal bedstead with plain chintz bedclothes and a dressing table. But, most importantly for May, two large wardrobes were filled with her ever-expanding accouterments. I never knew a woman who loved pretty things more than May. Dresses in the newest colors and styles, coats, hats, wraps, purses, shoes. She even made sure I had the most dapper fashions in menswear too. I daresay we made a striking couple going out for Sunday strolls.

The little cottage was complete with an indoor bathroom. This was the one thing May had insisted on. After becoming accustomed to the modern plumbing at Maude's, no way would she even consider less. As a man, it was convenience I could take or leave, but May was adamant and would not give in. Her years of bathing in that cold spring back in the country and trips to the outhouse were over and done with.

We spent some happy days in that little cottage, each of us preoccupied with our own comings and goings. May would occasionally have her mother or one of her sisters come in from the country for a visit, usually when I was away. Fine with me. I'd just as soon not be under anyone's scrutiny.

After a couple of years renting the little cottage at an appallingly low rate thanks to Maude's generosity, we had stashed away enough money to become full-fledged homeowners. In fact, it was Maude's astute real estate knowledge that helped us buy our first house. Maude knew the property business well and was always knew what was available. With her help, we purchased an even newer home.

The newer place had an additional bedroom, as well as a separate breakfast room and butler's pantry. The extra space was sorely needed since May seemed to buy new dishes and dresses nearly every week. It didn't bother me too much; I was glad to keep her happy and out of my business. As long as I made sure there was plenty of money in our accounts she did not seem to mind my being away. It was not things that interested me, just my freedom to come and go and do as I pleased.

I enjoyed seeing Amanda and the children on a regular basis and even visiting her kinfolk some when I was up that way. The children were growing. Little Mandy was a beauty just like her mother, and little John was shooting straight up like a bean pole. I had a couple of other lady friends in outlying areas I enjoyed spending time with too. That little Ludie Anderson down in Crawford County was one of my favorites and quite a looker too. I surely did enjoy some fine evenings with her when I was down that way.

Meanwhile, business was booming. We had several moonshine suppliers. Between May's family, Amanda's kin, and occasionally a few others, we had a steady supply coming into town. If any one of them had an incident with the authorities we could always turn to the others to make up the difference. It was just good business sense not to put all your eggs in one basket. They'd make their weekly runs to Atlanta, make their drop-offs, and be nearly back home before daylight hit. My network of way stations and deliverymen made sure to cover their tracks and never use the same routes twice in a row. Most law officials looked the other way anyhow. Shoot, some of them were our best customers.

The tonic business was a bit more complicated. May knew I dabbled in this, but I kept her in the dark about the enormous profits. I depended heavily on Jim Willis, but I did have a couple of other pharmacists, and even a chemist I could call on if needed. All in all, it was riskier but the profits more than made up for that. Every once in a while I'd feel a pang of guilt if I heard about a death from an overdose, supposedly accidental, but for the most part, I felt like we were providing a service for folk dealing with aches and pains. Most were the result of military service or industrial accidents anyway. I supposed one could justify it as a type of humanitarian service. If a rich society dame took a little too much now and then, that was her fault, not ours.

Yes indeedy, life was easygoing and I was enjoying myself until things came to a head one day in 1904. I should have heeded Maude's warnings and known I'd get found out sooner or later. A fateful event was about to change my life forever.

12
MAY

    I can't believe I've been a married woman and lived in Atlanta almost five years now. I loved our first little cottage on Blackgum Street and set about fixing it up with a fervor. It was so nice to have our privacy. I furnished the modest white frame house in the latest fashions. I had already accumulated some housewares while we were at Maude's, but mostly I focused during that time on building my wardrobe. I was beginning to realize a few of those big dreams I had that first day in Atlanta when I saw the beautifully dressed ladies about town. Fashions were changing at a dizzying pace and I was continually amassing new things. Our little room at Maude's was overflowing with just my dresses.

    John and I were making money hand over foot and lived well, but there were some disturbing issues. I thought John was away far too much and often disappeared for days at a time. He provided well, but I had the nagging feeling there were things going on that I didn't know about. He was so vague about his whereabouts and his business endeavors. He always seemed to have plenty of cash and was generous, and I had more than enough money to get pretty much whatever I wanted.

In the beginning, he included me in arranging for his special deliveries. I knew the moonshine came in from the North Georgia Mountains where John had lived and where Uncle Wash kept several stills running. Bootlegging illegal liquor was considered a necessary evil and most officials looked the other way. Why, in Atlanta, the Law was some of our best customers! With rumblings all over about possible prohibition, the success of this part of our business was assured.

I wasn't so sure about the other dealings John was involved with, but I had a suspicion it had something to do with tonics. Good tonics were getting harder to find. I was especially fond of my DeepSleep Sweet Dreams Tonic. It was an essential part of my daily routine. Big Jim the pharmacist and Maude both cautioned me often about taking too much of the stuff. They knew I loved my Coca-Colas too and said that mixing the morphine-laced tonic with the cocaine-infused soft drink could be dangerous. I just laughed them off and went on about my own business.

Maude and I had grown to be quite close. I considered her my one true friend in the city. Oh, Mama or one of my sisters might come to visit for a day or so, but Maude was always up for some hen talk. I eventually figured out she had known about the pregnancy ruse all along, and we eventually laughed over the pretense we'd kept up those first few weeks John and I were in Atlanta. Maude was always game to help me find the best bargains. She'd rented us that first little cottage at a nominal rate and then helped us find our newest home to purchase. She was quite the businesswoman and never ceased to amaze me with her knowledge of folks and goings on in the city.

There were occasions now and then when she seemed a little distant. She'd get a faraway, wistful look if I mentioned I was in no hurry for a baby. She'd say houses and clothes might be nice, but eventually, women needed a good man and a soft, warm little baby in their arms. I'd always pass it off with a laugh, but sometimes I wondered about her past life. She never mentioned family or kinfolk and seemed to be all alone in the world except for her many business associates.

I was sometimes suspicious she knew more about John's background and business than I did, but as long as I had plenty of money to do as I liked I didn't let it bother me too much. John, Maude, and I seemed to all go about our daily lives carefree. Perhaps if I had known what the future held I would have taken some of those misgivings more seriously, but at the time it did not seem worthwhile. And then…

One gray winter day in 1904 while John was away I went to the post office to retrieve the mail. It was usually John who did this, but since he had been gone over a week I decided to get it myself. I was due a letter from Daisy, one of my younger sisters back home. The clerk handed over the packet and I spied Daisy's letter right off. I was so excited I didn't even look through the other letters. I ripped open Daisy's letter and read all the news from Covington.

When I got home I went through the letters, sorting them out. I noticed a letter addressed to John, posted from Ellijay, Georgia. I knew John had vaguely referred to some relatives living near Ellijay. This letter might be important news! If it was news of the bad sort, it might actually be good for us; if someone had died, maybe there was a will with something for John! He had never been specific about his parents or siblings, and I always attributed that to his wanting to move on with business in the city. As I turned the letter over in my hand, I noticed some differences about this letter from some others he'd shared with me. The handwriting was very fine, and I thought I detected the whiff of a flowery scent. I wanted to know the contents of the mysterious letter and my curiosity soon got the better of me.

I carefully opened the paper envelope without the slightest tear and pulled out two sheets of stationery, both covered with the same fine handwriting as the address. I could tell the letter had been scented, and there was something slightly familiar about that perfume-like smell: I knew I had smelled it before. No family news, good or bad, would come in a scented envelope. The first three words were enough to set me off….

> *My Dearest John,*
>   *It has been days seen we've last seen you, and I am missing you terribly. The snow up here has kept us inside, and the*

cold that seeps into my heart cannot be warmed in your absence. Little Mandy is beginning to read her letters and write her name, and she is quite the little mother to John. The dear children always ask, "When is Daddy coming home again? Whys does he have to work far away in the city?" I try to soothe their pleas, but even a mother's gentle touch does not quench their desire for you, my love.

I suddenly felt faint and sank to the divan. Should I go on? I couldn't stop myself and turned to the second page of the letter.

John, I fear we cannot go on like this. I must continually call on your father or mine for help with the household. I have tried to do both the chores of a husband and wife, but I find myself unable to physically continue, and, with trepidation, I add that I find myself not only unable but unwilling to continue such an arrangement. Please come home soon and let us resolve this matter.
Your Loving Wife,
*   Amanda Wright Collis*

My emotions ran the gamut from disbelief to astonishment, to hurt, to anger, to rage, and back to disbelief. I reread the contents of the letter, and my wrath began to pour forth. I was now pacing furiously from room to room. I picked up a glass vase and threw it against the floor. Then another, and another. How dare him! I would not be made a fool of! After stomping around and raging like rapids of water over huge boulders in the river after the spring rains, I began to realize I could not let him get away with this. But what was I going to do about it?

Slowly, I calmed down. This Mandy, obviously a child, had to be at least six or seven years old if she was learning to read and write! That meant, I determined as I ticked off on my fingers, the child had to have been born close to the time we were married. Did Uncle Wash know about this? Was that why he had mysteriously whisked John away to Stansells? This could explain John's days-at-a-time absences. It might also explain some of the reticence I sensed in his business associates to make conversation. I grew more incensed by the second. Maybe he had arranged for this Amanda to come to Atlanta and that's why he was at the Kimball Hotel that first day in town! Did this explain his frequent week-long business trips? All this time, had I been cast into the role of mistress? Had I been made a fool of? I cared for John, yes, and we enjoyed each other's company immensely, but I would not be made a fool.

I had to think and plan carefully if I was to going to do to John what he deserved and show him he would never get the better of me. I began to develop a plan. I would have to be extremely clandestine over the next few days as I plotted and wreaked my revenge. I knew enough about how John managed his money to get what I needed in financial support for a few months until I could untangle the sidelines I had established running off of John's business. Did Maude know about this? If she could be persuaded to see things my way, she might be useful. I had to get busy.

I sat down and began to make a list. I had places to go and things to take care of. After an hour of planning, I threw my wraps back on and headed out into the cold.

13
MAY

    I made my way to the Kimball Hotel and purchased a newspaper. While sipping tea in the lobby café, I scanned the advertisements, looking for rooms to let. There were several possibilities, all within close range of the Blackgum Street house. Just two streets over, a room in a house on Pittman Place sounded ideal and I was soon on the way. The location was perfect and the house looked clean and well-kept from the outside. When I rapped on the door with sharp knocks, the landlord answered immediately. I wasn't really expecting a man, but that was not going to stop my inquiry.

    "Good day, sir. I understand you have a room available for board?" The man appeared to be perhaps 50 to 55 years old, slightly stooped, with graying hair. He was dressed nattily in shirtsleeves with a tied bow at his neck. He smelled of shaving soap, and although his chin was bare he did have a dashing long handled mustache.

    "Why yes, Miss, I do have a room available. I was hoping to accommodate a quiet young man, but I might consider a woman.

Would you like to come in and see the room? My name is George Clark."

"Yes, thank you, Mr. Clark. I would like to see the room. I can assure you I am an independent woman and would not be a bit of trouble. You would barely even know I'm here. This is an ideal location and I am most interested if the price is right and the room acceptable."

"Certainly, Miss…"

"It's Mrs. Mrs. May Collis, but my husband and I have decided to live apart for the time being. No trouble mind you, just a temporary situation, perhaps a year. He is going to be away on business and we just could not see maintaining our home for just me. But I do want to stay in the city and not go back to my family in the country."

Mr. Clark was leading me into the front parlor. It was modestly but comfortably furnished and clean as a whistle. I wondered if there was a Mrs. Clark, but did not want to seem so forward as to ask.

"Oh, I see, Mrs. Collis. Well, sometimes business requires a man to be away. I can understand your predicament. I can understand you wanting to stay in the city. I came from the country years ago myself and would not give up my city conveniences, especially now that it's just me. My wife passed several months back. But don't let that concern you. I'm not looking for another. I have a housekeeper and another boarder, and I like to keep to myself and they do the same. I hope you're not looking to socialize. I like to keep a quiet, private house."

"Why, Mr. Clark, that sounds ideal. I'm exactly the same. I want a comfortable quiet place to keep to myself. I assure you I would not be a bother."

"Well, all right then. Let me show you the room and see what you think."

Mr. Clark led me through the dining room, also comfortable but modest. Off a small vestibule were several doors. He opened one and showed me a large bedroom. An iron bedstead, two wardrobes, a dresser and mirror, a side chair, a small writing desk and chair completed the furnishings. The room was light and had a faint lemony smell.

"Mrs. Smith, my housekeeper, has kept this room up. It's

clean and ready for occupancy. Her services would be included, of course. There's also a modern bathroom just next door you would be welcome to use."

"Oh, it's lovely, Mr. Clark. Just what I'm looking for. And having housekeeping services is very convenient. Just to let you know, I won't be in much during the daytime as long as the weather is pleasant, and I'm often out at supper too, so I won't require much in the way of board. I can always let your housekeeper know if I will be here for meals, and I promise I won't be much of an imposition."

"That sounds satisfactory, Mrs. Collis. If the cost is agreeable would you want to take the room right away?"

I responded as we started back to the front parlor.

"Yes, Mr. Clark. I would like to move in later today if that suits, or first thing tomorrow morning. I'm sure your cost is fair."

We concluded our business in the parlor. I was pleased with the arrangements and bid Mr. Clark good-bye, letting him know I would not be there for supper but would have some things delivered and then be back in the evening.

My next stop was the mercantile. I purchased a few household items I would need for the rented room and arranged to have them delivered to my new address on Pittman Place. Once I was satisfied with everything, it was time to be off to the bank for a key part of my plan.

The First Bank of Atlanta on Peachtree Street was imposing. I entered through the massive front doors and made my way to the teller bar. The marble columns and rich wood oozed the wealth of a city burgeoning with growth. Most bank employees recognized me, as I often made deposits and withdrawals for mine and John's various businesses. I mused that they were probably expecting me to make another large cash deposit, as I often did, but smiled to myself as they were going to be sorely disappointed.

Mr. Long greeted me. A weasely looking fellow with beady eyes and sharp features, he wasn't my favorite banker. He employed a pompous manner, probably in an effort to make up for his small size and high voice. Suspicious of his confidentiality, I asked to come around and meet with him privately at his desk. He showed me through the gate with deference and offered me the hard wooden chair across from his broad desk. Once seated on the other side, he arched his hands pretentiously on the desk surface as if to make himself appear larger. I assumed an air of superiority myself and did not hesitate to announce in a clipped voice that I wished to withdraw a large sum of money from our account.

Mr. Long's eyebrows shot up. "Oh! Mrs. Collis! I hope our services have been satisfactory. I do hope this is a temporary condition."

"We'll see about that," I replied curtly. "Just give me a withdrawal form, please."

We did not speak while I neatly inked an amount that nearly emptied the account, save for a small token amount just to keep it open.

As I handed the form back over, Mr. Long appeared not just surprised but shocked.

"Why, Mrs. Collis!" he exclaimed. "Are you and Mr. Collis about to make a large purchase? A new home maybe? This is quite a bit of cash. It leaves your account nearly empty!" Mr. Long said this lightly as if he were just making conversation, but I knew full well the garrulous banker was fishing for gossip. I wasn't about to be sweet-talked into revealing my plans for the cash. My reply was sharp.

"Let's just say there are some transactions in the works that require cash. It's really none of your business. And please, Mr. Long, I'd rather it not be announced to all of Atlanta!"

Mr. Long looked rather chagrined and nodded as he counted out the bills. His face was now white as a sheet, his lips pressed into a pale, thin line.

"As you wish, Mrs. Collis."

With no reply but recounting the bills, I stashed the cash safely in my fashionable new leather pocketbook with the clasp. So much roomier and more practical than those silly cloth reticules! I nodded curtly. "Good day, Mr. Long. And if you ever wish any of my money to be back in this bank you will not run to your cronies announcing this withdrawal."

Poor Mr. Long looked stricken. "Of course, Mrs. Collis, of course. Good day to you too."

I walked out the door and headed for Gilmer Street, arriving just in time for tea. Dear old Maude, she insisted on keeping this quaint custom even for just herself. I had to admit it was a delightful respite and could be just the right atmosphere for some girl-talk. I knocked lightly at her door.

Maude cracked the door then opened it wide for me to enter.

"Dear me, get yourself inside here May; you'll freeze to death out there on the doorstep!"

"Be glad to, Maudie. Am I in time for tea?"

"You certainly are. Right on time. Let me take your coat and you go on in the dining room. The tea table's all set."

Shrugging off my coat and closing the door I said, "Thank you kindly, Maudie. Are you expecting other company? Maybe John? I know he stops by sometimes."

Maude raised her hands in the air and said, "How should I know? I wasn't expecting you, and here you are! But seriously, as far as I know, it's just the two of us. I'm happy to say so, too. We're overdue for a nice private visit."

Although Maude and I had grown fond of each other, I wasn't totally convinced where Maude's allegiances would lie in a standoff between John and me, but I knew I needed to find out, and soon.

Maude said, "I'm sure not expecting John since he's been gone all week. I expect he would have sent word if he was coming to tea today. He usually will send word if he's stopping by. Before he left last week he said he had some business out in the country to attend to and might be gone for several days." Although Maude was looking at me innocently, I returned her look with a piercing stare. I knew my black eyes could be intimidating, and I often used them along with a hard look on my face for that very purpose. John had not even told me that much!

"Is that so? Just what do you think that business might be?" I asked as Maude poured the tea. I was trying to suppress my anger. My stern expression never wavered, but I was sure Maude could tell there was something different about my demeanor. I knew she had to know more about John's shenanigans than she let on.

Maude set the teapot down and looked me directly in the eye. "I'm not sure I understand, May. Is there something you want to ask me?" It was Maude's turn to put on a blank face and a rigid gaze.

"Well, Maude, is there something I should be asking? Is there something I should know?" was my pointed response.

The old woman sat back and sighed. She wiped her mouth delicately and set her hands on the table.

"If it's what I think it is, I wondered how long it would be before you caught on. I told John this was a dangerous path. I didn't much want to go along with it, but he paid me well. I've grown quite fond of you, May, and I don't want to see you hurt. I made sure he took care of you first."

I sat back too, relieved to have it out in the open. I asked questions and Maude responded. Before long I had all the answers I needed for now. It was almost amusing that here I had been using John for my own schemes and he had pulled the wool over my eyes. It would be rather funny if I wasn't so mad. I told Maude the story of how I had seduced John just so I could get to the city. Another surprise to me was that John had already told her all of that! We compared notes and stories, and it didn't take long before we were both laughing hysterically, as only two women who are formulating revenge against a man can do.

I explained how I already made plans to leave John, having taken a room and emptying his bank account. "That's it for the immediate future, but I'm going to give some thought to my long-term schemes. Can I count on your wisdom, Maudie?"

"Of course, dear. I consider it a matter of friendship. I like being of some use to somebody, especially a woman with the pluck you have. We womenfolk have to stick together if we're going to make it on our own."

"You are absolutely right about that, Maude. We women have to take care of ourselves. There's more than one way to skin a cat, and I've got my mind on several possibilities. Well, I'd best be on my way. I need to get settled in my new place. This tea and biscuits will do me for supper."

"Are you sure May? Let me wrap you up a few bites to take with you. You need to keep up your strength."

"Oh, all right, Maude. I'll take a few bites with me. I don't know what the food in this new house will be like, but I suspect it will do fine. Everything else appears to be in good order. I'll be back around tomorrow to let you know how things go."

Maude waddled off to the kitchen to wrap up some food

and I gathered my coat. We met back at the front door. "Thank you so much, Maudie; you are a dear friend. What would I do without you?"

"Oh, go on now, May. You'd do just fine. Anybody would be a fool to cross you. You take care in that new place and sleep well. I'll be wanting to hear all about it tomorrow."

We hugged and I went back out into the cold, facing unknown prospects yet again. *Lord, would I ever be at peace?*

14
JOHN

"Where the hell is she? Where's she gone? I demand to know the whereabouts of my wife!"

Maude gave me a steady look, but she had a slight grin and her eyes were twinkling with amusement. "Now John, which wife would you be referring to?"

It slowly dawned on me what must have happened. I sank defeated onto Maude's divan. "Aww Maude. I was a fool to think it could last much longer. How did she find out?"

Maude silently held out a letter addressed to me, postmarked Ellijay, Georgia. I immediately recognized Amanda's handwriting and scent. With dread, as if were a serpent, I took the letter from her hand and slipped out the scented pages. I smiled to myself as I read the first page, thinking of my darling Amanda, Mandy, and John. As I turned to the second page, however, my smile faded. I rubbed my face doggedly. This did not bode well.

"I've got to think this through," I said to Maude. "If you hear from May, and I know you're in touch with her, tell her I want to talk." I gathered my hat and headed out. I made several visits about town, making inquiries and trying to get clues about May's whereabouts. I might be needing a new residence myself and I knew I'd need cash, so I headed over to the bank.

"Good day, Mr. Collis!" Mr. Long greeted me cheerfully. "And how is Mrs. Collis today? Such a fine lady. Nice seeing her in the bank yesterday."

What? My suspicions were immediately aroused. What would May have been doing at the bank yesterday? My stomach began to knot and the blood drained from my head as the possibilities emerged in my thoughts. Apparently, this did not go unnoticed by Mr. Long.

"Are you all right sir? May I get you anything?"

My reply was terse and I began to regain some composure. I couldn't have it look like I was worried, upset, or ill. That wouldn't be good for business. I reassured Mr. Long. "I'm fine, Mr. Long. I'd like to have a little review and reckoning of my accounts. I'm going to need some cash funds for a few temporary endeavors."

Mr. Long looked a little surprised and somewhat confused. "Well, that's interesting, Mr. Collis. Come on around to my desk where we can speak privately." Mr. Long busied himself in his files. I had a sense of apprehension as I made my way to Mr. Long's desk. I did not think his rummaging in his files was a good sign. Finally, Mr. Long produced a ledger. He silently slid the ledger over towards me and turned it right side up so I could see for myself.

Immediately, I saw the $2,000 cash withdrawal made the previous afternoon. I also saw the balance line - $25.00. I pushed the ledger back to Mr. Long, sat back in the chair, and sighed. I had originally had second thoughts about allowing May access to the account, but I had become confident as we forged a partnership that seemed to meet both of our requirements. And here I had thought I was the more devious half of that partnership! I had to give May credit – she was no fool. I knew she had been skimming the account for some time. I chose to ignore it and attributed it to her frivolous purchases of clothing, personal items, and, of course, her precious DeepSleep Sweet Dreams tonic. I knew she also imbibed a little product at times too. Her penchant for treats and Coca-Colas was no secret either. But had all those small withdrawals gone towards such frivolities? Or had she been secretly squirreling away funds for some time? As I thought about the possibilities, I was finally able to respond calmly.

"Thank you, Mr. Long. It looks as if my wife has already taken care of the situation. Please give me the remaining $25 and close the account."

Mr. Long began to splutter, but I took my hat and stood up with my palm out, indicating there was to be no more discussion of the matter. Mr. Long walked to the drawer, took out $25 and handed it over. I pocketed the cash and stuck out my right hand. We shook hands solemnly. I'd let Mr. Long draw his own conclusions about our transaction.

I walked towards the depot. I began to scheme and devise my own plan for the future. Maybe I'd be better off without May. Let her go her own way. She wouldn't be able to skim money off my accounts and I wouldn't have to put up with her. The more I thought about it, the more comfortable I became with the idea. Oh, it would take a few months to make up the $2,000, but things were going well and money was coming in steadily. I'd just call in a few debts and be on my own two feet in no time.

I made arrangements to sublease the house on Blackgum Street. I had no interest in staying there among May's fancy furnishings. I stayed at Maude's a few days now and then when I was in town, but I was out of town quite a bit and managed to avoid running into May when I was there. For all I knew, she had gone back to the country. Well, good riddance. I wouldn't have to bother with any formal proceedings. Any wife who ran off and left her husband would not care about legalities and was considered a deserter. I knew May would not let marriage or divorce get in the way of whatever plans she'd made. Eventually, I avoided Maude too. I could sense she naturally took a woman's side in this. I would miss her jovial company but there were plenty enough places a man could find pleasant female companionship; you just had to know where to look.

15
MAY

    I spent my first few days on my own getting settled in my new room, meeting with Maude several times, and making my own business arrangements with numerous contacts throughout the city. Together, we established quite a network of associates. The illegal whiskey business, as well as the tonic business, provided more than enough for both of us to live comfortably, although the income could at times be sporadic. Maude had her already established real estate enterprise that supported her well and didn't really need the extra income, so she gave me the greater portion. Still, I was a tad anxious about all these changes. I cunningly convinced Mr. Willis to increase the amount of morphine in my DeepSleep Sweet Dreams tonic. He was reluctant but seemed sympathetic. I knew I was increasingly dependent on the tonic but justified it to myself in light of recent events.

    John seemed to have disappeared from the city. At first, Maude had allowed him to stay in her boarder's room when he was in town, but then one day he left and was not seen or heard from for months. I secretly followed his former business partners from time to time, but there was never any sign of John. Maude investigated too, but neither of us could find out anything about his whereabouts. I was conflicted. I wanted to remain angry at John for his deception, and I wanted revenge, but it was hard to stay mad when he wasn't around to remind me!

    Maude and I were bringing in plenty of money. I was sending cash home to Ma and Pa, who were barely managing. It helped that my sisters were all married off now except for Ola, the youngest. My only brother Oliver had not married yet, and he was a big help to Ma and Pa. They were living next to my sister Sadie and her husband and daughter, and they all were dirt poor. I wanted to be able to do more, but I needed to build up some reserves first.

    Now that I was on my own, I missed John. There was that small part of me that cared for him. I missed our companionship, the fun banter, the collusion in questionable business dealings, the generous income he produced, and, to my surprise, I missed having a lover. I could remedy that part easily, but I was wary and put off from men. I would not jump into any arrangements so quickly again without knowing the man's background.

    I went about my daily work. I had been able to convince several of John's contacts to transfer their dealings to me and Maude. It didn't take too much convincing, considering John was hardly ever in town. Mr. Willis and I were getting increased interest in the tonic. As the rumors of regulation grew, folks seemed to want to stock up. The same thing was happening with the moonshine. Calls for some type of prohibition were becoming more frequent.

    I was living comfortably, although a step down from our last home. I had left my housewares and furnishings but brought my clothing and accessories with me. I had a beautiful wardrobe of the latest fashions and paid Hattie well to keep me in new styles. Skirts had begun to rise, younger women were showing their ankles and there were more choices in colors. I was fairly conservative, but I did like having more choices. I especially liked the accessories. Fancy hats, furs, shoes, purses, and jewelry. I had accessories to go with all my dresses and outfits. Atlanta was booming with retail shops and I could spend a whole day shopping. Many women were buying ready-to-wear garments now. I liked having Hattie make my dresses, skirts, and shirtwaists, but I shopped the stores for coats, underthings, and all the accouterments. I still had my slim figure, and I enjoyed dressing like the ladies I'd first seen when I came to Atlanta. That part of my dream had been fulfilled.

But I wasn't satisfied. There was still the desire for a fashionable home. I was still boarding, although in a bit nicer area of town. Without a house of my own, I couldn't purchase furnishings or housewares. I longed for a place of my own to set up housekeeping. Not that I wanted to be my own housekeeper, but just so I could have visitors and entertain. I roamed the furniture and department stores, mentally furnishing a place of my own. Hopefully it would not be much longer before I would be arranging furniture in a real house.

Making business arrangements, shopping, and visiting with Maude was just about my only social contacts. I did read voraciously and would occasionally write letters for pay for those associates who were illiterate. Little did I know then what an important role letters would play in my future. Thank goodness my mama and daddy had not kept me from learning. School was a luxury back in Newton County, and usually, only boys had the opportunity for an education. I didn't let that stop me. I about drove Ollie mad having him tell me everything he learned at school. I practiced on my own with whatever I could get my hands on. I even tolerated the uppity folks at the Baptist church so I could read the Bible and the hymnbooks. When I was little, I spent hours at the store in Covington looking through newspapers, almanacs, and whatever else they had on hand. The advertisements of the latest fashions and the news from the city opened my eyes to the world beyond dirt-poor rural Georgia. That's where my dreams were born.

And now those dreams were coming true. At least partly. And yet, I couldn't say I was happy. I tried to put it out of my mind that here I was, getting exactly what I'd wanted, but somehow it wasn't enough. I went on, day by day, with the help of my tonic. Sometimes I wouldn't even remember if I'd taken it or not, so I'd take another dose. I was sinking into a melancholy unlike anything I'd ever experienced, and I doctored it with increasing doses of good ol' DeepSleep Sweet Dreams Tonic. Something was missing in my life but I just couldn't put my finger on what it was.

16
MAUDE

Unlike May, I cared nothing for material things. Oh, I enjoyed being comfortable, and I had enough legal rental properties for me to be satisfied even without some of my less-than-legal business ventures. If there was one thing I'd learned in this life, things and people could be taken away in an instant. I didn't like to talk about what happened so many years ago. It only dredged up terrible memories. There didn't seem to be enough sweet ones to outweigh the horror of that one night, and I didn't like to dwell on what might have been. Instead, I chose to live a meager existence and try to help other women out however I could. If it involved a little hanky-panky to get them on their own, then so be it. I didn't create the social order that only recognized women if they were attached to a man, but I sure could ease the way for smart and persistent women to become independent within that order. Women like May.

I had grown very fond of May. She was like the daughter I never had, or perhaps I should say the daughter I *almost* had. Oh, I knew some of my more clandestine activities were not considered moral by the society crowd, but there was a whole lot of them who liked to enjoy the benefits of such goings-on. And there just weren't many opportunities for a woman to make it on her own in a city like Atlanta these days. I had seen some progress in my years here, but if you considered only legal business, opportunities to become an independent female entrepreneur were still almost non-existent. I hated to see a sharp mind go to waste. When I realized May's determination and cleverness, I knew she could be my ideal protégé. I just hoped I could convince her not to repeat mistakes I'd made.

I had carefully built my relationships and hidden my secrets. In that respect, May and I were much alike. At one time, at a much younger age, I was like her. I craved the finer things of life and I managed all right to achieve that desire. But I also wanted a family, someone to love me and someone I could love. Children. I thought I was well on my way to having it all until that fateful occurrence. I never knew such pain existed until I lost those I loved. I tried to give May some insight without revealing the skeletons in my wardrobe, but she never took me too seriously. I hoped that she would eventually come around.

For now, I could only encourage her and help her be independent. There was no pushing a woman like May, once she set her mind to something. Without that rogue of a husband, she would probably do better on her own. That is if he had ever been her legal husband. I knew too well how men could come and go. For all I knew, John could have other supposed wives. Maybe even children, though he did seem genuinely smitten with little Mandy and John. Yes, May would make it. She might have some rough patches, but I believed that in the end, she would come out all right.

Still, I did not know what a precarious state of mind May was in, but I was about to find out.

On a hot July afternoon, I called at May's boarding house on Pittman Place, hoping to find her there to discuss some possible clients. She had told me she'd be home by early afternoon, and it was two o'clock when I got there. I knocked and knocked on the door to her room. I wasn't terribly concerned, but something told me not to walk away. I got the landlord, Mr. Clark, to unlock the door. He was hesitant at first, but when I explained that I had a prior arrangement to meet May, he obliged, then he stood by the door as if to make sure I wasn't up to anything as I walked in.

"Oh! My Lord a mercy! Help! Mr. Clark! Help me, please!"

May was sprawled on the floor of the room between the bed and the door. Her hair was tumbling from its bun and the hem of her shirtwaist was pulled out from her skirt. She was in her stocking-feet. She did not respond as we called her name and shook her. I even slapped her face. Mr. Clark put his head to her breast and declared that her heart was beating, but only faintly.

"We need to get her to the Grady," I said desperately. I was sure he didn't want one of his rooms tainted by a death. People had funny ideas about that sort of thing, as I well knew. Mr. Clark scooped up the slight May in his arms. I was close behind as he headed out the front door to the street. The Grady Hospital was just a few short blocks away.

"I'll just carry her there," Mr. Clark hollered. "She don't weigh no more than a feather!"

That was fine with me. I figured he'd make the distance more quickly on foot than by the time we found a wagon or carriage. May, so tiny, was not a burden at all.

By the time we arrived at the hospital, May was gray and limp. I feared she was already dead. She was quickly taken away by the nurses, and I followed right after them, ignoring their orders to stay put. Mr. Clark made a hasty retreat – he didn't want to be involved. A doctor was quickly called in. Now, with an audience of only the doctor, I told him what I suspected: an overdose of morphine, accidental of course, though one could never be sure. I knew May had been increasing her tonic, and she wouldn't be the first young woman to die of an accidental overdose, or worse, be left in a state that required constant care. It was common for women to become addicted to their tonics.

May's condition was precarious and for a while, her life hung by a thread. After a few hours, the doctors were able to get her stabilized. She was still not conscious, but no longer on death's door, and the doctors assured me she would survive. Once I was convinced of this, I instructed them to provide the best of care, and I would be responsible for any charges.

Oh Lordy, what should I do now? Poor May had no one in the city. I thought things through as I started home. I realized that as fond as I was of May, I could not take on the responsibility of caring for her. And who knew if this was just a stroke of luck that she survived? What if the next time she did end up dead? I surely did not want another death on my hands either. I decided to let her family know she was "ill," and that I was going to send her home to the country. Although it was nearly dark, I headed straight to the telegraph office, addressing the message to Sanford T. Wheeler, Stansells, Newton County, Georgia:

> **Urgent... STOP... May ill... STOP... Sending her home... STOP...**
> **Train arrives Covington depot 2 pm July 5... STOP**

The doctors had told me May could leave the hospital the next day if she continued to improve, but that she should not be left on her own. I figured I could bring her home and stay with her overnight. I would gather a few of her things and send her home on the train the next day. If I didn't hear from her family or if she protested, I'd just have to get more creative. It was home to bed for me. I was going to be plenty busy the next couple of days.

17
MAUDE

When a telegraph arrived the next morning I was relieved to read that May's brother Oliver would collect her at the depot. I hoped this did not mean her ma or pa were unable to come for her. I knew they had little to live on, and her pa especially had not been well, but I couldn't worry about that right now. I had my hands full just getting May taken care of.

I got to The Grady about noon. May lay expressionless in the bed and did not acknowledge my presence. I assured the staff I had made arrangements for her to be taken care of for a few days. A nurse stepped out and returned with permission from the doctor for May to be released. Still, May's expression did not change at this news. The doctor himself stepped into the room. We endured his lecture about the dangers of tonics and his warning that the next time she might not be so lucky. He advised her to quit the tonic altogether. May remained blank and did not speak a single word. She just stared at the wall. I was hoping this was just her fierce independence and not an indication that she was going to be impaired. I'd heard tales that you never could tell what a person might be like after such a brush with death involving morphine.

I got May dressed in her street clothes and walked her

slowly out of the hospital. She allowed me to lead her like a docile sheep. I chatted brightly, but she only nodded or uh-huhhed in response. "I declare, May, isn't it a pretty day? Not too hot for the beginning of July, just pleasantly warm. I imagine out in the country at your folks' it's even a touch cooler."

"Uh huh."

"As a matter of fact, I've taken care of all the arrangements for you go home for a spell. I know you miss your sisters and your ma and pa would love to see you!"

May nodded.

"Now don't you worry about a thing. I'm going to stay with you today and tonight. We'll gather your things and let Mr. Clark know you're going away for a bit so he can let your room. I've already got you a ticket for the one o'clock train to Covington tomorrow, and Ollie's going to be meeting you there. Now, how does that sound?"

We were at the walkway up to the Pittman Place boarding house. May stopped and turned to me. In a tired voice, she said, "That's just fine, Maude. That's just fine. I'm so tired. Thank you for taking care of everything."

Those were the last words she spoke that day. When we got in her room, I put her to bed where she immediately went to sleep. I started packing up her things. I would store her personal housewares and her winter clothes, but most of the warm weather clothing I packed in her valise. As I went through her belongings I found tonic bottles stashed away in every nook and cranny. My lord, how much was she taking? My first impulse was to pour out the poison, but on second thought I put the bottles in my own bag. One never knew when one might have need of a good strong dose. I stepped out of the room briefly to inform Mr. Clark that May would be leaving. I daresay this produced quite a look of relief on the landlord's face, and I couldn't much blame him for it.

May did not awake all that evening. She slept straight through until morning. I did not sleep and checked on her often, making sure to listen for her breathing. She seemed a bit restless, tossing and turning, but she never came fully awake. When she finally awoke the next morning, she still appeared tired, but was a bit more conversational, although not her usual prattling self. Our conversation was still mostly one-sided.

"Why, good morning May! I hope you're feeling better this morning. I've got some good tea and biscuits here for you. Try to eat – you're going to need to build your strength back up."

"Thank you, Maude," was her only response, but she did drink the tea and eat every one of the biscuits.

"Now, I've got everything packed that you'll need back home. I'll take care of your winter things and housewares while you're away. Everything will be safe and secure until you're ready to retrieve them. I had a porter bring over my trunks. He'll pick them up and get them back to my place. He'll deliver your valise to the train station too and have it checked. I thought we might take a nice stroll, do a little window shopping, and then have lunch out at a café before we get you settled on the one o'clock train. How does that sound?" I knew these were May's favorite activities and hopefully would keep her mind off more trying matters.

"Whatever you say, Maude. Whatever you say," May responded. I had to hold back tears as I observed this unknown creature. I had never seen May like this. She was usually the one making the plans and flitting about, the very essence of vivaciousness. It was so sad to see her act like a lost soul that needed leading about. Hopefully after a stay in the country, the old May I knew and loved would return.

We took our stroll and window-shopped. May had only the briefest responses to my attempts to engage her in conversation. After a while, I gave in and we just strolled in silence. She made a few polite comments over lunch. I waved her off as the train pulled out, but she only gave the merest hint of a raised hand then stoically turned her face away from the window.

I went back home, exhausted from trying to put on a cheery façade for May and sick with worry about how she would actually fare. I was getting too old for such drama. I took care of a few business necessities and got May's things stowed away for safe-keeping. I thought about letting John know what had happened, but then I thought better of that idea. I didn't really know how to get a message to him anyway. Even if I did know how to reach him, he would not care. Having missed tea time, I had a light supper and went to bed. My days of sitting up all night with sick folk were long gone, and my soul was as weary as my old bones.

The next morning, feeling well-rested, I made plans to take

care of further business. I thought I might make the rounds of May's usual associates and let them know she was going to be away and if they had need of anything they should contact me instead. I thought that would be best; no need of announcing her true circumstances. When I started out, my first stop was usually to buy a paper and find a comfortable spot for reading and watching passers-by. When I got to page nine in The Atlanta Constitution, I realized my plan would be impossible.

> **The Atlanta Constitution**
> Miss Willie Collis, 30 years old, of 17 Pittman's Place, was sent to Grady Hospital yesterday afternoon suffering from an overdose of morphine taken accidentally. For a time the life of the woman was despaired of, but hard work on the part of the hospital physicians had her out of danger in a short time.

    I did not know how serious May's addiction was. Her brother, Oliver, wrote me from time to time. Occasionally the letters were encouraging; May had seemed like her old self, May was helping her mama with the household duties, May was infatuated with her sister Sadie's children. But more often than not, there were dark tones to the letters; May had not gotten out of bed in three days, May had destroyed one of her favorite dresses, May had played mean tricks on Sadie's daughter, scaring the poor child half to death.
    I wanted to blame these behaviors on her morphine addiction. I did not want to think that May was going mad at such a young age without some specific cause. True, there were more and more reports of the dangers associated with the tonics and the long-term effects on those who took morphine for legitimate painful ailments, mostly the Confederate veterans. The soldiers' homes were full of old men gone raving mad or, perhaps worse, catatonic, from the effects of their medicine. It seemed from Ollie's letters that May alternated between the two states of mind.
    From time to time, Oliver would write to say he was sending May to me in Atlanta for a visit when her strangeness was getting on everybody in Covington's nerves. I had taken on her clients and

when she was in town, we would make business calls. The clients and I never let on that she was actually not the one in charge. It was a silent agreement that seemed prudent at the time. Of course, I made sure May had income, and we often shopped and dined out. May rarely mentioned John on these visits, but I knew from some of her infrequent comments she had not forgiven or forgotten. When she did mention him, it was with bitter vengefulness. It seemed she was still so caught up in that, she could not move on. Things went on like this for months and eventually stretched into a year. About a year and a half after her overdose, May came to town for a visit. This time, she announced she would not be returning to the country.

"Maude, I believe I'm ready to move back to town. My welcome's wore out back home. Have you got anything suitable?"

I was not really surprised. May had stayed away longer than I'd thought she would. I knew she had become accustomed to the advantages the city offered and would not tolerate a rural existence indefinitely. She had seemed more stable during her last couple of trips to town, so it seemed as good a time as any for her to make her stay permanent.

"Well May, I might have just the spot over on Bush Street. Let's go look at it this afternoon. It's real clean and close to the streetcar line. Got lots of conveniences nearby too."

"I just knew you would have a place, Maude. I'm ready to move in. I'll send for my things back home and then get the belongings you've been storing for me. Who knows, once I get re-established, I might just find me another man. Just for companionship, mind you. Gets pretty lonely sometimes for a gal on her own, if you know what I mean."

"I do know what you mean May, but you just take your time and be careful. Last time you jumped from the frying pan to the fire, and you sure don't want that to happen again. Be sure any fellow you meet up with is on the up and up. You don't want what happened with John to happen again, that old snake."

May smiled knowingly. "Oh, you don't have to worry about that Maude. I'll be careful. As for John, he'll get his comeuppance. Just you wait and see. I heard he's married another woman! Likely she doesn't know what she's gotten herself into, poor soul. Oh well, she'll find out soon enough." May sat back and smiled to herself as if I wasn't even in the room.

I felt a bit uneasy. May could be just talking, but I didn't like her expression or the insinuations she seemed to be making. I recalled her brilliance at manipulating people and getting what she wanted at whatever cost. The hard glittery look in her eyes didn't seem quite right. In fact, it was downright frightening. I'd have to keep an eye on her.

"All right then, we'll go over to Bush Street and have a look this afternoon. We can get you moved in over the next few days. You just concentrate on getting settled and don't give that scoundrel John or his new wife another thought." I had heard that John was married again, but I was not about to share that with May. Should have known there was no keeping secrets from her. I'd just have to try and keep her preoccupied with other matters.

Within the week, May was settled in her new place. She seemed happy enough there. It wasn't the fanciest place in town, but it would do for now. It was on the fringes of the old Hobo Hollow, once an extremely disreputable part of town. The police had cleaned out that notorious domicile of drunks and women of the vilest nature. Those who remained were down on their luck poor folks who couldn't afford much better. At least Bush Street was a few blocks over from Haynes and Markham, the heart of the Hollow. It would do for May until she could build back up some resources, and she would be close to her clientele.

I kept a fairly close watch on May. All seemed pretty normal, or normal for her, anyway. She was gaining back the confidence of her clients, and I slowly released contacts back to her. It was slow going though, and her status was nowhere near what it had been when she and John were together. I just hoped she could stay clear-minded enough to manage on her own.

18
MAY

    It felt good to be back in the city. I enjoyed getting out and about, reconnecting with my business associates. I knew the time was ripe for the moonshine customers. Lots of folks wanted to have a supplier established in the event prohibition was instituted. I'd heard stories about back in 1885 when some do-gooders attempted to pass it for Atlanta, but couldn't get enough popular support to maintain their campaign. But now, twenty years later, the rumblings were getting louder. The church folks and the officials who curried public opinion were becoming much more vocal. I could see the writing on the wall, and I intended to be in a position to take full advantage of a ban on liquor by the drink. If the saloons were run out of business, I was determined to oblige those who thought it a man or woman's right to take a nip if they wanted it.

    While I worked diligently to establish suppliers and runners, I was also carrying out a sideline of a different nature. I had learned my lesson with the tonic, and although there were times I still craved the release it gave, I had curbed my intake substantially. Between that, calls for prohibition, and the Coca-Cola Company no longer putting real cocaine in their drinks, it was quite a challenge to find legal ways to address one's nervous conditions. I managed to find a way, though. Revenge was sweet and went a long way towards making up for the mental effects of pharmaceuticals. It did not matter one speck to me that my plan for revenge was not legal; at least not in the beginning, anyway.

I kept my secret from Maude, knowing she wouldn't approve of my scheme. I had mentioned to her that John was back in town and had a new wife. I tried to make it sound matter of fact and not act like it bothered me at all. But it did. I wanted John, and if I couldn't have John, I wanted his money. I was entitled! After all, he owed me. I swore that no other woman was going to have him and his money, so I plotted my revenge.

It didn't take much to find out where John and the new missus were living. I frequented some of his old haunts and eventually, he showed up. I followed him to where they were living on Tennelle Street. It was clear across town from me, but that made no matter. It was a step up from where John and I had last lived together. That just made me more determined. Who did he think he was, throwing me off for some biddy, then moving her into a place nicer than what we'd ever had? I would show him.

First, I'd have to take care of him. My scheme was to make him sick, then light into his new wife, Ludie, while she was distraught. With John sidetracked, she would have no choice but to give in to my demands for money. I spent several days watching their comings and goings. After learning their routines, and when I was sure they were both out of the house, I made my way around back. Not many folks kept doors locked in that part of town.

I left various poisons in provisions and products that I suspected only John would use or eat. A little arsenic powder in his tobacco tin, a little camphor oil in his pomade, a touch of this and a touch of that. I kept this up for several weeks as I watched and waited for some results. Just when I was about to despair this wasn't going to work, I began to see results. It was March of 1905. When John was out, he did not look well. His skin had a sallow tone. He walked with an unsteady gait. He just didn't appear to be his usual jovial self with a spring in his step. I stepped up my doses considerably over the next two weeks.

By mid-March, John rarely left the house, but Ludie would come and go often. It was harder now to keep up with the poisoning since John was always home. When Ludie was out, I would follow her and eavesdrop on conversations with her acquaintances. By the end of the third week of March, I learned that John had been taken to Grady and was considered seriously ill. I almost laughed out loud at that. Seriously ill! Oh yes, he was ill all right. I decided it was time to put into play the second part of my scheme, and it was not a minute too soon.

    Back at my own house on Bush Street, I sat down to pen a letter. The fact that I learned to read and write had served me well. Many women never became literate, and as a result, their opportunities for independence were very limited. Of course, I counted it inconsequential that my skills were often used for less than moral purposes. In my mind, if it moved me toward my goals it was moral enough for me.

Dear Mrs. Collis,

    I use that title doubtfully. You should know that your husband, John, has had several women go by the title, and sometimes more than one at a time. I know this from personal experience. However, I am the true and rightful Mrs. Collis, having married John on September 10, 1898, in Newton County, Georgia, and never having been legally divorced from him. It did not matter that another woman had claimed the title before me or even that she had children with John. I was and am the true and rightful Mrs. John Collis.

    I am now demanding that you release my husband from his supposed marriage with you. You are nothing but a whore as was that silly bitch Amanda. John owes me a great deal of money. If you cannot arrange to pay me $1,000 within the next week, I will find you and kill you.

> *I warn you that I will find you and hunt you down. I will murder you as the harlot you are deserves to be murdered. Your guts will spill onto the street and your blood will flow into the gutter.*
>
> *If you do not release John immediately and get me the money, I swear I am going to kill you and then get the money to pay my way to hell.*
>
> *Signed,*
> *Willie Collis*

    I went immediately and posted the letter. If John was really seriously ill, I did not want to delay. Although I felt sure he would recover, I did not want to take any chances on losing out on the money. I figured Ludie would comply with my request, then head back to wherever she had come from. John would recover and find that Ludie had abandoned him, and I would be right there to comfort him. We would once again be business partners and lovers.

    I kept up my watch at the house on Tennelle Street. After two days had gone by without a sign of anyone leaving the house, it crossed my mind that my plans might not go as I had anticipated. Apparently, John was still in the hospital, and Ludie was either staying there with him or was afraid to step out of her house. The next morning I stayed home, thinking on what my next step should be.

    My mid-morning biscuits and coffee were interrupted by a loud banging on the front door. I didn't have many callers, and those who did come usually weren't so boisterous. I jerked the door open angrily, ready to light into whoever was causing such a commotion. I was surprised to find myself face to face with not one, but two police officers.

    "Mrs. Willie Collis?" The larger of the two men spoke loudly.

    "Who wants to know?" I asked.

    "Don't get smart with me, lady. We've determined this is

the residence of Mrs. Willie Collis. We also have it on good word that you are the aforementioned Mrs. Collis."

"Oh, you do, do you? What if I am? I haven't done anything illegal. Why would you be wanting me?"

The more reticent officer spoke up. "Well, Mrs. Collis, we beg to differ with you on that account. Seems a Mrs. Ludie Anderson Collis claims you have threatened to kill her and have sent obscene letters through the United States Mail."

"I don't know what you're talking about, officer. Now, I've got things to do." As I tried to close the door in their faces the larger man stepped into the way and prevented me from shutting the door.

"You're right about that, Mrs. Collis. You do have something to do. You're under arrest and you're coming with us down to the station house."

"Well, I never!" I blustered.

The quieter man spoke. "You can tell it to the court, Mrs. Collis. Now come along peacefully. We're sure you don't want to cause a scene here on your front stoop. Might scare off some of your regulars, if you get my drift."

I gave him a cold stare. It seemed these officers were aware of some of my illegal dealings, which was really no surprise. Most of the force and elected officials in the city were on my client list. If they weren't on mine, then they were on Maude's or John's. "Just let me get my handbag," I said as I left the door open and stepped into my bedroom. "I'll be right out."

Think, May, think! What are you going to do now? I had no choice but to go with the police since I didn't have enough cash on hand to bribe them. Of course, I would deny everything; it was that whore Ludie's word against mine! I was well connected with some of the officials and there was not a chance this was going to amount to much more than a little misunderstanding. I tucked at my hair, put on a hat and light wrap, and gathered a few items in my handbag. I rejoined the officers and said cheerily, "All right gentlemen, let's go."

19
MAUDE

It was a Friday in late March. About mid-morning I was looking over the Atlanta Constitution. I enjoyed reading the paper and it kept me up on the latest news around town. Not only that, but the Constitution had a state and national presence. Sometimes it was amusing to read about the wife in Nebraska who tried to sell her husband for $300, or sad to read about two children that died in a fire in New York City. It was concerning to read that the peach crop was nearly wiped out in the last cold spell. That did not bode well for some of my business associates who were planning on the peaches to bring in a good amount of cash this year. And there were always plenty of editorial opinions too. Today, Mr. Howell, the editor, was blasting the Federal courts and judges.

I had not heard from May since earlier in the week but wasn't worried about it. I just figured she was busy. She seemed to have a renewed vigor since she'd moved back to town. I attributed this to her wanting to move on and get over the past. As I moved over to the right side of page six, an interesting headline caught my eye:

Janet Hogan Chapman Ed.D.

HIS TWO WIVES FIGHT OVER HIM

Just below that, the sub-headline read:

John Collis' Present Wife Prosecutes his Divorced Wife

Oh Lordy – what had May gotten herself into now? I read on…

> Lying ill at the Grady hospital, John Collis is not aware of what a terrible row is going on between his two wives, one of whom was divorced from him two years ago.
> The row has reached such a stage that now wife No. 1 is now held in the tower on complaint of wife No. 2.
> Wife No. 2 had wife No. 1 arrested on the charge of writing to her obscene letters through the mail. The prisoner was arraigned in the recorder's court yesterday afternoon and the case was transferred to United States Commissioner Colquitt's court, and the commissioner held the woman in a $200 bond, which she was unable to give.
> John Collis first married Miss Willie Wheeler, and about two years ago he was divorced. Last fall he married Miss Ludie Anderson and went to keeping house at 69 Tennelle Street. The first wife was living in the country but recently moved to Atlanta and has been living at 18 Bush Street.

> A short while ago Mrs. Collis No 2 received a letter with the signature of "Willie Collis" in which the writer said she wanted her husband back again and she proceeded to use some very abusive language to wife No. 2.
> Wife No 2 stated to the recorder that she was afraid to walk on the streets as the first Mrs. Collis had threatened to kill her on sight.
> One of the expressions used in the letter was "I am going to kill you and then get the money to pay my way to hell."
> Wife No 1 denies writing the letter.
> Collis is very ill and so far knows nothing about the trouble between his two wives.

I sat back and sighed heavily. I had been so wrong in assuming May was moving on! Apparently, she had been plotting all along and it was no wonder I hadn't heard from her as much lately. Now, I knew May had access to $200 even if she didn't have it on her person, and who in their right mind would go to The Tower with money in their pocket? The Tower had quite a reputation. It was the third building to house the Fulton County Jail and had been completed just eight years ago. At the time it was said to be an "elegant" building, which I always thought was an unusual choice of words for a prison, but it did have indoor plumbing, heating, an elevator, and several wings. It became known as "The Tower" because of the 138-foot tall rounded tower on one corner. The massive structure of gray granite nearly had the appearance of a castle, and if you didn't know it was a prison you might think it "elegant." Knowing its true purpose as a prison gave it a dark air of gloom. I'd never been inside even though I'd known plenty of folks who had. The story on the street was that although it had started out clean, inside and out, the interior was already run down I was trying to imagine May being locked up in a filthy cell in the cold gray building. I would see to it she wasn't there long.

But before I headed out, I read the article again so I would know exactly what I was up against. I surely did not put it past May writing such a letter. I had seen glimpses of her vengefulness and I shouldn't be surprised she would go to such an extreme. And what was this in the piece about a divorce? As far as I know, May never received word of any divorce. Knowing John, I doubted this was true. He probably just told Ludie a made-up story, in case she found out about a previous wife. Most likely, he didn't want her to be surprised like May had been when she learned about Amanda. I was also concerned about John, so sick in the hospital. If he was too ill for Ludie to even tell him about the letter, then he must be real bad off. Not that I had much fondness for him anymore, but I didn't wish him such ill will that he should die. I even had a niggling thought in my mind that it sure did seem odd that John should be so ill just at this time. I would not put anything past May. Could she have something to do with John's illness?

I dressed warmly and headed out. Although it was late March, spring had not come to Atlanta yet. I figured I'd nose around a bit, talk to some of my detective and court clerk friends. Maybe I could find out which way the winds blew with this Judge Colquitt and see if I could do anything to remedy the situation. Since it was Friday afternoon, I didn't know if I could get much accomplished with most offices closed for the weekend. Maybe I should try to talk with Ludie first?

I made my way to Tennelle Street. There was no one home at number 69. Perhaps Ludie was at the hospital? I could go there on the pretense of visiting John. I had no idea if Ludie knew that I was an acquaintance of John, or of May for that matter. It was just a short walk to Grady. I made inquiries at the desk and was directed to the second-floor ward. As I was going up the stairs, The Grady seemed a busy place. Nurses scuttled back and forth. A few visitors were making their way down as others made their way up. A clerk or two hurried by with arms of papers or supplies. The hospital smelled antiseptic and appeared to be clean. It had opened in 1892 and recently been remodeled with the addition of an operating theatre.

There were several men folks in the second floor waiting lobby. Most had worried expressions on their faces. If you were sick enough to be in The Grady you were seriously ill, or even close to death. Folks sick with run-of-the-mill maladies were kept at home. Only those with the direst emergencies or illnesses were admitted to the hospital, usually brought in by a rubber wheeled, horse-drawn ambulance and unloaded at the front portico. A nurse was speaking in low tones with the only woman present. The woman looked very distraught. I edged closer hoping to overhear mention of a name.

The nurse, who looked rather young to me, was saying, "We just can't say if Mr. Collis will recover or not, Mrs. Collis. But please don't give up hope. It's in God's hands now. Dr. Elkin himself has been in to see him. You can't get any better doctor than that."

The now tearful Mrs. Collis said, "Thank you, nurse, thank you. I do hope the good Lord sees fit to bring my husband back to good health. May I see him?"

The nurse looked hesitant, then replied, "I guess a few minutes wouldn't hurt. He's not conscious anyway. Just don't disturb any others on the ward, please."

Mrs. Collis stood to go into the ward. Although her back was to me, I seized my opportunity.

"Mrs. Collis? Mrs. Collis?"

Mrs. Collis turned with a confused look on her face. I'm sure she wondered who in the world I was. My readily apparent age should reassure her that I couldn't be Willie Collis!

"Mrs. Collis, my name is Maude Cox. I conducted business with your husband when he was in Atlanta a few years back."

Mrs. Collis stiffened. I had no idea what John had told her, but I'm sure May's letter had raised questions about John's recent past. "Yes, what can I do for you?" she answered coldly.

"Well, I just read in the paper today that Mr. Collis was seriously ill. I was quite fond of John at one time. In fact, he was a frequent boarder at my house. I just wanted to express my condolences."

"Condolences? I don't think those are in order yet, although the doctors say he may not recover. I appreciate your expression, but I need to get in to see my husband. I don't think anyone from his past should be nosing around. I've had quite my fill of that." Mrs. Collis' tone was clearly a dismissal.

"Ah, well, from what I read in this morning's paper I can understand that. Just so you know, I wouldn't take the first Mrs. Collis too seriously. She's been ill herself. Her tonic use sometimes makes her say or do things she would never do in her right mind. But I won't keep you any longer. I do hope Mr. Collis recovers. Quite a charmer, he is."

Ludie's face perked up at the mention of May. "Do you know May Wheeler?" she asked.

"I met her a time or two. Mostly I heard about her through John. She was quite the riddle, she was. But like I said, I don't think she'd seriously harm anyone, poor lost soul. After John left her she was destitute. Had to go back to the country and work on her pa's farm a while. And she was in such a state, I feared for her life too." I was hoping that if I could soften up Ludie's attitude towards May she might relent in pursuing her charges.

Ludie looked wary. "Well, whatever you say, but I really do need to get in and see John now. Good day, Mrs. Cox."

"Good day, Mrs. Collis. I do hope John gets better." I made my way out. Mrs. Ludie Collis didn't seem so threatened to me. My guess was she was just overwhelmed when she got May's letter, what with her husband lying at death's door. I figured I'd best get on my way if I was going to make those other calls. I had to get May out of that Tower.

20
MAY

Of course, I actually had the $200, but I wasn't fool enough to bring it to jail with me. I'd never been in jail before, but I wasn't going to take any chances. How was I going to let Maude know where I was? Would she be able to get me out? I thought to keep my eyes and ears open so I could learn everything I could. Even though it was my first time in the pokey, it might not be my last.

First, the officers took me by the recorder's court. I learned this was the first stop for anyone being arrested. Like a clearinghouse to decide who should go on to jail and who could be let loose. The city official apparently didn't take too kindly to murder threats, so he bound me over and sent me to jail, and here I was.

That first cell was cold, dark, and smelled terrible. Just about made me retch. I was happy to be moved to a cleaner cell the next day where I met two whores, Bessie and Addie. They seemed pleasant enough even if they were practicing the world's oldest profession.

Bessie was the first to strike up a conversation. "So who are you and what brings you here? Don't think we've run into you here before."

I wasn't quite sure how I should respond and I didn't want to reveal too much information. "Oh, I just got in a minor scrap and didn't have access to my bail money. I've never been here before. Sounds like you're a regular resident."

The older of the two women spoke up. "You might could say so. My name's Addie and this here's Bessie. We provide comfort to lonely fellows, if you get my meaning. The money's good, but every once in a while some new do-gooder official gets pressured to clean up the streets and we have to spend a night or so here. It's not too bad though. They know to treat us well."

I didn't want to seem surprised and I wanted to learn more about their goings on. "Oh really, you don't say! How is it you manage to get such special treatment? The cell I was in before they moved me over here with you two was awful."

It was Bessie who responded, with a little laugh. "You really are a novice here, aren't you? Why, this whole town knows us. Half of the officials are regular customers of ours. This city has quite a burgeoning underside. Most times they look the other way, but like Addie said, every once in while they have to make it appear they're cracking down. Just goes with the territory."

It was my chance to not come off as so naïve and hopefully learn a little more about their business. "Well, I dabble in some illegal business deals myself. That's what landed me here. I just haven't gotten into your particular trade, but I have been giving it some thought. What advice would you give to someone just starting out in the business?"

Addie and Bessie exchanged glances, then Addie spoke. "Hmmm. That all depends. Me and Bessie are getting on all right, but it's the young ones who bring in the most money. Course experience is worth a lot too. My advice would be to start small, be discreet, and start building a client base."

Bessie chimed in. "If you ask me, the real way to do it is have people work for you. If I was just starting out that's what I'd do. Not dirty myself with the actual work – just reap the profits."

I nodded. "That's certainly something to consider. I just may call on you girls in the future if I end up going that route. Hopefully we'll all be out of here soon. How can I get in touch with you?"

"Just strike up an acquaintance with John Dodgen, Justice

Puckett's bailiff. He's got all kinds of connections. He'll know how to find either one of us. Just keep it on the low. There's plenty of business to go around, but no use diluting our profits if we can help it. Might be we can all help each other out a bit." Addie seemed to be the more business-minded of the two.

Soon after this conversation Bessie and Addie were released. I had plenty of time to think about my plans for the future, but first I had to get out! I had the warm cell, clean linens, and decent food all to myself. I tried to be polite and nice to the guards and the matron. When the deputy came around, I asked him how I was supposed to go about getting out of here.

Without looking up, he replied, "There seem to be some behind the scenes negotiations going on for just that purpose, Mrs. Collis. Just be patient."

My eyebrows shot up in surprise. "How can that be? I haven't even been able to let my clients know where I am!"

Now he did look at me with more interest. "Well ma'am, it seems you don't need to worry about letting anyone know. That newspaper article pretty much told it like it is. Seems you're in a heap of trouble. But like I said, you've got somebody in your corner."

"Newspaper article? What newspaper article?"

"Oh, the one telling all about you and Mr. Collis's wife. How you wrote that obscene letter and threatened to kill her! You didn't think something that juicy would be kept under wraps, did you? My, my, you're quite the feisty one. And poor Mr. Collis lying there in the Grady 'bout to pass on, not even knowing he's got two women fighting over him."

I sank down on my cot and wept into my hands. "I didn't know about that! Please sir, can you manage to get your hands on one of those papers? All of Atlanta is going to denounce me. Why, I just wanted my husband back, and now he's nearly dead and I'm jail."

"I'll see what I can do, Mrs. Collis. Don't you worry yourself none. This town's used to all kinds of scandals. We rather enjoy most of them, and you're a nice addition to our underdog heroes. Mr. Collis himself is a well-known scoundrel, and it seems you've got some powerful friends working on getting you out of here. I wouldn't be too concerned if I was in your shoes. It's just the weekend that's got things bogged down a bit. I imagine you'll be out of here first thing Monday morning."

He managed to get me the paper with the article. After reading it several times over, I got back to thinking about my future, and it sounded like John might not be around to be a part of it. I had some serious planning ahead of me. The deputy's talk had been very educational about the possibilities around town. And true to his word, first thing Monday morning he showed up to take me to be discharged.

There was my dear friend Maude, only she didn't look so friendly. Her firm frown and wrinkled brow indicated she had quite a bit of consternation regarding my circumstances. I smiled sheepishly, but soon as we were out of there I was again in good spirits and full of bright ideas for the future.

Over lunch, which I dearly appreciated, I told Maude about my experience. "I declare, if I'd had to stay in there one more day or night I really would be stark raving mad! I thought I'd seen some characters in my life, but those women took the cake. It was actually quite interesting to meet some of 'em. Gave me something to think about."

"Seems to me, May," Maude started, "You'd best be thinking about how to avoid such an experience in the future. It took me quite a bit of sweet talking to convince Judge Colquitt your mental condition was at the root of your evil deed. He was kind enough to let you go when I promised to look after you. And that was after I'd already got Ludie to drop the charges."

"I do appreciate it Maude. But I did meet some most enterprising young ladies. Why, Bessie and Addie were most charming, and smart too. Said they turned over $500 the night before they were brought in early that morning. That's more money in one night than tonics and moonshine together!"

"Well, maybe so, but those kind of women can be dangerous, May. Disease, theft, looney men fighting over them," Maude replied.

"Oh Maudie! I wasn't talking about me! I would never put myself in such a profession, even if it is the world's oldest. But I do say I know a great deal more about it after spending time with those two. Why, I think it could be quite a profitable enterprise."

Maude conceded, "Well, I'm glad to hear that at least. And

it is the world's oldest profession. The law in Atlanta does tend to look the other way from it unless things get rowdy. Why, I dabbled a bit with it myself years ago. Takes a smart woman to run a house like that."

"Well, well, if I'm not the cat's pajamas! Maude, you're just the person I need to help me get set up!"

Maude was quick to reply. "Hold on now, missy. I just got you out of the pokey and here you are planning illegal business already. I promised Colquitt I'd look after you. Even those bailiffs, Dodgen and Jordan, helped me out and made sure you were taken care of. Not everybody at the Tower gets clean linens or decent food."

"Oh, so that's why they moved me! That cell I was in first was downright awful. Green slime on the floor, damp, and cold too. I was happy to be moved come suppertime."

"That's because I made some rounds on Friday. I didn't even know you were there until I read it in the paper. I made visits to some of my insiders. Even then, there wasn't much to be accomplished over the weekend. It wasn't until I could see Walt Colquitt himself early this morning that arrangements could be made for your release."

I hadn't realized all the trouble Maude had taken. I would have to repay her some way, and I'd have to be careful not to get in such a situation again.

"Maude, if you'll help me get back on my feet, I'll make sure you're repaid for your trouble, and more. I really think running a house would be right up my alley."

"Well May, if anybody could do it, you could. But I think it best you lie low for a while. You probably need to think about changing your name too. That newspaper article was pretty severe, and I don't think most folks would want anything to do with anybody named Collis. Considering John's past indiscretions, you'd be much better off without carrying around his name as baggage."

"Oh, that shouldn't be a problem. If I can't get it changed legally, I'll find some other way. As you know by now, I'm pretty good at persuading folks to see things my way. I don't know what got into me, writing that letter. I guess it was the tonic talking. I'll take your advice and try to stay on the up and up for a while. But come this time next year, I want to be in business!"

21
MAY

I kept my word to Maude. I stayed at my little Bush Street house and minded my own business. I kept any business dealings I had to make undercover and was careful not to do anything that would draw attention. I figured after about a year I would be ready to move on.

But my plans changed. One afternoon in June, Maude turned up on my doorstep unexpectedly.

"Well, howdy do, Maude! What brings you over my way? I know I'm as clean as a whistle, so it can't be because of any trouble I'm in."

"No May, it's not because of any trouble you're in, at least I don't think so. But it's not just a pleasure visit either. May I come in?"

I noticed Maude had the newspaper under her arm. "Of course, come on in. I'll get us a cold drink. Sure is hot for June."

When we had settled down in the parlor, I saw that Maude had the paper turned out. Without saying a word she handed it over to me and pointed her finger at two lines about mid-way down the left column: the list of death notices. I was leery, but I took the paper from her. A name lurched out at me, and I read out loud:

> **COLLIS:** The body of John Collis aged 31 who died Monday morning at the Grady hospital of meningitis will be taken this morning to McDonough for burial.

"Oh, dear me." I sank back against the divan. I put my hands to my head and did not speak for several moments. Maude broke the silence.

"I thought you'd want to know, May."

I shook my head and sat up straight. No one must ever think that I had anything to do with John's death. And perhaps I actually hadn't. Oh, the poisons had definitely made him sick. But meningitis? How could the doctors tell, anyway? If they said it was meningitis, they would not be looking for anything further. If the poisoning was ever found out and then tied to my letter to Ludie, I would surely be put away forever. I might even swing from the gallows in that tall tower at the very jail I'd been in! I decided right then and there that no other living soul would ever know what I'd done.

"Oh Maude, thank you. I didn't know he was so seriously ill. Meningitis? How does one contract such a thing?" I asked innocently.

"It's usually an infection picked up somewhere. The way he traveled around all the time, there's no telling where he got it. I just hope that new wife of his didn't have anything to do with it. Or any of his other wives for that matter." Maude gave me a sideways glance.

"Oh, what a horrible thought, Maude Cox! John was a rascal but he was charming. I'm sure no one would want to seriously harm him. Like you said, he probably just picked it up somewhere, God Rest His Soul. Well, I'm sad to hear the news, but at least that horrid Ludie won't be trotting him out around Atlanta anymore. What a fool!"

Maude did not appear to disagree with me. "Yes, it's a sad passing, that's for sure. I wonder why he's being buried in McDonough? I never heard of any connections he had there."

"Me either, Maude, me either. Unless of course, he had another wife over there we don't know about. At least maybe now he can rest in peace."

"I suppose so," Maude said. "Well, I guess I better be getting on my way. I just thought I ought to be the one to tell you about this." Maude stood and gathered her things. She chuckled lightly.

"What? What is it?"

"Oh, nothing, May. I was just thinking what an enchanting scoundrel he was. Maybe he did have another wife in McDonough. Not surprising he wasn't long for this world."

"Well, you're right about that Maude. And there's plenty more out there just like him. The trick is to find 'em and use 'em to your own advantage before they find you and do the same." I was becoming rather cynical these days, after all, I'd been through. I'd decided one just had to look out for one's self. That was the key to a good life.

Maude looked at me a little strangely but then said goodbye. "Be seeing you real soon, May. You take care now."

"Oh, I certainly will Maude." With John gone, I was more than ready to move up my plans for the future. I had best be getting busy!

22
MAY

It was hot as blue blazes, reminding me of the time when I met up with John Collis. It seemed like a lifetime had passed since then, but it did make me itch to get back to my plans to be an independent businesswoman. I'd pretty much given up my tonics, but staying out of trouble was enough to drive anyone mad. Maude had helped get me set up at the small house on Bush Street, but someone who had been arrested on murder threats did not go unnoticed and the police were keeping a careful eye out, expecting me to return to my old ways. I had traded favors with policemen before but didn't know the local cops over here quite as well. I was determined to get by on my moonshine money and the pocket change I could get for writing letters. I went on living quietly, stashing away my earnings. I moved over to Mechanic Street, a slight step up from Bush Street, but still bordering on the rougher areas around the railroad tracks.

Maude and I visited often, and I could tell she was slowing down. I had learned by now that she was in her 70's. Many women, especially those who bore child after child, were dead in their 50's, like my poor old Aunt Mannie. I suppose that was in my favor, and I planned to live a long life. Not that I had totally ruled out ever having another husband or even having a child, but I sure didn't want to end up like Uncle Wash's wife that died in childbirth with a twelfth baby when I was 45 years old.

Several days later Maude came to visit. I could tell right off she was up to something.

"Hello May, how are you? Hot enough for you?"

"Why, yes indeed Maudie. What brings you out in this heat? You usually stay in when the weather's like this. You must have some pretty important business or else some spicy gossip to tell!"

Maude looked a bit sheepish, knowing she hadn't fooled me one bit. "Well, I suppose you could say it's a combination of both, in a way."

I was all ears. What was she up to now? "Let me just get us a cold drink and let's set down. I want to hear all about it."

Maude settled herself on the divan. I brought in the tray and sat down too. "All right, Maudie, what's on your mind?"

"I declare May, this cold Coca-Cola just hits the spot. Cools me right off."

"Come on, stop putting me off Maudie. I know you're here for a reason. Now what is it?"

Maude was in no hurry. She sipped her drink, patted her lips with her napkin, and arranged her skirts.

"Maudie!"

"Oh, all right. I'll get on with it. I received a surprising letter the other day. Postmarked Ellijay..."

"Ellijay! Who do you know in Ellijay .. No! You can't mean . . ."

"Yes, I do mean, May. It was from Amanda of all people. She's remarried and didn't do so well picking this one either, it seems. She married a man named Ponder and had a couple of more babies. Said John's little Mandy was a big girl now. She wanted to get her out of Ellijay and find her a place working in town. One less mouth to feed and away from some of the less than honorable men up there. Said she's quite a beauty, and she fears for her virtue. I figure if she's so big and a beauty, virtue is most likely no longer an issue, but that's just me. Anyway, in the letter, Amanda wanted to know if I could find her some work and a place to stay in Atlanta." Maude paused, letting this statement sink in.

I was dumbfounded. "Why, of all the nerve. I can't believe it!" But I was intrigued. Here was a young girl in need, even if she was that scoundrel's daughter. She had nothing to do with that – she was just an innocent child at the time. Maude was looking closely at my face. I was sure she was reading my mind.

"You know, May, Amanda and I were right close at one time. She knows, just as you do, that I'm resourceful in helping out younger women in difficult circumstances. She says Mandy's a smart girl, can read and write, and is good with figures too. I shouldn't have too hard of a time finding her something. And I suppose she could stay in my boarder's room, although it's been closed up so long now it'll need a bit of airing."

Maude let her voice trail off, and I knew she was just waiting for me to step right into her scheme. Just as a tease, I thought I'd let her wait it out a bit.

"Well, she could be some company for you, Maude. You might enjoy having the girl around. I imagine she could be a bit of help to you. I don't mean to be unkind, but you are slowing down."

Maude looked haughty, straightening her shoulders and sitting up straight. "Harrumph! Me? Slow down? What do you mean? I'm just as spry as ever." Suddenly Maude's eyes shifted down and her expression turned more dubious than indignant as she slumped. "Well, I'm not as young as I used to be, that's a fact. Maybe you're right. I just don't know about having someone else in my home though. I'm pretty set in my ways. I'm used to being by myself these days. I wouldn't want it to be a boarding arrangement. I'm way past cooking and cleaning on others' account." She sat quietly, sipped her drink, and glanced around my little parlor.

I didn't respond and we both sat quietly. She'd turn her rheumy eyes on me and they looked so tired. She'd let out heavy sighs in between sips of Coca-Cola. She'd shift on the divan as if her bones were aching. I could recognize all the ploys.

"Oh, all right Maudie. I might consider letting her stay here. Might be interesting to have her around. Almost as if we'd had a child of our own, me and John . . . " I wasn't totally heartless.

Maude broke out in a big grin. "I just knew you'd see it that way, May! I just knew it! She'll be here in a week or so and I've already got her a job with Mr. Mitchell's grocery. If she's all her mama says, she won't be staying long. Some young fella will snap her up. We'll just have to find the right one!"

"I'm not making any promises, Maude. Let's just see how it goes."

Mandy Collis proved to be all her mama had said. She was polite and kept pretty much to herself. She went off to work every morning and came in early every evening. We'd share a light supper, exchange pleasantries, and that was about as far as it went. I never could get her to open up about her mama or daddy, and frankly, I didn't know how much she knew about her father's shenanigans. As far as I could tell, she just thought Maude was an old friend of her mama's and I was a woman with an available room.

Atlanta kept growing and got busier and noisier. Automobile registration was required, the Metropolitan Opera came to town, and the northern suburbs of Collier Hills, Peachtree Heights, and the Brookhaven Country Club were established. The city limits were extended in all directions, even as far south as McPherson Barracks. Prices had gone up on everything, and although Mandy's little bit for room and board helped, at times money could be tight. I tried to keep a low profile but bad luck just seemed to find me, even when I had the best intentions. It didn't take long before a bushel of trouble appeared on my doorstep.

23
MAY

    The young girl knocked on my door early one morning. "What can I do for you?" I asked through the screen.
    "Mrs. Collis? I heard you sometimes helped out young girls like me that need a place to stay a day or so. I'm really down and out and need a place to rest my head," stated the girl, who didn't look to be more than 12 or 13 years old. I was a fairly good judge of age and character, both good and bad. I narrowed my eyes at the girl. She appeared to be scared. Kept shifting her eyes up and down the street, as if she was afraid someone might be looking for her. Like I said, I wasn't heartless, but I sure didn't want to invite trouble either. "You wouldn't be trying to get me in trouble, would you? I keep a clean house here. I don't want any police coming around looking for a girl that's caused some trouble somewhere else." The waif looked stricken as her eyes widened and began to brim with tears.
    "Oh no ma'am, I'm not in any trouble. Just need to be somewheres else than my mam's and pap's for a day or two. My name's Mary, and I can take on any chores you got. Please give me a chance!" begged the girl.

"Well, I guess it won't hurt for a couple of days." I wasn't going to take any chances. I laid down the rules. "You're to stay inside and work. I don't want anybody noticing you're here, and this ain't no hotel. There'll be plenty of chores to keep you busy." Despite sounding harsh, I had developed a soft spot for such girls who needed a hand up since Mandy had come to town. It wasn't so long ago I myself had been in a similar situation. I could see the desperation in her eyes, and it could have been me in the same circumstances a few years back. I knew better than most that a girl sometimes needed to escape the harsh realities of her own home.

"Oh, yes ma'am. I'm a hard worker and I won't cause any trouble. I promise nobody will ever know I'm here."

So it came about that Mary Hutchins came to stay a few days. I put the girl to work cleaning, cooking, and doing the laundry. We got along well enough. She was fairly quiet and didn't talk much about her family or home. I let sleeping dogs lie and figured she'd open up if she wanted to talk about it.

I suppose she just got tired of being cooped up or maybe she was thinking about going home, but one morning I noticed Mary was nowhere to be found, inside the house, that is. I happened to glance out the front window and there she was, sitting on the doorstep. What in the world had come over her? Little did she realize the consequences of such a simple act. I couldn't see down the street from the window and Mary didn't notice the policeman approaching. Before I could get her back inside, it was too late.

"Young lady?" The officer addressed Mary.

Mary looked up and turned to run back inside. In what seemed like two steps the policeman was banging on the front door.

"Open up! Open up, Mrs. Collis! I know you have a girl in there, now open up!"

I hissed at Mary, "Now look what you've done. They'll never believe you're just visiting here! Get out of the way!"

Opening the door, I turned a sweet smile on the officer. I noticed he was one of the regulars on this beat.

"How do you do, Officer Morris? I won't deny I do have a girl in here, but she's just visiting and helping me out with some chores. Poor thing, she needed a little extra money for her starving baby brothers and sisters, and I just couldn't turn her away!"

Policeman Morris looked at me shrewdly. "Mrs. Collis, I

know all about you and you can't fool me. You've been in trouble with the law before. You and that girl come on with me down to the station house and we'll get this straightened out. Somebody may be looking for that girl."

"Oh, dear me!" I said. "We'll certainly come along. Just give us a minute. Mary, get your things!" I invited the officer to step inside while I got my pocketbook. "I'm sure we can clear this up," I warned Mary not to open her mouth and let me handle things.

I kept up a pleasant conversation and acted like we were just out for a stroll as we walked with Officer Morris down to the station. He asked us to wait and disappeared behind an office door. Next thing I knew, we were ushered into the clerk's office where a rough looking fellow stood off to the side. As it turned out, it was Mary's brother-in-law. From the looks of him, he was none too kind or brotherly. I thought he might be the very reason the girl ran away. We were all hustled into the adjoining recorder's office. The clerk read out the record on my previous troubles with the law and declared my home was "not of good character." I knew better than to protest. Mary was remanded to her brother-in-law, who promised to send her to the country until she learned better than to run off from home. Since I suspected he was the very reason she had run off, I knew sending her back with him would be sentencing her to more abuse. Well, if that was the case, so be it. I couldn't save the world, and I had to look out for myself.

I wasn't arrested, but I was fined $10.75 cents for allowing the girl to stay at my house and no formal charges were filed. I had to pay the price just for having a bad reputation. After all, I hadn't broken the law. I promised to never allow another child in my home. Although I was relieved that nothing more came out of the episode, I felt bad for the young Mary. I felt sure she was heading back to an intolerable situation and knew it would only be a matter of time until she ran away again. I wished there was some way to help such girls, but it seemed my past would always dog any sincere effort I made to do good. I felt hopeless to improve my lot without resorting to the unsavory activities I knew best.

24
MAY

I'd tried to stay on the straight and narrow, living off just the moonshine and tonic money. Most folks didn't even consider bootlegging a real crime, it was so commonplace. Just like those whores in the jail, I had contacts and many prominent men were glad to have a reliable source for what they considered some of the best spirits available, especially after Atlanta enacted a local prohibition law. There were a few loopholes in the law, but mostly it served to increase the business and profits of illegal whiskey makers, runners, and providers like me. My earnings were slowly but surely increasing, yet I craved the finer lifestyle I'd had with John. I had managed to stay out of trouble for a while until that little Mary girl showed up.

Returning from the police station that day, I was surprised to see Mandy. "Why Mandy, what are you doing home this time of day?"

"Oh, May! I've been worried sick about you. I'm so glad you're home!"

I gave Mandy a hug and told her what had happened.

"Here I was, just getting back on my feet and making more money when that Mary just about did me in!! That little episode cost me nearly eleven dollars! Being brought to the attention of the law just wasn't worth any do-gooder feelings I might have had regarding that girl. No-siree, it was just not worth it."

I went on to explain, "Course, that doesn't mean I can't conduct any business. I'll just have to be a little more careful about it. Maude and I have an idea about some younger girls but we'll put it on hold for a while. That escapade with Mary may stall our plans temporarily, but we can build back up eventually. We'll just take a little vacation time and then we can rustle us up some new business."

I hadn't always been so forthcoming with Mandy, not knowing if I could trust her completely. But bits and pieces of information had leaked into our conversations that let me know she knew more about Maude's side businesses than she let on. And she'd been staying out later in the evenings recently. I was sure her few months in the city had provided quite an education, and she was no longer the innocent she appeared to be.

"Whatever you say, May. You know I'm indebted to you for taking me in, but I would like to git back up home and see my mother and brother. Be nice to be in the cool of the mountains, too, instead of the heat in the city."

If I was going to eventually expand into more risky business, I sure didn't need an extra boarder underfoot. Although I'd grown to enjoy Mandy's company, it might be best if she moved back to Ellijay.

"If that's what you want, Mandy. I'm sure your ma can use the help more than me. If you let Mr. Mitchell know you've had an emergency at home and need to get back to Ellijay as soon as possible, he would probably let you go with no notice. You might even be able to get on the train as soon as tomorrow and head on home if that's what you really want to do. While you're up there you could check on our 'shine suppliers; this 'near beer' ain't hitting the spot with too many fellows. And that Coca-Cola's tasty but neither one substitutes for a good hard drink. Here, take this twenty dollars. Go see Mr. Mitchell, and if it suits him, go ahead and buy a train ticket." Mandy would be better off if she didn't know the schemes I planned to start. Even better if it could be sooner instead of later.

Mandy returned about an hour later. "You were exactly right, May. Mr. Mitchell was fine with me leaving. Said he could always find help if he needed it. So I did just what you said and got me a train ticket for tomorrow morning."

"I'm not surprised to hear that, Mandy. There's plenty of good folks looking for jobs. He'll find somebody in no time. After supper, I'll help you get your things together. Don't you worry about letting Maude know. I'll be talking to her tomorrow and will let her know you decided to get on back home."

"Thank you so much, May. You've been so kind to help me out while I've been here in Atlanta. I have been homesick, and I'll be sure to check on things up there for you. I truly do appreciate all your help."

"Oh, don't you go on about that, girlie. You've been a bit of company to me in return. I'll miss you being around, but I could tell you were a bit homesick. Maybe it's not just your mama you're missing? You've probably got a special beau up there, pining away for your pretty face." Mandy's face turned pink when she started to stammer out a rebuttal, but I just shushed her and patted her arm. "Now, now, let's get some supper together and then we can get on with your packing."

We had supper and spent the evening getting Mandy's few belongings together. She seemed lighthearted like she'd been toting around a big flour sack and now her burden was laid down. Maybe she had been brooding about whether to leave or not and was fine with it now she was as good as gone. Well, she was young and had a whole life ahead of her, so I was glad to help her on her way.

Once Mandy was gone, Maude and I were keeping our distance while I decided it was time to scout out some new locations for a 'house.' I tried to stay out of trouble and only provide my best and most appreciative customers with a drink. Then I started arranging a bit of female company for them from time to time. If I was going to get to a higher standard of living, I needed to make a lot of money in a short amount of time, and this was the best way I knew how. I made sure to stay with the most trusted and vulnerable men. I learned the power I could hold over men of substantial standing in the community, and I wasn't ready to give up that power just yet.

Several months went by and soon it had been nearly a year since me and Maude first began to discuss our plan. We each felt enough time had elapsed to revive the plan, but with a twist. Atlanta had plenty of young women who wanted to make a fast buck. If I couldn't save 'em, I might as well make money off 'em. After morphine, poisoning, bootlegging, and murder threats, it was hard to imagine I could sink deeper into the underbelly, but that is exactly what I was about to do.

Once again, Maude helped me get set up in a house, this time on Johnson Street. I hired a new assistant, Miss Louvine 'Lou' Bryant. Being down on her luck, Lou was glad to find a position and was willing to help however she could. She didn't seem suspicious at first when I began to invite some young ladies to stay over the weekends. But Lou began to grow uneasy when gentleman callers, if you could name them that, also began to make weekend visits. Lou tried to just do as she was told and keep her mouth shut. She cooked, cleaned, did laundry, and delivered messages at my bidding. I was making money hand over foot and paid her well. Most of the girls would just come in for one or two weekends and I'd never hear from them again. I liked to think I was just helping them out in a way, getting them over a rough spot.

Had it not been for Nellie Lewis, this lucrative trade might have continued indefinitely. Nellie showed up on a Saturday morning. She was the daughter of G. P. Lewis of Kirkwood, an area just barely outside the city limits to the east of Atlanta. Nellie was a striking young girl; pretty, and very mature physically for her tender age of 14. She said she had run away from her abusive father many times before, but this was the first time she came to my house. She said she'd heard about me, was "experienced" and needed to make some quick cash so she could get out of town and away from her father. She begged me to take her in, if only for a few days.

I knew that Nellie could bring top-dollar, and the girl admitted she already had a loose reputation, so it wasn't like I would be responsible for the spoiling of a pure child. Nellie seemed quite agreeable when I had Lou get her dressed up in some finery.

"Oooo Mrs. Collis, I just love this red satin. And the

feathers really set off my white skin. I never wore anything like this!" Nellie exclaimed as she turned in the dress.

"You just take care of that outfit, Nellie, or you won't be getting a dime of your share, understand?" I warned.

"Oh yessum, Mrs. Collis. I know how to take care of myself and my outfits. I'll make sure nothing happens to this fine dress. I do declare I think it's the prettiest thing I've ever worn. You won't have any problem out of me, I promise!" replied Nellie.

But there was a problem. Nellie's father wanted her back home. He reported her missing that Saturday afternoon, and the police knew just where to look. Two detectives appeared on my doorstep that Saturday night. Once again, I turned on my deceptive charm.

"Why, it's so nice to see you again, Detective Coker and Detective Norris. It's been quite a while, hasn't it?"

"Yes, it has, Mrs. Collis. Yes, it has. But we're not here on a pleasure visit," said Detective Coker.

"Oh? Why I'm sure I can make it a pleasant visit. Why don't you two just come on in and make yourselves comfortable?"

Detective Norris squirmed a bit but entered the small parlor. "Mrs. Collis, I wish we was here for some pleasure, but we've been sent to look for someone. Just a girl, in fact, only fourteen years old, and her name is Nellie. Her pa is awful worried about her."

I masked my face with concern. "Oh my! I can certainly see why her pa would be worried. Imagine a fourteen-year-old child out on her own. Anything could happen to such a sweet young thing."

Lou was just coming in the parlor and overheard this last bit of conversation between me and the detectives. I turned to her and said, "Did you hear that Lou? These fine lawmen are looking for a mere child of fourteen named Nellie. Isn't that a shame? I certainly hope they find her soon before she comes to any harm."

Lou looked down and answered, "Yes ma'am. I hope so, too. I better get back to my chores." Lou turned and went out of the parlor towards the back of the house.

Detective Coker spoke up and said, "Mind if we take a quick look around?"

"Of course not," I replied, "And you don't have to be too

quick about it. I love having men about the house, especially on a Saturday evening." I winked as I smiled at the two men.

"Well, we'll only be a minute," Detective Norris said. The two men headed leisurely in the same direction Lou had gone.

"Be my guest," I said, as I bowed and waved them onward with a sweep of my arm.

After about ten minutes, the two detectives returned to the front parlor. Detective Coker spoke, "Well, we didn't find Nellie Lewis, so we'll be on our way now."

"I do hope you find her, the poor thing. Y'all come back when you can stay awhile. I'll be sure to make your next visit real pleasurable." Again I smiled warmly at the men as I closed and secured the front door.

I went straight to Lou and instructed her to keep Nellie out of sight, and that we would let the girl stay for Saturday and Sunday nights, but she would have to leave on Monday morning.

"Nellie," I said to the girl, "you can stay tonight and tomorrow night, but I want you out of here on Monday morning. Your pa has the law out looking for you. Now, I don't blame you for wanting to get away from him, but I don't want to get into any trouble. When you leave here, keep your mouth shut or you'll be sorry you ever met me. I'll give you $50 to get out of town. Do you understand?"

"Yes ma'am, I understand. I just appreciate you letting me stay. I promise I won't cause any trouble. I'll be out of here come Monday morning and you won't ever hear from me again," Nellie tearfully agreed.

On Monday morning Nellie was leisurely sauntering away from my house with money in her pocket while I peeked out from behind the window curtains. The detectives had not entirely given up on the idea that I knew something about Nellie, and I noticed they had kept a lookout all day Sunday, but I saw no sign of them this morning.

"Miss Lewis?" Detective Coker said as he and Detective Norris stepped from behind a wall, directly blocking Nellie's path. I couldn't believe it! They'd been hiding, lying in wait like wolves. I hadn't seen them at all until they stepped right in front of Nellie, not 20 feet from my front door. I could plainly hear their conversation.

"You are Nellie Lewis, aren't you?" Coker continued. Nellie looked startled. Apparently, she knew who the men were. Maybe she recognized Coker's voice from my house on Saturday night, or maybe she knew who he was from some other escapade. Nellie answered sweetly in a child-like voice,

"Yes, I'm Nellie. What's the matter?"

"Your father has been looking for you since Saturday, Nellie. He's been very worried. You better come on down to the station with us and we'll let him know we found you. Are you all right? Where have you been? Well, time enough for that when we get to the station house. Let's go."

Nellie did not resist when Detective Norris took her arm and the threesome went on their way. Norris and Coker must have thought they knew exactly where Nellie had been and what she had been up to. In their experience, her shy little girl pretense was all part of her act. I was a bit anxious but hoped for the best. Maybe she would not implicate me, and maybe the detectives would choose to overlook any suspicions they had that she had been at my house. Once again, luck was not to be on my side. Within the hour the two men were back at my house.

"Sorry to bother you again, Mrs. Collis, but you're wanted down at the station for questions. Do you mind coming on with us now? We'll need your assistant to come along too."

I knew there was really no choice. I got my things and hurried Lou along, telling her to just keep her mouth shut and let me do the talking. After arriving at the station, just like before, they took us next door to the recorder's court and it didn't take long for the proceedings. Judge Broyles heard the story. Nellie's father had come to get his errant daughter and looked none too pleased. Nellie gave the story that she had been held against her will at my house! *That little witch! Just see if I ever tried to help any girls out again.*

Judge Broyles was newly appointed; I didn't know him and he didn't know me. He was appalled at Nellie's story and was loathed to release us after being told of my past record. Lou and I were bound over to state court on bonds of $1,000 and $500, a huge sum, even for me. Once again, I found myself headed to The Tower, with Lou as my companion this time.

"Oh Lou, I didn't mean to get you into this mess. That Nellie is a sly one, she is. Not telling us she'd been running around town for months. After all, we were just giving the runaway girl a place to stay. It's not like we started her on the road to ruin. She did that all by herself. We may have even saved her from a worse fate." I talked to keep Lou calm as we were led away. I might be used to this, but Lou was a first-timer. The matron leading us over, like Judge Broyles, was another new face.

"I just hope this is not going to be a long stay," I chattered on. "I got things to take care of and business to attend to. 'Course, my friends on the inside take good care of me, but some of them have moved on. I don't relish the idea of being behind bars again."

"That's fine and dandy for you May, but I haven't ever been to jail! I'm scared near half to death!" cried Lou with great big sobs and wails.

"I'll put the word out to treat you nice, Lou. Don't worry. Now you need to hush up or some of the meaner folks will smell you like new blood. Just pretend you're going on a little visit away from home for a few days." I passed a hanky to Lou, who used it to blow her nose and gain her composure.

"If you say so, May. I just know when I get out of here I'm leaving town and going back to my folks in the country if they'll have me. I don't really take to this city life anyway."

I just clucked over her and said, "Well, you just do that. It takes a tough hen like me to hold her on in this town. I might try to settle down someday myself. Been thinking about it anyways. Get me a little house, find a man that will marry me for real, maybe even have me a baby. Can't keep doing this forever. Maybe run a little moonshine, but that ain't no big deal."

We were soon at our destination. The Tower was an imposing structure, and just looking at it about started Lou off again. I just hoped they'd give me the same cell I'd been in before. I planned to smile kindly at the intake clerk and I was confident that was all it would take.

It turned out to be about a three-week stay. When the case came up in criminal court I was delighted to see Judge Calhoun on the stand. I'd had no use for that Broyles man who thought he was such a goody-two-shoes, but Judge Calhoun was my kind of adjudicator. Never mind the fact he was a frequent customer too.

During the trial in Judge Calhoun's court, a different

picture of Nellie Lewis was portrayed. What had appeared on my part to be a flagrant disregard for a girl of such a tender age turned out to be not so far from reality. I had indeed been right about Nellie Lewis. Detectives investigating the case uncovered witnesses who testified to shocking behavior by the young Nellie. Her father claimed he knew nothing of her immorality. Huh, I thought. He probably taught her everything she knew.

Judge Calhoun pronounced, "Mrs. Collis, I know of your past record, and I really should be hard on you. I can't be too light, but it does appear this girl misrepresented herself and tried to cast most of the blame on you, so I'm not inclined to be as harsh as I could have been under other circumstances. I'm fining you for operating a disorderly household, reducing your bond to $200, and time served sufficient. I also strongly suggest you try not to bring further speculation on the legality of your businesses." Judge Calhoun peered over his spectacles at me with a look that bordered on kindness. To Lou, Judge Calhoun said, "Miss Bryant, you are dismissed also with time served and no further bond." I was fortunate indeed. $200 was an amount I could easily produce. Staying three weeks in the Tower was an easy off too, especially after Judge Broyles wanting to put me away for years.

Back in the comfort of my own home, I gave a great deal of thought to my business plan. This young girl trade was just not working out. It was too risky. There were other ways to make money. I pictured Maude, old and sick and alone. I did not want to end up like that. I thought more seriously about what to do. I would need once again to transform myself. I had money put away. Dressing the part would not be a problem. Living arrangements might be another matter entirely. I needed to be in a better neighborhood. Somewhere my past would not be so noticeable. I needed more acquaintances too, in respectable circles, not my usual crowd. *But how? How could I accomplish all this?* As soon as I asked myself this question, I had the answer. I turned again to my old friend Maude. I made my way over to Gilmer Street, just as I'd done years ago on my first afternoon in Atlanta.

25
MAY

    Maude once again found me a new place to live, this time over on Mechanic Street. I continued my moonshine trade but shied away from providing female favors. I had quite a few friends and clients among law enforcement, and they had no problem looking the other way when it came to bootlegging. I was quite the businesswoman. I even supplemented my income writing letters for folks since I had excellent penmanship and grammar skills. That was not too common for lots of folks, especially women, in those days. Crime in Atlanta continued to be rampant, but I managed to stay out of trouble for the most part. I read the papers and kept myself informed about all the goings-on around town.
    One day there were newspaper headlines about a man named William Holland who was murdered at the Atlanta Coal and Ice Company where he worked as a night guard. I didn't know the man, but I did know of his wife, Lucy. She had quite an unsavory reputation about town. I'd seen this woman on occasion and didn't think she was much to look at. I felt sorry for the two young children, their father dead and their mother openly cavorting about town with a number of men. I did not give the matter much more

thought for several days until an old acquaintance by the name of Jim Nation showed up at my door. "Well, howdy-do, Jim. What brings you my way? You know I try to maintain a respectable home these days, even if it is hard to get by."

Jim, responding politely, said, "Miss May, you know me and Bill Black always counted you as a good friend. We heard you were in need of a little extra cash, and Bill says if you will come to meet him down to the corner of Marietta and Spring Streets he might have a small business proposition for you."

My wary reply went something like this. "Business proposition? Is it on the up and up? I haven't had any trouble with the law in a while now and I'm not looking for any." I knew Jim and Bill were fairly straight, but they had been known to have some questionable connections from time to time.

"I don't think it's illegal if that's what you're asking," said Jim. "Why don't you just come on down there with me and find out?"

I thought for a moment. What could it hurt to find out? I answered, "Let me just get a wrap and I'll go down there. But I'm not making any promises until I know what this proposition is and how much cash is involved."

When we got to the appointed corner, Bill Black was waiting. I said, "Bill, let's hear it. What is it you have for me? I don't want any trouble."

Bill Black started explaining the situation. "I heard a man shoot another man. I was within 20 feet when he shot him. The man told me he was going to do it but I didn't believe him until I heard gunfire and then he came back and told me it was done."

I stepped back and put my hands over my ears. "Oh Lordy. I don't want to hear any more. I don't want to be mixed up in no murder."

Bill and Jim moved closer and shushed me. "Just hear us out, May. You won't be involved in a murder. The murder's done took place. We're just trying to help out a friend. He had good reason to shoot that man. We don't want to see him put away. He's a good fellow."

"I don't want anything to do with this!" I stated emphatically, and turned on my heel, leaving the two men standing there. As I made my way back to Mechanic Street, I stewed. *The nerve of them! I don't want to take any chances now. Still, I like to help out somebody in a tight spot. And the money might come in handy....*

I had just about put the matter out of my head when two days later Bill Black showed up at my door. "Can I come in May? I've talked to Maude and she suggested I come to see you. I'd like to explain the situation a little more thoroughly."

I didn't respond for a moment or two. Finally, I stepped aside and motioned Bill inside. He proceeded to explain. "Well, May, you know David Phillips, that old friend of ours?" I nodded, and Bill continued. "He's in quite a spot of trouble. He's the man who killed William Holland. He shot Holland because he's been laying up with Lucy, Holland's wife. Holland found them out and was set on revenge."

I put my head in my hands. I remembered David Phillips well. He was a heavy-set man with a full round face, reddish hair and a tawny mustache. He didn't have the appearance or demeanor of a Don Juan. Still, he was a pleasant fellow. Rather quiet and very polite. He was a frequent visitor to my Johnson Street house. Still, I couldn't imagine him a murderer.

That trollop Lucy must have enticed him. The poor widow is usually thought to be the heroine in the case of a murdered husband, and heroines are usually portrayed as pretty in such a romance, but Mrs. Holland was not pretty. She might have been said to be fine looking, but the compliment could go no farther. She had light brown hair and gray eyes, was above average height and walked with an air of superiority to which she had no claim. All of this was going through my mind but I still didn't understand how any of it could have anything to do with me or making money. Bill Black proceeded to explain.

"What we want to do, May, is help out Phillips by laying this killing on Will Ellison." At the mention of that name, I immediately looked up. Will Ellison was well known to have many enemies in the underbelly of Atlanta. No one would doubt that he could, indeed, be the murderer of William Holland.

I said, "Well, certainly there is no more of a scoundrel than Will Ellison. And Mr. Phillips always seemed like a nice enough fellow to me. I imagine that floozy Lucy Holland enticed him. She always did seem to be conniving. What I still don't understand is what you want me for."

Bill went on, "In order to put the finger on Will Ellison, we need a way to implicate him. We need someone to write a letter saying Will committed the murder, and sign it with a made-up name. That should take care of it. I've already laid it all out for Maude, and she's agreed to her part in mailing the letters. We just need you to write 'em. What do you say?"

I studied Bill Black's face. "You say Maude has agreed to this plan?"

"Yes, May, she has. And she sent me straight away over here. We all know you're good at your letters and write as well as any man. That's why so many folks come to you. We need you to write the letters, sign them 'Otis Speer', and then let Maude mail them to you. Then you can inform the police when you receive the letters." Bill knew I often got paid from folks who needed something written out who didn't have any learning. Not that I had any formal education, but I was good with business affairs and prided myself on my penmanship.

"And how much is in this for me?" I asked.

"There's a reward being offered by the guard company for information leading to the killer's address. And I'm sure Jim, me, and David can put together a handsome sum once this is all over," explained Bill.

I continued to study Bill's face. I was trying to read him and contemplate my own risks at the same time. Finally, I rose from my chair, walked over to a small chest, pulled out pen and paper, and sat at the parlor table. "Tell me what you want me to say." Soon, the deed was done. I handed the letters over to Bill and he took his leave. I returned to my chores, but could not shake the uneasy feeling that this might not turn out so well.

A few days went by with nothing out of the ordinary occurring, and I began to relax. Then the letters that I had written came in the mail, addressed to me. I opened the letters as planned and saw the words I'd penned. Maude, as planned, was visiting for the day, and made the prearranged phone call to the police station. "If you will send an officer to number seven Mechanic Street, he can find out something about the murder of William Holland." I knew it would not be long before the police would once again arrive on my doorstep.

Detectives arrived in less than an hour. I turned over the letter supposedly written by Otis Speer stating he had seen Will Ellison shoot William Holland. The detectives thanked me and Maude, and took their leave with the letters in hand, setting out to find and arrest Will Ellison.

We both breathed huge sighs of relief. Maude turned to me and said, "May, I think we've just helped spare a poor dupe a murder rap, put a man behind bars who has long deserved it and earned ourselves a tidy sum all at the same time."

But I was still uneasy. "I hope so Maudie, I hope so. I'm pert' near tuckered out with worry over this whole affair. Let's us go out for some refreshment."

Maude heartily agreed and we went for stroll. It was a beautiful spring day. We enjoyed cold Coca-Colas and shared a handful of penny candy. I went on back to my house and Maude departed for her own house. I settled in for a quiet evening, glad to have the whole business behind me. Still, I was looking forward to the extra income and was already planning how to use the unexpected funds. A couple of ladies, one I knew and one I did not know, came by and paid me to write letters for them. I had a meager supper and a nip of white lightning. I felt like I needed it to calm my nerves. I even took a dose of Dream tonic, which I hadn't had in weeks, and turned in for the night.

The next morning I felt well-rested and took a leisurely breakfast. Maude arrived mid-morning. We were enjoying discussing what to do with the money when we were interrupted by a banging at the door.

"Open up! We know you're there! Open up!"

We exchanged glances and ceased our conversation. I could feel my face fall and worry lines crease my brow. "I knew this was too good to be true!" I seethed under my breath and went to the door. I opened it just a crack and looked out at the two police officers standing on the porch.

"May, you're wanted for questioning down at the station, and Mrs. Cox too. Now y'all come on peacefully. We don't want any trouble."

"I beg your pardon? Questioning? Questioning what?" Maude stepped up behind me.

"We're not going to discuss that here on the doorstep,

ladies. Now you two just come along with us and we'll get this all straightened out," said the younger of the two officers, who I recognized as Officer Morris.

"Well, just give us a minute, officer. We'll be right out," I responded. We gathered light wraps and our pocketbooks while we whispered to each other. Maude suggested we just play dumb and deny anything to do with the whole letter situation. I agreed.

As the officers led us into the station, Maude seemed unfazed and greeted everyone warmly. "Good morning Captain Smith! It's quite a fine spring day outside even if it is a little nippy, don't you think? And Officer Parker, I heard about that new little baby at your house, I know you must be busting with pride to finally have a son. Why, Miss White, you look pretty today. I always admire a woman who can look pretty and carry on her professional responsibilities as admirably as you do." Maude made a point to compliment everyone she saw and acted as if she were there for a social visit.

I was pleasant, but mostly kept to myself as my dread increased. I had much more at stake here than Maude. I just couldn't be as relaxed as her. I exchanged nods with some of the officers and gave a brief "Good Morning" to Miss White. *How could Maude seem so relaxed?* She doesn't know what it's like to be in The Tower. I knew what that hell hole was like and I didn't intend to go back there.

We were led back to a closed office where Captain Smith proceeded with the interview. "Good morning, ladies. I appreciate your coming down here. I have just a few questions I'd like to ask about an unfortunate event that took place a few days ago. We have reason to believe you two ladies might be able to shed a little light on the situation and help us with the detective work." Captain Smith smiled broadly.

Maude continued her goodwill campaign. "Why certainly, Captain. You know we'll be glad to help if we can. I just can't imagine though, what unfortunate business you might be referring to."

I said nothing, just nodding in agreement with Maude. The Captain looked more intently at me. "You got anything to say? You wouldn't be knowing anything about the Holland murder case, would you?"

I stared straight back at him. "No, Captain Smith, I don't know anything about that. I don't know any of those people involved and I just think it's a shame about those poor little children being left without a father. Whoever done that murder should be put away for good."

"That's our feeling too, Mrs. Stamper," continued the Captain. "But someone seems to want to protect the evil fellow that committed this murder. Someone's been trying to mislead us in the investigation. Would you know anything about that?"

I felt a small rivulet of sweat trickle down my back and shifted in my seat. Maude shifted too and cleared her throat. "Why Captain, we wouldn't know anything about that, now would we May?" As she glanced in my direction, I just shook my head.

The Captain sighed heavily. "I was hoping you ladies would make this easy on yourselves, but I guess you're going to play hardball." He opened a drawer, pulled out several envelopes and pieces of paper, and spread them on the desktop. He did not speak for several seconds. At first, I glanced at the letters then looked around the room, disinterested. Maude let her eyes rove over the letters, then looked directly at the Captain and lifted her eyebrows in question.

"Been getting some kind of clue?" Maude asked casually.

"As a matter of fact, we have, Mrs. Cox." Then he drew forth one more piece of paper, turned it towards me, and slid it over the desktop right in front of me. My eyes lowered to the paper and I immediately recognized the letter I had written the previous evening for the unknown woman. Although my insides were churning, I tried to appear undaunted, letting my eyes roam the paper briefly before glancing up at the Captain and nonchalantly responding.

"Is that so, Captain? It certainly is good that your detectives are making progress on this horrible crime." I sat back in my chair and did not look again at the letters. "Maude, I think we've made it clear we can't be of any help here. Let's us make our way home." I made a move to rise from my chair, as did Maude.

I knew Maude did not fully understand my suddenly taking the initiative, at least not until she glanced at the letter the Captain had placed directly in front of me. I knew she could recognize my handwriting, exactly matching that of the other letters, supposedly from Otis Speer. Now she understood the need for a hasty departure.

"Not so fast, ladies," the Captain said as he too rose from his desk chair. "I believe there's more to this than meets the eye." He strode to the door and motioned to someone. As he opened the door wider, I was stunned to see Matron Sanderson step inside the office. Maude and I both were speechless.

The Captain proceeded. "Matron Sanderson, will you please escort these ladies over to The Tower. As of right now, they are being held as uncooperative witnesses in the Holland murder case."

"Yes sir, Captain, Sir." Matron Sanderson looked apologetically at us as she placed cuffs on our wrists. I had never been cuffed, even in my previous arrests! I was mortified. And poor Maudie, the cuffs pressed into the soft fatty flesh of her wrists, but her eyes remained passive.

As we headed out the door the Captain called after us, "When you ladies are ready to cooperate, just let us know!" We could hear him chuckle to himself as he closed the door.

When we had cleared the precinct building, Matron Sanderson struck up a conversation. "Now what did you two want to get mixed up in this for? You've kept your nose clean a while now. May, I was hoping I wouldn't have to see you again under such circumstances."

Maude responded, "Well, of course, we didn't plan it this way. Just tried to help out an old friend that was an acquaintance of the real murderer and make a little money on the side while we were at it."

I chimed in, "I certainly had no intention of ever being in this situation again, either. Just got a little greedy I guess. Times is hard when you're trying to stay on the straight and narrow. I'm just going to keep declaring my innocence."

"Might not be the best tactic," replied the Matron. "Some of these new folks in charge are trying to make it look like they're taking a hard line. Might be best to just tell it all and get it over with. It's not really y'all they're after anyway. It's that sleazy wife and murderer they're going for."

We had arrived at The Tower. Matron Sanderson walked us

to the receiving area. She whispered to us that she would do what she could to look out for us. Then she spoke to one guard in particular. He glanced over towards us and nodded his head. He gave a wink to the Matron and she went on her way.

"Well, hello ladies. I'm Mr. Ford and I'll be looking out for you two." He turned to the intake guard and said, "Jim, I'll take care of these two. Just leave 'em to me. Go on and take your break." Jim just shrugged and walked away. He was probably used to all kinds of goings-on in this God-forsaken place and most likely thought we were in for a rough time with Ford.

With Jim well out of earshot, Ford said, "Now ladies, seeing as how you're special friends of the matron, and you two have quite a reputable past, and not to mention, May, that you supply some of the best white tiger and tonic in town, I'm going to look out for you. First of all, I'm going to claim crowded conditions, so's we have to put you two together in the same cell. Second of all, I'm going to make sure you get the good food, don't do any duties, and get some fresh clothes the matron will have sent over. How does that sound?"

I spoke up. "Why, that's very kind of you, sir. We just hope you put in a good word for us and help us get out of here. I don't relish this place. I've done my time here before. And Maudie here, I fear for her health in a place like this. She's gettin' on up in years and I'd hate for her to take sick."

Maude chimed in, "I am an old woman and I'm not too well. Please, sir, we can make sure you're kindly repaid for helping us out, once we're in a position to do so."

Ford just grinned at us. "Now don't you worry, I'll do what I can. Why, the entire law enforcement community knows May, and we know you're her silent partner, Ms. Cox. Times are a little tougher with the new powers that be, but we'll work on getting you out quick as we can. My advice is to give 'em what they want. They'll go easy on you if you do."

As Ford clinked the cell shut, we looked around and noticed it was fairly clean, had a window, and there were clean linens folded on the cots. Being the more familiar with Tower amenities, I told Maude, "He means it too, Maude. Most folks don't get a cell this clean or any linens at all. This shouldn't be too bad. I think I can wait it out for a few days and see what happens. But what about you?"

Maude said, "Well, May, if you can do it, I can too. Let's just hope it'll be only a few hours instead of a few days!"

It took exactly five days. We were treated well but were anxious to be released. We talked over prospects for the future and came up with some plans. But in order to proceed with the plans, we had to get out of The Tower. We informed Mr. Ford and he sent word we were ready to talk. Within the hour, we were once again seated in front of the Captain and confessed all.

True to Matron Sanderson and Guard Ford's predictions, the investigators were not that interested in us once they got our confessions. The law wanted the murderer brought to justice. Of course, our reputations were once again questioned in the newspaper, but we could each live with that. We once again decided it would be best to go our separate ways a while. Best to appear that each of us had nothing to do with the other's affairs.

26
MAY

  Maude and I did just that. We visited from time to time, but mostly I kept my business limited to providing white tiger to my most trusted clients and writing letters for people I knew well. I visited family some back in Covington. I did not dare to dabble in any other trade. I moved once again to another of Maude's properties, still not satisfied it would be the best location to establish a real business, but a step up from where I had been. Mostly I squirreled money away in preparation for moving to a better area of town and furnishing a nice place. Occasionally I would drop off a pie or some other delight to the folks at The Tower who had looked out for me and Maude. We developed an amiable relationship. I also made sure to get acquainted with any new deputies, judges, or police officers who came on board. Most of them wanted a good reliable source of information and moonshine anyway. I spent several months getting to know my new neighbors and biding my time.

  Even though most officials seemed tolerant and agreeable to my activities, there were a few do-gooders I still had not won over. Something Maude had said months before stuck with me and

I began to give it some serious thought. Perhaps a new name would erase any lingering suspicion. If I appeared to be a respectable married woman, maybe I had a better chance of pulling off my plans for the future. After several months of pondering this, I made up my mind. I was going to undertake a transformation, and in order to do that, I needed to find a husband.

Oh, we'd have to have some clear understandings right from the start. Whoever he turned out to be, I would be his wife in name only. After all, that's what I was after, a new name. I made a list of the possible prospects and was going to determinedly try out the advantages and disadvantages of each one.

One day, having lunch out with Maude, I noticed a pleasant enough looking gentleman standing nearby. I thought he looked vaguely familiar. "Maude, don't we know that rather tall fellow over there?"

Maude looked the man up and down. "Oh, yes. That's Wesley Stamper. Used to do some business with me and then John, back before you got to town. He's just a farmer but comes to town looking for a good time now and then. Nice fellow as I recall."

"I do believe I met him before. I think he and John had some dealings. Moonshine procurement mostly. I recall because he was one of the few suppliers from south of town instead of up in the mountains. I remember him as quite nice. A bit quiet, but pleasant enough. Rather simple-minded, though."

"Yes, he's that all right. Never married, lives alone down on his pa's farm in Fayette County. Bless his heart. Does pretty well for himself money-wise, just not much of a ladies' or family man. Shy, I suppose. Guess that's why he comes to town for some female companionship."

"Maybe he just hasn't met the right lady. He might just fit the bill!"

"Fit what bill, May? What are you up to?"

I finished off my Coca-Cola and made ready to follow Mr. Stamper, who was paying his check. "Just you wait and see, Maudie. Just you wait. And remember. You're the one who said I probably needed to change my name!"

Maude rolled her eyes. "Oh heavens, May. Please don't tell me you've got another scheme up your sleeve."

I grinned and batted my eyes at her. "Who? Little old innocent me? Whatever do you mean?"

"You know exactly what I mean, May Collis. Don't you go getting yourself in trouble again. I'm not sure I'm up to getting you out of it if you do."

"Dear, dear Maudie. Don't worry yourself about me. I'll manage. You'd best be preparing yourself for a wedding. I believe I can hear church bells ringing." With that, I sashayed myself out of the café and set out to follow Mr. Wesley Stamper, leaving Maudie with her mouth hanging open.

With careful deliberation, I set my sights on Mr. Wesley Stamper. I followed him to the Kimball House and managed to reach the door at just the same minute he did. Being a gentleman, he held the door for me to enter ahead of him.

"Thank you, sir. I do believe we've met before. Aren't you an acquaintance of Maude Cox?" We continued walking into the lobby.

"Why yes ma'am, I am. You look a bit familiar too, but I'm sorry to say I don't recall your name."

"I'm Mrs. May Collis, but I'm a widow now. Mr. Collis has been gone for a while. And aren't you Mr. Wesley Stamper?" I continued into the lobby and walked toward a divan. I sat down and patted the seat beside me, indicating for Mr. Stamper to sit and chat. He fidgeted and glanced around, then sat gingerly, a good two feet away from me.

"Yes, yes I am. I do remember you, Mrs. Collis. I'm sorry to hear about your husband passing. He seemed like a good enough fellow, John Collis did. I met him a few times at Maude's. Sure was young to have died. Do you mind my asking what happened?"

"Oh, dear me, Mr. Stamper. I've tried to put it out of my mind. Seems he contracted a terrible case of meningitis. The doctors offered no explanation of how he got it. By the time he was hospitalized it was too late." I fished a handkerchief out of my bag and dabbed at my eyes. Mr. Stamper leaned in a bit closer but still kept his distance. I sniffed and looked up at him. "But I've mostly got my grieving behind me now." I gave him my sweetest smile.

"Of course you do, Mrs. Collis, of course you do." Mr. Stamper relaxed his tense expression a bit and with a shy smile said, You're a young and pretty woman, Mrs. Collis, even if I do say so myself. It's good to hear you're getting on well."

"Yes, in fact, I have a little business I run, but I'm afraid a woman alone in the world is not taken too seriously. I've kept most of John's clients, but some have drifted to other suppliers. I fear I'll have to marry soon to make any progress."

"That shouldn't be too hard to manage, Mrs. Collis. Like I said, you're a pretty gal, if I'm not being too forward to say so. Any man would be glad to marry you."

"Why thank you, Mr. Stamper. And oh no, you're not being forward at all. Why don't you call me May? And while we're on the subject of marriage, is there a Mrs. Stamper?"

"Not at the present time, May. But I just might be looking to remedy that." Mr. Stamper gave me a wink and nudged closer on the divan.

"Oh? Would you now? Well, perhaps we should get together again soon if that's agreeable to you?"

"Why, Mrs.…er…May, that would be most agreeable. I'm in town at least once every couple of weeks."

"Oh, I didn't realize you didn't live in the city. I'm quite the city girl. Where do you live? Perhaps we could work out some arrangements. I take it you're a butter and egg man?"

Fully at ease now, Wesley grinned at my astute assessment. Butter and egg men, as they were referred to, were usually farmers from the country that liked to come into town every so often and spend their money on things they couldn't readily get in the more rural outlying areas. Things like fancy food and drink, and even fancier women. They were accepted as lucrative customers at establishments that provided such fare. In fact, many were regulars. They could be depended on to be discreet, clean, and pleasant. That's how they came to be called butter and egg men.

Wesley Stamper looked a little sheepish. "I guess you could say that, May. Just what kind of arrangements would you be talking about working out?"

"My, my, let's don't rush into anything. But I would love to become better acquainted." I didn't want him to think I was just going to tumble with him just like that. "When will you be in town next?"

"I can be here anytime you want me to be, you just name it."

"All right then. How about you come around to my place next Monday evening? I'm usually alone on Mondays. We'll have a nice supper and get to know each other a little better. Here's my address." I gave him one of the calling cards I'd had made up recently. Mr. Stamper looked a little confused as he took the card. "So I can expect to see you then? About six o'clock for supper?"

Although he still looked a little confused, he was able to splutter out, "Absolutely, why yes, Mrs. Collis, I mean May, I'll be there!"

"Good! Then I'll see you next Monday. Good day!"

I left Mr. Wesley Stamper looking like a stunned rabbit, still discombobulated as I patted his arm and rose to leave.

27
MAY

    The next Monday evening I made sure to look pleasing, but not too seductive. At precisely six o'clock there was a knock on my door.

    "Hello there, Mr. Wesley Stamper! Come right in. It's so good to see you again." I smiled my sweetest smile and took his arm to usher him inside. "You just take a seat right here and let me get you a drink. I have some North Georgia spring water shine that will tickle your fancy."

    "Why thank you, ma'am, don't mind if I do." Reaching inside his waistcoat and bringing out a flask, Mr. Stamper said, "And here's a little sample I brought you of my own goods. May not be North Georgia spring water-based, but it is pretty smooth if I say so myself."

    "Why thank you, Wesley. I might have to try a sip of this myself. I always like to try out my competition." I walked off to the kitchen to get glasses, leaving Mr. Stamper with a puzzled look on his face. Let him wonder. I wasn't ready to spill the beans just yet on what I had planned for him.

    Returning with two glasses, I sat beside him on the divan.

"Thank you, ma'am," he said as I handed his over.

"Oh, please don't keep calling me ma'am, Wesley. Call me May. I'm hoping we can be on a first name basis." He took a sip of his drink and smacked his lips.

"Mighty fine shine, Miss May. Mighty fine!" He took a more substantial gulp.

I took a small sip of his sample I'd poured myself. "This is pretty fine too, Wesley. I appreciate a small nip of a good beverage from time to time, but one does have to be careful."

"Oh, you're right about that, May. I take the utmost care in producing my shine. Certainly, don't want anyone getting poisoned on my account. By the way, I was wondering what you meant about competition. Your own product here is excellent. Where do you procure it?"

Hmmm. Maybe Mr. Wesley Stamper wasn't such a dullard after all. But I still wasn't ready to let him in on all my secrets just yet. "Oh, let's don't talk about that right now. Let's have a bite of supper, take a stroll, and get acquainted a little better." I stood and took his hand, leading him into the dining room.

I picked at my food as he seemed to enjoy his, wolfing it down in a rather slovenly manner. Maybe not too refined in the manners area, but I wouldn't be spending too many mealtimes or public outings with him if things went my way. I kept the conversation to light inconsequential banter. After clearing away the dishes we went for a stroll. The evening was beginning to cool and I nudged closer to Wesley's side, putting my arm through his. He prattled on, the shine having loosened his tongue.

When we returned to my little house, Mr. Stamper came on in and made himself at home. I made an obvious point to sit on the chair, not on the divan next to him. He looked a bit disappointed, but I didn't want things to move too quickly. As I'd hoped, he did not inquire more about my personal business. After some conversation, his eyes began to droop a bit and his incessant patter slowed up. Finally!

"Mr. Stamper, I do declare I have enjoyed our evening, but I am feeling rather tired. Why don't we call it a night? I would love to see you again, though. Would you like to come back on Thursday afternoon? I'll make sure to be well-rested so we can spend more time together.

"Certainly, Miss May. How about around three o'clock? I have some business in town and I'm more than anxious to see you again!" I led him to the door. He attempted to lean into me but I firmly turned my shoulder and bid him good-night.

Thursday was a gray, rainy day. True to his word, Mr. Stamper arrived promptly at three o'clock. I had made some inquiries and felt more secure about my plan to become Mrs. Stamper. Wesley had no family entanglements, and his business associates all seemed to feel he was a lonely farmer who just came to town now and then for a bit of entertainment. He seemed to be an honest fellow, even if he was slightly dull.

I decided to let things move ahead. I did not offer him a drink right off. I wanted him clear-headed when I made my proposal. We sat in the parlor and talked, him in the chair and me on the divan this time.

"Mr. Stamper, I do appreciate you visiting again. Even though I have some business interests, things can get a little lonely for a widow." I was testing him out to see if he'd dispute my marital state or had a clue about my past run-ins with the police. "I try to keep busy, running a little moonshine business of my own. I manage all right but am hoping to increase my earnings significantly. That can be hard for a woman on her own and whose name has been drug through the mud in the newspapers."

Mr. Stamper looked at me blankly even if a little confused. "May, I don't know what you'd be referring to. You seem to be a nice enough lady. And running a little white tiger trade is nothing to be ashamed of. Why, everybody's doing it. I don't even think the law minds a bit. Seems they pretty much look the other way, especially up here in Atlanta."

"Yes, that's true, Wesley. I know you're right about that." It seemed clear enough he had no idea about my other troubles. "It seems like most of the upper crust here are happy to look the other way when it comes to hard drink and women. Seems to be a lot of money to be made if you have something to sell."

"Oh, of course, there is, May. Always a market for such. I partake a bit myself when I come to town from time to time, but mostly I'm content on my little farm down in Brooks, even if money gets a little tight sometimes."

We talked a bit more and I made us a light supper. Then I

decided the time was right to seize the opportunity. Returning to the parlor after supper, this time I sat beside Wesley on the divan. I used my feminine wiles to be flirtatious and coy. It was obvious I had not lost my touch. After some giggles and playful bussing, just enough to get him hot and bothered, I brought things to a halt.

"Why Wesley, I do believe you could turn a girl's head. I better be careful to keep my wits about me."

"Miss May, I could say the same about you. I think the two of us are good company for each other." Wesley moved closer, and brought his face close to mine.

"Now, you just hold your horses, Mr. Wesley Stamper. Let's don't get ahead of ourselves. I've got plans for the future and I need a man who's willing to help me get those accomplished. You might be just the fellow."

"Why, sure, May. I got no strings to tie me down and could use a little excitement in life. What do you have in mind?

I pulled Mr. Wesley Stamper in like a fish on a line, just as I had with John. I got down to business. I informed Wesley how he could help me out, and make money too. I explained my plans for an exclusive boarding house that would cater only to law enforcement, government officials, and other professional clientele. Just to sweeten the pot, I hinted I would not object to carrying out wifely duties occasionally, but that wasn't my main purpose in marrying. I let him think it was for appearances, not just his name.

It wasn't long before I had convinced Wesley for us to get married. I assured him he'd have his freedom, and in return, I could have mine and the appearance of a respectable married woman operating a little boarding house in the city while her husband toiled away on the farm in the country. And I let him know I was willing to pay, giving him a cut of the profits. Other than that, we would keep strictly separate living accommodations and finances. I even offered to go to the ordinary to get the license, so he wouldn't have to make an extra trip back to town. So it was that I became Mrs. May Stamper. Men are so easy – just a little smooth talk, some good food and booze, and a nominal roll in the hay makes 'em happy and can get most women whatever it is they want.

28
MAUDE

    I hadn't seen May too often over the past month, since that day we had lunch and she spotted Mr. Wesley Stamper. I had been a bit under the weather and didn't go out much. It made me a little uneasy, wondering what she might be up to. I had not forgotten the gleam in her eye and the remark about wedding bells when we parted that day. I had a sense of dread about what might be coming next. I knew she wanted to make more money, and I didn't think she had given up the idea of the world's oldest profession as a means to get rich, but I couldn't figure out how Mr. Stamper and wedding bells might fit into her plan. I didn't have to wait long to find out. One afternoon May appeared on my doorstep.
    "Hey, Maudie! It's been a while, hasn't it? How are you? You taking care of yourself?"
    "I'm fair, May, I'm fair. Where have you been keeping yourself? Why haven't you been over to see me?"
    "Well, Maudie, I do apologize. You look tired. Are you well? I'm going to need you well. I've got news for you. I'm so sorry I haven't been over. I've been a tad busy."
    I stood back and ushered May inside. "Come on in and sit a spell. I want to hear all about it." I was suspicious of May's bright

eyes and fine outfit. Somehow, she seemed a bit crazed. Lordy, Lordy, I hoped she wasn't back on the tonic. "Let me just get us some tea and we'll have a nice long visit and catch up on all the news and gossip."

When we were settled, May began her explanation.

"Well Maudie, do you remember back several months ago when you said that Collis name was going to dog me? I gave that quite a bit of thought. And I've made a decision."

I stared at May incredulously. "Why May, whatever do you mean? You can't just up and change your name."

"Oh yes, I can, Maude. Yes, I can. There's one surefire way a woman can change her name. And I'm determined to do it."

"Oh, dear me, May, oh dear me. What are you up to now?"

"Maude, you know I've managed all right on my moonshine money, but I want more. You know I've been thinking about running a little boarding house, so to speak." May paused and sipped her tea.

"Yes, yes, I know you've been pondering it. Tell me more." I was still wary of what May's news might be.

"I've hit on just the right plan. You remember that Mr. Stamper we saw last time we were out to lunch? The farmer from Fayette County?"

"Yes, yes I do May. An old business associate of John's."

"Well, we've been seeing each other quite a bit these last few weeks. In fact, we've gotten rather close."

I raised my eyebrows. What? May and Mr. Wesley Stamper? I couldn't quite picture lively, conniving May dallying with that simpleton with dirt under his fingernails. "Go on, May. And?"

May avoided looking me directly in the eye. Staring intently into her teacup she said, "I've made up my mind he's just the right fellow to help me move forward. Next week, I am going to become Mrs. May Stamper!"

I nearly dropped my teacup. It rattled in the saucer as I set it down on the parlor table. "Oh dear God, May. What have you gone and done now?"

"I haven't done anything yet, Maude. That's why I'm here. I want you to come and stand up with me at the Justice of the Peace next week. We're going to be married!"

I crossed my arms over my chest. "All right May. Let's hear it. How did you manage this and what have you got up your sleeve this time?"

"Well, Maude, Mr. Stamper and I are going to have a business arrangement. I'm going to open a boarding house. Wesley is going to pretty much stay down in Brooks running his farm, but when he does come to town he'll have a place to stay with fringe benefits if you get my meaning. He won't interfere in my business and I won't interfere in his. He'll get a small financial cut in addition to his fringe benefits, I'll get a new last name, and we'll both be able to go about our lives on our own."

I thought about this scenario a few moments before I answered.

"May, this sounds too easy. What are you going to do with a husband you don't even want, much less love?"

May still didn't want to seem to look me in the eye. "Well, I've given that quite a lot of thought, Maude. When my house gets up and going and I don't need Mr. Stamper anymore, I'll just quietly divorce him. I have my ways, as you well know, to get just what I want of men and then dispose of them when they are no longer of any benefit to me."

I was still not completely sold on this idea. I had my suspicions about John's suddenly taking so ill, then up and dying. Although it was never suspected by any authorities that she had anything to do with his death, she might not come out smelling like a rose if she tried something like that again. I narrowed my eyes at May and decided to go straight to it.

"Just what do you mean, May, when you say 'dispose' of them? Surely you wouldn't sink so low as to actually make somebody sick enough to pass on, now would you?"

May did look directly at me now, with a shocked and hurt expression. "Maude! Whatever do you mean? Surely you do not suspect me of, of, actually causing bodily harm to someone! I can't believe you would accuse me of such a thing!" She covered her face with her hands, although I could tell she was just acting hurt for my sake.

"Oh May, come on now. Maybe I was a bit harsh. I was just testing you out. I know you would not intentionally hurt a flea. As long you're only talking about divorcing Mr. Stamper, this just might work."

May uncovered her face. "Of course that's what I meant, Maude!"

"May, you may have just come up with a plan that makes sense this time. It will give you a slight advantage in respectability to be a married woman. The officials around town don't seem to get too nosy when it comes to liquor and women. This may be just the ticket, but I still want you to watch out for yourself. There's no guarantee you won't run into trouble."

May was clearly relieved to have my grudging approval of her plan. Her face brightened and she returned to prattling on about just how careful she was going to be.

"Oh, I intend to be very particular about who I get to work for me and who I let in my new establishment. I've been talking with Bessie and Addie, those two, ahem, businesswomen I met that first time I was in the Tower. They're quite experienced and already have the preferred clientele, mostly lawmen and government officials. I intend to run the most exclusive house in town. That will give me protection and profits."

"And just where do you intend to operate, May? And can you afford it?"

"That's where you and Mr. Stamper come in, Maudie. Wesley has agreed to put up some capital, and I know you have your ear to the ground where property is concerned. I need you to find me a discreet but convenient location. I've been saving so I can furnish the right place just the way I want. I plan on returning to the high lifestyle John and I used to enjoy before his demise."

"Well, I'll have to give it some thought, May. Do you have anyplace particular in mind?"

"I'd like to move over towards the west side of town, but still be close in. I enjoy my conveniences, shopping, and the fancy goings on in town. Streetcar access would be an advantage too."

"And just how soon do you want to be in business?"

"The sooner the better as far as I'm concerned, but first things first. Wesley and I plan to get married next week, then I'll spend a few days down at his farm, just for appearance's sake. I'd say I want to be in the new place next month, then it'll take me about another month to get it furnished and in shape for business. Hopefully, I can be in full swing by fall. Does that sound reasonable to you?"

"I suppose so, May. Like you said, first things first. I'd say we have some shopping, property inspection, and a bit of public relations work to do. It's not too soon to get started. I think this new endeavor has me feeling better already. I always did need something brewing to get me up and going."

May jumped up and threw her arms around my neck. "Oh Maudie, I just knew you'd see things my way. When can we get started?"

"I've always said there's no time like the present, but I need to put out some feelers and get a few things in order before we get too busy. How about day after tomorrow? I should have something lined up for us to see by then. What do you say?"

"Oh Maudie, I'd say that's perfect. Just perfect."

"All righty then, sounds like we have a plan."

I bid May goodbye and shooed her out the door. Clearing the tea things, I chuckled to myself at that woman's spunk. This was the May I'd become so fond of.

29
MAY

    Everything moved quickly and smoothly over the next few weeks. I married Wesley Stamper and spent three days at his farmhouse. His house was pleasant enough, but I needed the city life. It was not much of a honeymoon, but that was the last thing on my mind. I was itching to get back to town and the new place Maude had found. The sooner I left quiet little Brooks, Georgia, the better.

    I was affectionate enough to Wesley. Even made meals, cleaned up the place a bit, and listened enthusiastically to his chatter about the crops and animals, and that was in addition to performing my 'wifely duties.' Wesley was not much of a lover, seeming very inexperienced. I did not mind though; I pretended a bit of naiveté myself just so as not to outshine his own performance. He was tender and almost apologetic. I felt a little guilty for taking advantage of him, but then again, I had my future to consider.

    Wesley would say something now and then to let me know he realized this was a marriage of convenience and he knew it would not last forever. One day after a hearty supper, he sat back and sighed. "May, I'll miss your company when we're not together. A man could get used to this. I know you will be moving on eventually, but I want you to know I appreciate your kindness. I just hope we can remain friends."

"Oh pooh, Wesley. Of course, we will remain friends. You come to town to see me anytime. I'll let you know as soon as I get settled in the new place. Maude will have something in no time at all."

"All right, May, if you say so. I'll be happy to drop in anytime I'm in the city. Maybe you can find it in your heart to come and see me down here from time to time."

"Let's just take it a step at a time, Wesley. It will require a lot of time and effort to keep a boarding house like I plan to have running smoothly. I doubt I'll actually get to leave town, but one never knows. You just don't dwell on that now. I assure you we can always be friends."

I hoped I sounded optimistic to him, but I knew I never planned to make this a long-term relationship. And it would be a cool day in hell before I came back to this farmhouse. I just couldn't take the peace and quiet! I packed my things that night and was on the train back to Atlanta the next morning.

Maude had been true to her word. The perfect location was right on Marietta Street, a nice, two-story brick building. The landlord was a former associate of hers and made arrangement to have the upper floor vacated by the end of the month. The first floor was occupied by a feed and grain store with a small restaurant in the back, and the tenant had six months left on his lease. It was all arranged for me to establish the boarding house on the second floor for the time being, while I paid a down payment, then purchase the building outright and expand to the downstairs when the present tenant vacated the premises at the end of his lease. The separate business downstairs would actually be an advantage, giving the place more of a respectable business location.

There were outside stairs on the north side of the building that led up to a landing where the second-floor entrance was. No one on the front street would see anyone coming or going on that side of the building. The railroad ran right behind the house and there were often cars sidetracked there, which provided even further protection from prying eyes. Perfect for what I intended to do. Maude set me up with the landlord and soon I was moving in. I was glad to be on this side of town, especially with the unrest and riots that had recently occurred over around Decatur Street. I had no case with the coloreds. In my mind, people were people, and I was willing to treat anybody nice who was the same way to me. I just didn't understand what all the fuss was about.

For about three weeks I lived on my own and got the place fixed up. It wasn't fancy, but it wasn't a typical bawdy house either. More like a home where the gentlemen and ladies could be at ease. I intended to run a respectable place. It might not be the most extravagant brothel in town but it would be the cleanest and most discreet. I furnished the parlor area with dark red settees and side chairs. There were lavish velvet drapes. I was especially glad to have electricity, so I installed fancy lamps with shades and fringe trim. For dining, I bought the latest style. The soft reddish cherry wood table, chairs, and sideboard were understated and elegant. My favorite furnishings were two bow-fronted glass china cabinets. I filled these and the sideboard with china and glassware. I finished off the bedrooms with high poster beds, chifferobes, storage chests, and dressing tables with huge round mirrors. The kitchen and bath were tiny, but at least they were inside on the same level and had hot and cold running water! Small but functional, they were kept so clean you'd be hard pressed to find a speck of dust. A few odds and ends completed the décor.

Wesley came once each week while I was settling in. I was pleasant but tried to be as preoccupied as possible. I believe he got the message clearly. When I told him at the end of his last visit not to try to come the next week, I was going to have my first "lady boarder" move in, he took it in stride.

"Of course, May, I knew this time would come. I'm going to miss seeing you, but like we said, we can stay friends." Wesley looked crestfallen but resigned to his fate. His chin even trembled a bit as we bade goodbye and I gave him a chaste kiss on the forehead. I would wait another few weeks before filing the divorce papers, let him get over missing me.

After getting the rooms in order, I let Bessie and Addie know I was ready. We had kept up with each other since our stay in The Tower, and eventually, I had let on what my plans were.

They were both keen to work with me. They were sweet ladies, and I knew we could have a pleasant working relationship. I would be helping them out too, providing a clean house, room and board, decent clients, and medical needs if necessary. They both had established customers among the very clientele I wanted to entice and were looking forward to moving into my place when all was ready. I had also been making the rounds of the neighborhood and getting to know my new neighbors. There was an unspoken understanding of the nature of my business and I received nothing less than a favorable welcome. The higher ups in Atlanta and Fulton County, as corrupt as they come, would appreciate my discreet but elegant place. It was to my advantage to have the law around and on my side. Bob Jordan, a bailiff in Judge Jones' court, lived just a few doors down. It was him, along with Judge Beckett's bailiff John Dodgen, who had made sure I got good treatment in The Tower. Both the judges and bailiffs were regulars of Bessie and Addie, and they would be good clients who would help look out for us.

By late November I'd sent Wesley Stamper back to Fayette County for good. Oh, he would stop in when he was in town, and I didn't mind that. Even though his largesse as a lover couldn't match John, I figured at least I owed him occasional conjugal rights. Before long, "Mrs. Stamper's Boarding House" was bringing in the dough big-time. Addie was especially popular, being just 17 years old. Bessie, although a little older than Addie, was still a beauty and had her own specialties. I took care of the place and the ladies with a little help from some young colored girls from time to time. I had good food and even better drink and made sure everything and everyone was clean. If any disease symptoms did crop up, I had a doctor client who provided services free of charge. Everything was going well and I was enjoying an easy and amusing way to make good money. I always knew I would enjoy entertaining, once I had the right place and all that went along with that. All was running smoothly, and we girls and the regulars were enjoying high spirits.

I was living comfortably, even if I found myself lonely from time to time. I had a beautiful wardrobe of the latest fashions. I paid Hattie well to keep me in new styles. Fashion was changing. Skirts had begun to rise. Younger women were showing their ankles. There were more choices in colors. I was fairly conservative, but I did like having more choices. I especially liked the accessories. Fancy hats, furs, shoes, purses, and jewelry. I had accessories to go with all my dresses and outfits. Atlanta was booming with retail shops and I could spend a whole day shopping. Many women were buying ready-to-wear garments now. I liked having Hattie make my dresses, skirts, and shirtwaists, but I shopped the stores for coats, underthings, and all the accouterments. I still had my slim figure, and I enjoyed dressing like the ladies I'd first seen when I came to Atlanta. That part of my dream had been fulfilled.

My side business continued to do well, too. Maude and I were bringing in plenty of money with the moonshine trade. Mr. Willis and I were making profits off tonics as more folks took an interest. As rumors of government regulation grew, folks seemed to want to stock up. The same thing was happening with the moonshine. The high and mighty prohibitionists thought they were so prim and proper, and federal prohibition was brought up from time to time. Even though I didn't take it too seriously, women were demanding more rights and some were even demanding the right to vote. Hell, I didn't need to vote. If you were willing to work hard and used the brain the good Lord gave you, even women could be successful in business, as I was proving more each day with my increasing income.

Of course, I wasn't totally cold-hearted. I sent money to Wesley each week, just as I had promised. In return, I would receive a polite thank you note wishing me well. It was always signed "Your friend, Wesley Stamper." I took it as a good sign he was not referring to himself as my husband!

I regularly sent money home to Ma and Pa. My sisters were all married off now and had a rambunctious bunch of young'uns, but they were still poor as church mice. Oliver helped our as best he could. Between us, we made sure they didn't starve and stayed warm, but that was about it. I would visit from time to time and dandle the babies, but it didn't make me want any of my own. I was proud I'd kept my promise to myself not to end up that way. Yessiree, things were going quite well.

By Thanksgiving, business was steady and I had filed for divorce. Wesley was kind enough to comply, even offering to let me out of our arrangement for sharing profits with him, just because "You're such a nice lady, May, and I want us to remain friends." Poor old Wesley, he was too kind and simple for his own good. As it turned out though, it was just as well. What would happen before the first of the New Year would make him more than happy he no longer had any official business with May Stamper.

30
MAY

On a cold December night, several "friends" had been enjoying themselves in the house, including police officers. We were well acquainted with the local law, and they with us, but the rampant corruption among police and judicial parties just made it that much easier to operate. We were all having a good time swapping stories, laughing, and the men enjoying their private time with my girls. I had several regular customers associated with law enforcement one way or another, and things had been going so well, I may have lapsed into a false sense of security. But I did keep a little pearl-handled pistol hidden away just in case any trouble should arise. Of course, I never intended to use it.

"Why Officer Jones, how good to see you again so soon!" I greeted Jack Jones warmly. "Your favorite, Miss Addie, is here tonight and just happens to need some company."

"Thank-ee, Mrs. Stamper. You know I like coming to your house. You have the best and the prettiest. And oh, by the way, Bailiff Dodgen said he and his cousin from Woodstock might be over later this evening too!" John Dodgen was also a regular visitor.

"Well, isn't this just the grandest night? You just come in

and get comfortable, Jack. There's some of the best shine from the mountains on the sideboard. Miss Addie will be right with you. It seems like I might need to be prepared for extra guests."

Policeman Jones helped himself to refreshments and took my advice to make himself comfortable. Presently, Addie came from one of the front rooms. After exchanging a few pleasantries, they retreated back to the front bedroom. In the meantime, I called up a neighbor, Bob Jordan, with whom I often traded favors, and who was a bailiff himself. The telephone surely was one of the most advantageous conveniences city life offered.

"Hello, Bob? This is May Stamper. Could you come over for a bit? I got word that John Dodgen and his cousin are coming by later this evening. You know how John can be, especially if he's had a little too much drink."

Even though John Dodgen was bailiff and his daddy was an attorney, he had a reputation. Jordan knew he could be heavy-handed at times. It was well known, too, that some of his friends and relatives were not very gentlemanly. Dodgen had been known to show up with several drunken men in tow. The later they came, especially if it was after the pool rooms and clubs closed down, the more likely there would be more of 'em and the drunker they'd be. It getting close to Christmas didn't help the situation either. Many men felt they were entitled to a little extra "Christmas cheer." Still, I needed to keep Dodgen in my good graces.

"I'd feel so much better if you'd come over and stay the night, Bob."

"'It's a fine night, Mrs. Stamper, even if it is near freezing outside. I'd be obliged to come over and stay with you."

About an hour later, after Policeman Jones and a few other guests had gone, Bob Jordan knocked on the outside landing door. "Oh, thank you so much, Bob, I feel much better with you here."

"You know I don't mind at all, Miss May. I'm just glad to help out."

"Well, things seem to have calmed down a bit, and maybe Dodgen won't even show up, but when Jack Jones says he might, he usually does. It's late and I'm not expecting any more visitors. You're welcome to go on ahead to bed in that second front bedroom if you'd like. Bessie won't mind you sleeping in with her tonight."

"Don't mind if I do, Mrs. Stamper. I've had a long day myself and I'm fairly tuckered out. Good night now, and you just holler if you need me."

"I'm heading to bed now myself. A lady needs her rest, you know? I'm just going to take care of a few things in the kitchen first."

Bob Jordan headed off to bed and I tidied up in the kitchen. Addie and Bessie had already cleaned up and turned in and I was heading to bed myself. In the wee hours of the morning, just as I was about to shut off the lights, I heard a commotion on the outside steps and there was a banging on the door.

"May! May! Let me in!" I recognized the voice of John Dodgen. He sounded pretty rough, and I could tell he wasn't alone. I really did not want to entertain him in the state he was in when I was all ready to shut down for the night. I walked to the door and talked through it in my most syrupy voice.

"Johnny love, why don't you go on home and sleep it off and come back earlier tomorrow night? We're all closed up for the night here." I was hoping to sweet-talk him into leaving.

"But May, I brought my cousin! And besides, you owe me! Now open this door!" The banging resumed along with boisterous demands from other unrecognizable voices. I was realizing he wasn't going to go away with just sweet-talk. In a firmer voice, I repeated,

"No, John, I said we're closed up for tonight. Come back tomorrow." More banging. Should I get Bob up? Maybe I could scare John off with my own gun and not disturb Bob? There was a lull in the commotion on the other side of the door. Had they left? Or were they deciding if they should make their demands even more insistent?

I got my gun from the drawer on the sideboard. In this business, you never could tell when you might need a weapon. Suddenly, there was banging and what sounded like kicking. John, or someone with him, was trying to break down my door!

"John! Settle down, now! There's no need for all that. Why don't you just go on home where it's warm and sleep it off?"

John replied with an angry bellow. "No, you damned whore! I said let me in."

Well, that really set me off. "John, you're not going to talk to me that way. Go home!"

"Hell no, May! I ain't going home. I'm going to get what I came here for, me and my cousins. Now open the door!"

"John, you listen to me. I'm not letting you in here, the state you're in, I don't care who's with you. Now you take your cousins and leave. You're drunk!"

The banging and bellowing grew louder and rougher.

"John, I've got a gun. Now go away or I'll shoot!" I shouted.

Suddenly, the door flew open and John Dodgen and two other men fell into my parlor with a blast of frigid December air. The ruckus awakened everyone in the house, and now Bob, Addie, and Bessie were emerging from the front bedrooms. Before anyone knew it, shots were fired and blood was flowing. John Dodgen lay dead on my parlor floor. His cronies high-tailed it back outside, half fell down the steps, and ran towards the back of the building, out of sight.

Oh my Lord God in heaven! What happened? There was a dead man on my floor!

I was in a daze. I hadn't intended to kill anybody! I suppose I went into a type of trance. In a steely voice, I simply said, "Get him out of here!"

The events of the next several minutes flew by quickly, and I can't rightly say I distinctly recall exactly what happened. I don't think any of us grasped the enormity of what had just occurred. It certainly appeared I had shot and killed John Dodgen. All I remember is that John Dodgen was put out on the landing, the door was closed, someone tried to wipe up the bloodstains, and we sat and looked at each other in stunned silence. None of us knew what to think, and we were all uncertain about what to do next. The only certain thing we knew was that John Dodgen was dead. What in high heaven or low hell was I going to do now? Addie, Bessie, and Bob Jordan just looked at me expectantly, like I could make it all go away. Although I couldn't do that, I would have to come up with something, and that's just what I did.

Sunday morning dawned cold, clear, and bright. Annie, the young Negro girl I employed as a part-time cook, was due to arrive about seven o'clock to get things started for the big Sunday dinner. The house was quiet on the inside. Addie, Bessie, Bob, and I were still sitting in the parlor in mute disbelief. Presently, we heard Annie's shrieks on the outside landing.

"Oh, my lawd! Oh, my lawd! Somebody help! They's a dead man out here! They's brains and blood all over the place! Aaaaiiiiii!" Annie's shrill, intense caterwauling jerked us out of our frozen state.

"Annie! What in the hell is going on? What are you carrying on about…" my question was suspended in mid-air as I opened the door on the scene of John Dodgen's dead body, almost frozen, with half of his head blown off. "Run for the police, Annie, run! Now! Don't just stand there wailing. Go! Go!"

The events of the next few hours were not surprising. Police and detectives swarmed the house. John Dodgen's near-frozen body was moved to Poole's undertakers, where the coroner would examine the body. Along with me, Addie, Bessie, and Mr. Jordan were all taken into custody. Although I couldn't trust myself to be absolutely certain of what had occurred that freezing December night, I feared I was going back in The Tower. Only this time, the charge would be murder.

31
MAY

At first, we were taken to the police station, just like every time. We were all together during this time and able to converse enough to get our stories straight. I steadfastly maintained this was a simple case of defending my house. After waiting several hours, the coroner arrived and we were all assembled in another room. There were others there that I didn't recognize. Who were they? What did they have to do with anything? I hoped there were no surprises that would cause problems with our version of the events. Then, the inquisition began. Detective Spradlin started with me.

"Mrs. Stamper," began the detective, "Would you please give us your account of the events that took place at your house last night, the night of December 15th and early this morning, December 16th?"

"Certainly, detective." I began my carefully crafted tale. "Between twelve and one o'clock, someone came to my door and tried to force an entrance. I asked who it was and there was no response except a command to open the door. I then threatened to shoot if the intruder did not leave. When an effort was made to force the door, I fired one shot through the door. I was afraid to look out and the door was not opened until daylight when the body of Mr. Dodgen was discovered on the landing."

Then Detective Spradlin moved on to Bob Jordan. "Now, Bailiff Jordan, I understand you were present at Mrs. Stamper's on the night in question?"

"Yes, I was."

"And do you concur with her testimony?"

"Basically, I do."

"Well, then," continued the detective, "How about you give us your version of events?"

"All right sir."

Bob went on with his version of my tale. "I dropped in to see Mrs. Stamper Saturday night for a few minutes, and she begged me to spend the night there as she was afraid. She told me I could have her front room and I agreed to stay. Sometime after midnight, I was awakened by a noise at the door, as though someone was trying to get in. I thought I heard two voices outside. I heard Mrs. Stamper threaten to shoot and a few seconds later I heard one shot. I did not get out of bed until the shot was fired. I did not open the door to see whether she had hit anyone. As the pistol fired I heard a noise outside but could not tell whether it was a body falling or someone running down the steps."

"Is that all?" Asked the detective.

"Yes, sir, that's it."

"Do you know anything about other guests Mrs. Stamper may have had that evening?"

"No, sir."

"Do you know about a fight that may have taken place in the house that same evening?"

"No, sir."

"Mr. Jordan, did you know Bailiff John Dodgen?"

"I knew of him, sir."

The detective turned to one of the men I did not recognize and stated he was calling as a witness a railroad worker who was in the railyard nearby at the time the alleged murder took place. Witness? This could be trouble. I never imagined anyone would be around that time of night in the cold, but apparently, I was wrong.

"Mr. Peterson?" Spradlin began.

"Yes, sir?"

"Were you in the vicinity of the rear of the building at 530 Marietta Street on the night in question?"

"Yessir."

"Did you hear or see anything unusual?"

"Yessir."

"Would you please describe what you saw and heard?"

"Yessir. I was in the railroad yard nearby at the time of the shooting. I distinctly heard two pistol shots and saw the flash of a gun at the last shot. Then I saw a man run down the steps to Marietta Street and vanish. I did not investigate further because I don't want to get mixed up in any bad business. No, sir, I was just doing my job and don't want any trouble."

"Are you certain you heard two shots, Mr. Peterson?"

"Yessir, I am certain. Two loud cracks that made me just about jump out of my skin. You know how sound travels when it's so clear and cold outside. I just don't want any trouble, sir. I need my job and I've got a family to support."

"Thank you, Mr. Peterson. I can assure you are in no trouble as long as you're telling the truth. You can go on home now."

Next to be questioned was the Negro man, Frank Lawrence, who operated a small restaurant in the back of the feed store on the first floor of the building. His face was familiar, and we only exchanged polite nods in passing, but I'd never known his name.

"Now, Frank," the detective began again.

"Yessir?"

"Were you in the vicinity of the rear of the building at 530 Marietta Street on the night in question?"

"Yessir, I was cleaning up my restrunt downstairs."

"Did you hear or see anything unusual?"

"Well, I guess you could say so, yessir, I did. I don't want no trouble either sir, I'm just tryin' to make a-livin'."

"Would you please describe what you saw and heard?"

"Well, 'bout 12:30 I heard three pistol shots. I looked out the winder toward the outside stairs but didn't see a soul. Not a soul."

"And what did you do then, Frank?"

"Well, sir, I jes' finished my cleanin' and got on out the

front door and went home to my wife and chillren. Yessir, thas' what I did. Like Mr. Peterson, I don't be wantin' no trouble. No sir, I don' want nothing to do wit any kind of shootin'."

"Now boy, you're sure you heard three shots?"

"Yessir, I'm purdy sure. Sounded like pistol shots to me, and I could tell they was close by."

"All right, Frank, you're not in any trouble either, long as you're telling the truth. Now you get on home."

I was a little squirmy after Frank told his version. In the different testimonies, we'd heard one shot, two shots, and now three shots. Who was going to be believed? Bessie and Addie told their stories identical to Bob's, but none of us were told we could go home. The four of us were led back to holding cells. Before the afternoon was over, we'd all been booked on suspicion of murder. I was not fancying the idea of returning to The Tower, but to no avail. It was back to The Tower for me.

On our arrival at the fortress, I was pleased to the see the intake deputy was Warren Brown, with whom I had become familiar with my last stay. He remembered me well, mainly because of Maude's influence on my behalf. It had only been about ten months since I was there last. Right off, I asked Deputy Brown, to please let Maude know what was going on, and that I was here, and he assured me he would get ahold of her. Maybe at least she wouldn't have to find out by reading it in the newspaper this time. I guess they figured Maude would be back around and they'd save themselves some trouble if they went ahead and gave me the first class treatment, to begin with. I was supposing Bob would get special treatment too, him being a bailiff and all. I didn't know for sure about Bessie and Addie, but I was hoping they'd be given some consideration, being my cohorts. Each of us was registered and led away to separate cells. It would be days before I saw my cohorts again, and when I did, it would be in a courtroom at my own murder trial.

32
MAUDE

It was about seven o'clock when there was a knock at my door. I thought it unusual that anyone would come calling this cold, dark, Sunday evening. I opened the door slightly to see an old friend, Deputy Warren Brown, standing on my doorstep. He was alone, and I bade him come in out of the cold.

"Evening, Mrs. Cox. It's been a while."

"It certainly has, Warren. Get on in here and warm up. What in the world brings you to my house on this cold night? Can't be anything good."

"I'm afraid you're right about that, Mrs. Cox. Ain't nothing good going to come out of this."

"Well, what is it? You're not in any trouble, are you?"

"Oh no, it's not me, Mrs. Cox. It's your friend May Stamper. She's done gone and got herself in a heap o' trouble this time."

"Oh Lordy, what is it now? Come on back to the kitchen and let me get us a warm drink. I might need some fortifying to hear this."

"Well, I can't stay but a few minutes, I got to get on home to my family. But Mrs. Stamper asked me to let you know she was back in The Tower so's you wouldn't read it in the papers tomorrow. And I'm sure it'll be front page news."

Oh Lordy, what had May done now? I bustled around and put some warm milk on the stove. With a little cocoa powder, a little sugar, and a shot of whiskey, it would warm up the insides of an icebox, not to mention a person's stomach. While we waited for the milk to get hot, I had Deputy Brown sit down at the kitchen table with me. "Well, go on. Let me hear it."

"Well, um, er, well, it appears a bailiff was over at Mrs. Stamper's after midnight on Saturday, so it was really early this morning, and um, another bailiff was already there, and um,…"

"Lord, man! Just tell me!

"Well, um, you know John Dodgen? Judge Puckett's bailiff?"

"Yes, what about him?"

"Well, he's dead. Shot to death and his body near froze on Mrs. Stamper's stair landing."

"Oh, my lawd, my lawd! What has that woman gotten herself into now? Is she ever going to learn her lesson?"

The milk had started to roll. I got up and poured two cups and sat back down. Warren Brown was holding his hat in his hands, eyes downcast.

"Mrs. Cox, I don't want to be such a messenger of bad news, but it don't look good for Mrs. Stamper. It don't look good at all. And they's two other ladies, er, women, locked up too. And worse than that, Bob Jordan, Judge Jones' bailiff, is locked up too. No, ma'am, it don't look good for none of 'em."

"Oh mercy me! That surely does not sound good. What else do you know, Warren? Do you know anything about the circumstances?"

Warren sipped his hot cocoa.

"No'm, Mrs. Cox, I don't know nothing else. Just that Mrs. Stamper asked me to let you know she was there. I really do need to get on home. This sure is a good hot drink. It'll warm my insides til I can get to my house."

"All right, Warren. Thank you for coming by. Swallow down the last of that and you can be on your way."

Warren gulped the rest of the drink, stood, and headed for the front door. "Thank you again for the drink, Mrs. Cox. And I'm sure sorry about Mrs. Stamper, the other girls, and Mr. Jordan too. I'm right fond of all of 'em. I sure hope this all gets worked out soon. Not a good time to be in that Tower. It's cold and damp in the winter."

"I'll take care of 'em, Warren. You just do what you can while they're all in there, and I'll make sure you get a little extra Christmas cheer. Thank you again for stopping by. You tell Mrs. Brown and the children hello for me, now."

"I surely will, Mrs. Cox, I surely will. Good night now."

"Good night to you too, Warren. You get on home."

I shut the door and went back to the kitchen. Lord God almighty, how was I going to help May this time? Without knowing more details, I couldn't even begin to know how to help. It was Sunday evening anyway, so not much could be done. I'd just have to wait for the morning paper and see what slant was put on the story. I took another swig of whiskey. I wasn't much of a drinker, but it sure did warm up one's gullet as it slid down. I tidied up the kitchen and started to head back to my room for bed. I knew there wouldn't be much sleep for me. Maybe one more swallow…

I woke up the next morning with a dreadful headache. At first, I thought a case of apoplexy might be coming on, but then I remembered: Warren Brown, May, murder, whiskey. Oh, my Lord. I had to find out what was going on. I got out of bed and put on some coffee. The boy I'd been paying to bring me a paper was soon knocking on my door. It was a cold morning. I opened the door as slightly as possible, dropped coins in his hand and pulled the newspaper back through. "Off with you now!" The boy stared at the coins I'd handed over: two nickels instead of one. He broke out in a big grin, said "Thankee Miz Cox!" and ran off down the walk.

I settled at my kitchen table and unrolled the paper. There it was. Smack at the top of the front page.

    I read the entire article and sat there in disbelief. This was not going to be easy. May admitted she fired her gun and was claiming she shot through the door as an unknown person was trying to force entry into her house. That might be perfectly excusable in some cases. But this was not just any house. While not your run-of-the-mill can house, it was a house frequented by corrupt officials who wanted more discreet yet chippy female companionship and stronger liquor than they could get at other places. And it was not just any victim; it was a bailiff whose father was an attorney. And it was not just any alleged perpetrators, but women who'd already had run-ins with the law and another bailiff. Mercy me!

    I needed to see May and hear her version of the story. I dressed quickly and set out with the newspaper tucked under my arm. It was cold and blustery, but at least it wasn't raining. I could take cold, and I could take rain, but not together. It was only about ten blocks, but by the time I got to The Tower, I was near freezing. In the lobby, I warmed myself a bit before approaching the reception window. There was no one else around and the place was quiet. I approached the window hoping to see a familiar face on the clerk at the desk. Fate was not on my side. I did not recognize the clerk, who seemed engrossed in his own copy of the morning paper.

    "Uh, hum-mm." I cleared my throat loudly.

    The startled clerk jerked his head up. Apparently, he had

finished reading and was catching up on extra sleep in the quietness of the prison this early morning. He looked at me with an annoyed expression. I stared back and waited for him to address me properly. We were stock still in a standoff for several moments. The clerk finally snapped his paper noisily and folded it. He lowered his spectacles and looked over his nose at me.

"Yes?" was his single word greeting.

"Yes? Yes to what? I don't believe I've made any inquiry!" was my tart reply.

"Yes ma'am?" he forced begrudgingly.

"Sir, is that how you have been instructed to greet visitors?" I replied archly.

"Visitors? They ain't no visitors allowed until two pm on Mondays. Got to get the place cleaned up after the weekend rush."

"Do you mean to tell me that I, a well-known citizen of this city, am not allowed to visit my dear friend who has been so unjustly imprisoned?"

"Not until two pm today." The clerk picked up his paper and was about to resume his indifference.

I reached over and snatched the paper from his hands. "In that case, I am not here to visit after all. I'm here intending to see the authorities. I believe I shall meet with the warden himself. Please let him know Mrs. Maude Cox is here to see him."

The clerk looked astonished for a moment. Then he broke into a wide grin. "Well, I'll be a monkey's uncle if ain't Mrs. Maude Cox herself. I've heard about you. My super told me you'd probably be here first thing this morning, trying to get May Stamper some special attention. I'll be danged if he wasn't right on the spot!"

"Then I suggest you get yourself on the spot and get me in to see someone with some authority. I'll be sure to let your 'super' know how on top of things you are here in the reception office."

The clerk rose and ambled off. I sat in one of the uncomfortable wooden chairs lining the wall. It was chilled in the reception area. I could only imagine how it was in the cells. I took the opportunity to reread the article about Dodgen's murder. I waited for several minutes. The building was as quiet as a tomb. After a while, I heard doors opening and shutting and muffled voices. The side door to the clerk's office opened and there stood none other than Deputy Warren Brown.

"Good morning, Mrs. Cox. I told Oscar here you'd probably be here first thing this morning. Seems like I just left your place an hour or so ago."

"Well, good morning yourself, Deputy Brown. I'm glad to see that someone here knows how to address visitors. I daresay Oscar was not so welcoming. In fact, I believe I awakened him from his sweet repose."

"You don't say? I'll just have to remind him of his duties. Come on in and have a seat." He cast a disappearing frown toward Oscar, ushered me through the door from the reception room to the office area, and indicated a more comfortable chair by a desk off to the side. "What can I do you for? Visiting hours are not until two pm on Mondays. We have to get the weekend rush discharged and do a little housekeeping before we're very presentable."

"I would dearly love to see May." I lowered my voice to keep our conversation from Oscar's prying ears. "But if that's not possible, I'll come back this afternoon."

"You know I'd do anything for you, Mrs. Cox, but the powers that be have a tight watch on that one. I don't think I could get you up there without raisin' suspicions."

"Oh, dear me. I was afraid of that. Could you just tell me how she is? Is she holding up all right? And what about the others that came in with her?"

"Well, I don't rightly know about the other girls, but I know Mr. Jordan will be doing all right. We take care of our own. And so many of us, uh, er, I mean, so many fellows are fond of Mrs. Stamper and the other girls I'm sure they're fine too if you get my drift." Deputy Brown looked a little sheepish.

"I suppose I'll just have to take your word for it, Warren. Will you be sure May's got enough warm things and gets something decent to eat? A person could catch their death of cold in here."

"Oh, I'll be sure to take real good care of Mrs. Stamper. You don't worry one bit about that. She's gettin' top-notch treatment."

"Well, then, that'll have to do for now. Will I be able to see her this afternoon?"

"I don't rightly know that either, Mrs. Cox. That all depends. Sometimes with more serious charges, they don't allow any visitors at all. I'm supposing you could come back and try. The offices back there are humming this morning. My guess is there's going to be quite a bit of interest in this case, considering that front page this morning." Deputy Brown nodded towards my folded newspaper.

"Yes, I suppose so. Well, thank you, Warren. I'll be back this afternoon."

"You're welcome ma'am, come back to see us!"

I readied myself to face the cold again. I hesitated in the vestibule to gather my thoughts before going out onto the street.

What now?

33
MAUDE

When I left the jail, my thoughts were in turmoil. May was likely in more serious trouble than I'd suspected. One thing seemed clear. She was going to need more help than I could give her on my own. May was going to need an attorney and a damn good one at that. I thought I knew just the man to turn to.

I went straightway to the offices of John W. Moore, Esq. Moore was well known and handled high-profile cases involving officials. I did not personally know Mr. Moore, but I did know he and some of his partners were political enemies of some of the more conservative prosecutors. What's more, with John Dodgen's own father being one of those more conservative attorneys, I hoped Moore's firm would be more amenable to defending May against them. I desperately prayed Moore would be willing to take on May's case.

When I entered the luxuriously appointed offices of Moore and Partners, LLC, I sucked in my breath. Would I be able to afford them? The offices were paneled in rich, dark wood. There were carpets an inch thick on the floor. Velvet draperies hung on the huge windows looking out on Peachtree Street. Leather side chairs and an ornate coat rack graced the other side of the room. At a massive desk sat a pretty young lady. She didn't look terribly busy, but there was a morning newspaper on her desk. She looked up from her reading. "May I help you? I don't believe we have any appointments scheduled for this morning."

"Oh no, honey, I don't have an appointment. But I am here on behalf of Mrs. May Stamper," I said as I jabbed my finger at the front page story. That got her attention.

"Oh! Oh, I see. And just what is the nature of your call, Miss Ummmm…"

"Cox. Mrs. Maude Cox. And the nature of my business is really none of your business. I should like to speak with Mr. Moore as soon as possible."

The girl's smile faded and she became quite business-like. "Just let me see if he's available. Take a seat, please." She walked off to a side door and knocked. I heard a male voice tell her to come in. The girl disappeared through the door and closed it behind her. In less than thirty seconds a distinguished looking man I assumed was Mr. Moore came out, followed by the girl.

"Mrs. Cox?" The man spoke. "Please come into my office. We can discuss your business there." He motioned for me to go before him into the office. He followed me in, indicating a comfortable leather chair across from his even more massive desk, and closed the door behind him.

"May I take your coat?" said the handsome, youngish-looking man. Far too young to be the esteemed Mr. Moore, in my humble opinion. I gave him my coat and sat in one of the big leather chairs. The man went out to the reception area and asked the young lady to please hang my coat. Then, turning back to me he asked,
"Excuse me just one moment please, I'd like to call my partner in, if you don't mind?"

"Of course not," I replied. "The business I have could probably use several attorneys, so the more the better I always say."

"Of course, Mrs. Cox." He reclosed the door to the reception area and strode over to a large paneled door near the corner of his office. He knocked and I heard a deeper, older voice say "Yes?" The young man opened the door.

"John, could you come in here? There's someone I'd like you to meet. And, I think we'll need both of our heads together on this."

Momentarily, a distinguished appearing man joined him. They walked over towards me, and the younger man said, "This here is Mrs. Maude Cox." Then they introduced themselves. The more mature looking fellow put out his hand.

"I'm Mr. John W. Moore, Mrs. Cox, and this is my junior partner, Jack Branch." Branch put his hand out too. I took this as a good sign. Some men didn't deign to shake hands with women. I firmly shook both of their hands. I was correct about the young fellow not being Mr. Moore, and now I had been introduced properly to the dapper younger partner as well as the older more distinguished Mr. Moore. That receptionist had certainly been remiss in her professional duties, not even introducing me to Mr. Branch when she led me in. The men took seats, not behind the desk but catty-cornered to me, another sign that these men did not treat women like second-class citizens. Moore proceeded. "My secretary tells me you're here about the Stamper case. Is that correct?" He held up a morning paper he had tucked under his own arm.

"Why yes, Mr. Moore, and, Mr. Branch. I appreciate you two seeing me without an appointment, but I fear for the state of my good friend, Mrs. Stamper."

"Why would that be, Mrs. Cox?" asked Jack Branch.

"Well, I know May is not a paragon of virtue, but it wouldn't be like her to shoot a man in cold blood. With all the comings and goings at her place, someone must be setting her up, that's all I can think. And you men, of all people, should know there's plenty of shenanigans in Atlanta. Some fellows would love for a seemingly less than reputable woman to take the rap for some of their own misdeeds. I just think I smell a rat in this whole affair."

Both men exchanged looks and broke into smiles. Mr. Moore spoke next.

"Why, Mrs. Cox, you seem pretty astute. How come our paths have never crossed before?" Moore smiled and wagged his head. "Well, in any case, you just may be on to something. Just from this morning's paper, it is clear there's more to this case than meets the eye. I suspect there'll be more information coming to light, and very soon."

Was it my imagination or did Mr. Moore and Mr. Branch already have some opinions about what happened at May's? Not that it mattered, but it seemed like they were already leaning favorably toward May, and like me, admitting they thought there was likely more to the tale.

"Yes, sir. I'm just sure there must be. I know that May is going to need some legal representation. I'm here to ask you to consider taking on her case. She doesn't know I'm here – they wouldn't let me see her at the jail – but I will vouch for her and take care of any financial issues."

The men exchanged glances again, and Moore nodded silently. It was Mr. Branch who spoke next. "Mrs. Cox, I believe we will be glad to represent Mrs. Stamper. As a matter of fact, we'll also represent the others arrested in this case. As for payment, we can discuss that at a later time. I think we need to get right on this and see what we can find out."

Mr. Moore affirmed Branch. "I agree wholeheartedly with my partner, Mrs. Cox. We need to get started right away."

"Oh, my, my! Thank you so much, Mr. Branch, Mr. Moore. I just knew you'd be the right firm to handle this. I do appreciate it so much. Do not hesitate to bill me as needed. Now, what can I do to help?"

Mr. Moore spoke. "Mrs. Cox, you've already done a lot, just coming to us. I think right now the best thing is to just lay low until we know more. One thing for sure, though, now that we're Mrs. Stamper's counsel, we'll be able to get in to see her, and the others too. We can see that she's taken care of well, and she's allowed visitors. Try again later this week and you shouldn't have any trouble getting in to see her."

Both men stood, clearly bringing our meeting to a close. I felt a tremendous relief.

"Thank you so much, gentlemen. That's just what I'll do. You won't be sorry you took us on, I promise. You will be well rewarded."

"Certainly, Mrs. Cox, certainly. We have no doubt of that. Good day, now. You keep out of this weather and stay warm. Let us handle things for the next few days. We'll call on you if we need to."

"I will, sir. I will. Good day to you."

As I left the office, I couldn't help but notice the receptionist did look quite busy now. She looked up. Such uppity young women these days! Showing no respect for age or importance. I gave her a rather smug look and said, "Good day, Miss," and left the reception area without waiting for a reply, closing the door firmly behind me.

34
MAY

What in hell could be taking so long? I paced the cell restlessly day and night. I had not heard from Maude or anybody else for that matter. Two days had gone by and not a word. Oh, Deputy Brown had made sure I had heat, clean linens, and food, such as it was, but he did not have any news. I knew nothing much happened quickly in the justice system, but damn, I had not even been formally charged! How could they just hold someone without a charge or legal representation? And here it was nearly Christmas!

By late Monday afternoon, I was exhausted. I had not slept. I had to get some sleep, but my jangled nerves just would not calm down. Oh, what I would give for some tonic about now. Tonic! Maybe that could be arranged? I called out for a guard.

"Yes, Mrs. Stamper? What can I do for you? Are you all right? Anything you need or anything I can get for you?" The young man was quite anxious. I suspect he'd been given strict orders to take good care of me.

"Yes, there is something I need. Louis? Your name is Louis, right?"

"Yes ma'am, I'm Louis. I'm assigned to take good care of

you, so what is it you need?"

"Well, Louis, when I was brought here it all happened in such a rush. I didn't have a chance to bring any personal items. Do you suppose you could arrange to procure a few things for me? When I get out of here I will make sure you are richly rewarded, either in money, goods, or services, if you know what I mean." I gave the young Louis my sweetest smile and a wink.

"I'll do my best, ma'am. Just what is it you want?"

"Oh dear, you are such a sweet boy. I'm wondering if the infirmary has anything in the way of feminine supplies? I know this might be embarrassing, but I am in dire need. And some tonic. I have such a terrible case of nerves, given what's happened. Tonic truly helps during such a time, and I am in near constant distress right now. Do you think you could find out if I could have such things? I would be forever in your debt."

The young Louis stammered a bit and a slight blush came to his cheeks. "Well, ma'am, I'll see what I can do. Maybe one of the matrons can arrange it. Are you sure that's all?"

"Oh, that'll be all I need for now. Just enough to get me through another day or so. Some tonic will get me a good night's sleep and that will make all the difference in the world. I would so appreciate it, dear boy."

"I'll get right on it, Mrs. Stamper; don't you fret. I'll get those things to you as soon as possible. You just hold on. I'm sure the uppers want to make sure you're as comfortable as possible."

"Oh, thank you, thank you, Louis. I'll be waiting anxiously."

It didn't take long. Within the hour, Matron Sanderson appeared with a small bundle.

"Here you go, May. My, my, what a tale. I must say you're one of the most inventive ladies I've had the honor of looking after. Now, just tell me, did you really need supplies or is it the tonic you're wanting? The Matron gave a sly smile and a wink.

"Well, whatever do you mean, Matron? Of course, I need them both! I am, after all, a woman." I grinned back. The matron and I were on friendly terms, and we both knew what I really needed.

Matron Sanderson chortled. "Why hell yes, May, I do know what you need, and I've got it right here. Now you just keep it on the sly and don't be overdoing it. I sure don't want to hear you've gone and overdosed again. They don't get in a hurry to get prisoners over to the Grady. And I want to see how all this business turns out. You're providing quite a bit of entertaining gossip around town, and especially here at The Tower."

I pretended demureness. "Yes, Matron, I'll be sure to be careful. I wouldn't want to deprive anyone of their entertainment. I just hope the powers that be will feel the same way."

We both laughed, and Matron Sanderson went on her way. After supper, I did the best I could with my toilette. Feeling a bit more hygienic, I was planning to get a good night's rest. I took a big swig of tonic, careful not to overdo it, and settled in. Next thing I knew, clanging pans awakened me and a fine breakfast was presented. I was refreshed and ready to take on whatever came my way.

It did not take long after breakfast until some good news indeed made its way to my humble presence.

"You've got visitors, Mrs. Stamper. My, you're looking fine this morning. I can tell you're feeling much better." Young Louis smiled as he unlocked the cell. "I'm to escort you down to the conference office."

"Visitors? More than one? Oh my goodness, it's about time. But who would my good friend Maude be bringing with her to see me?"

"Oh, it's not Mrs. Cox. In fact, it is two rather distinguished looking gentlemen. Attorneys, I suspect. They look like the lawyering type."

"Praise God! Perhaps someone finally sees what a big mistake this all is. Thank you, dear Louis. Hopefully, I'm on my way out of here."

"I wouldn't know about that, ma'am. I was just told to bring you down. But I surely do hope it's a good sign."

I felt confident and near giddy as we made our way downstairs. Unfortunately, it was not long before my hopes were dashed. I was ushered into the conference room where Mr. John Moore and Mr. Jack Branch introduced themselves. I'd heard of these two men, though I'd never met them and they were not customers. I surmised they were very wealthy from the appearance of their fine suits, and also figured they must be quite morally upright since I'd never had the pleasure of making their acquaintance. Mr. Moore proceeded to explain how Maude had come to him and procured their services for my defense, even though I had not been formally charged with anything yet.

"Oh, gentlemen, I can't tell you how relieved I am. This is all just a big misunderstanding. I'm sure you will be able to convince the authorities of that. How soon can I leave here?"

Mr. Moore shifted and spoke up. "Whoa now, let's don't get ahead of ourselves. We have to go through all the proper channels. I'm sorry to say it may be a lengthy process."

I slumped in my chair and tears began to unwillingly fill my eyes. I did not cry easily, but this was quite a blow. I had counted on being back in my house. Why, I even wanted to have my ma and pa up from Covington for Christmas! Mr. Branch leaned forward and patted my hand. "Now, now, don't despair. We're confident we can resolve this; it just may take a little while."

I sniffed, regained my composure, and sat up straight. In my most businesslike tone, I said, "All right, just tell me what I need to do. Let's get this taken care of."

Mr. Moore shuffled some papers and responded. "First of all, we need to hear your version of what happened that night at your place. Then we'll talk with the witnesses and compare stories. The elder Mr. Dodgen wants answers too, and that's to our advantage."

I cleared my throat and told my tale, sticking with my original story: I shot through the door at someone trying to break into my house.

Mr. Moore then told me about those other versions in the newspaper, but also told me not to worry – not a chance in the world a jury would find any of us guilty. And I could have all the visitors I wanted now. He was sure the "esteemed Mrs. Cox" would be by to see me within a couple of days, and the two of them would be back soon.

In the last hour, my emotions had swung from optimism to despair and finally settled into guarded encouragement. I just had to be patient. I thanked Mr. Moore and Mr. Branch, and the sweet young Louis escorted me back to my cell.

35
MAY

"Just who do these people think they're dealing with?" I stewed to Maude, "I can't believe they've got us locked up in here and won't even charge us yet. If they can't charge us they should let us go!" It was later in the day and indeed, Maude was admitted for a visit.

"I don't think it'll be long now," replied Maude. "I haven't spoken with Mr. Moore since Monday, but nearly every day there's something more in the papers about this whole affair. Seems like there're conflicting stories, some talk about other men who were at your house that night, and something about a fellow that supposedly ran away right after the shots were fired."

"Well, when Moore and Branch came by early Tuesday, I stuck with my story: I shot through the door at someone trying to break into my house. Mr. Moore told me about those other versions in the newspaper. They didn't tell me much about what's going on with the case, but told me not to worry – not a chance in the world a jury would find any of us guilty. And now I can have all the visitors I want!"

Maude chuckled. "Considering a majority of the jury-eligible men in Atlanta have spent time at your place, he's probably right about your chances of being convicted being next to nothing. But on a serious note, I do have some bad news."

Oh Lordy, what had happened now? "How could things get any worse? Go ahead Maude, spill the beans. I can take it!"

"Well, you know Griffin Freeman and his buddy Charles Jones?"

"Yes, what about 'em?"

"They're both in jail too."

At this news, a niggling worry started. "Both of 'em? What did they do?"

"They set a house on fire. Charged with arson."

"Now why in the world would they do something like that?"

Now Maude looked even more distressed. "Seems they are also charged with destroying evidence."

"Evidence? What kind of ev . . . oh! My Lord – Maude! My house?" My gut was wrenching. "Oh Lordy, Lordy Maude, not my house?"

"I'm afraid so, dearie. The building is still there, but that's all. Just about everything inside was ruined. If the fire didn't get it, the smoke or water did. I'm really sorry to break it to you."

"But when? When did this happen?"

"Just the other night. The house was discovered on fire about three in the morning. With nobody being there, the inside had burned pretty good before the flames blazed out enough for anybody to see. By then it was too late to save anything."

"Oh, Maude – I worked so hard. That place was furnished with the best things I've ever owned in my life. I'll have to start all over."

Maude looked reticent. "Oh, I wouldn't worry about that just yet. Things are just that: things." Maude had that disturbing faraway look in her eyes that I'd seen before, but she went on. "You can replace things. It's people you can't replace. I've learned that the hard way." Maude shook her head as if clearing a bad memory then continued. "What you need to be worried about is why Griff and Charlie would want to set that fire. They've got to be mixed up in this somehow. They're trying to protect somebody. Whoever the 'mysterious' companions are that rag, The Georgian, keeps referring to, I hope they find 'em. That paper may be mostly a gossip sheet, but sometimes that's what it takes to uncover the truth. The Constitution just prints the facts about what's already happened, but the Georgian's speculations might flush out the culprits."

I wasn't so sure I agreed with Maude about the Georgian. What if they uncovered something that wasn't in my favor? Those writers over there sometimes liked to make things sound worse than they really were, and their conjectures might turn out to cause even more trouble. "Well," I told Maudie, "I can't lean on the press too much – I need them on my side, and I'm ready to get out of here. I sure don't want to spend Christmas in this place."

"Don't worry about that, May. You just take care of yourself and let me do the worrying."

"Oh, I'm taking care all right. And everybody in this place is taking care of me too. Seems I've become quite notorious. Doesn't hurt that I could tell stories on half the people in here – and not just the prisoners. The officials will do just about anything to not let word get out they were frequent visitors to 'Mrs. Stamper's Boarding House'. Gives me quite an advantage. It's actually quite amusing. All I have to do is mention it was a tad cold last night, or that soup at lunch was awfully thin, and next thing you know I've got extra blankets and meat in my soup."

"Well, May, you just watch your step. From what I'm reading this could go pretty high up. You don't want to get in over your head."

"Over my head? No such thing, Maudie dear. Anyways, I can swim just fine." We both laughed, but I was growing more concerned each day. I figured the longer I was in here the more complicated things must be on the outside. I was going to have to tell Moore and Branch I wanted to see some progress.

"If you say so, May. I just don't like the way they keep coming up with witnesses and folks who said they were with Dodgen that night. You know the senior Dodgen's determined to get to the bottom of this. He's pulling out all the stops. Got detectives running all over the state of Georgia tracking down folks. I have a feeling there's much more going on here than meets the eye. I know you paint a pretty simple picture, but you're not the only one talking."

This didn't sound good, either. "Let 'em talk. I've got my story and I'm sticking to it."

"All right, honey, I just hope you're not the one ends up stuck. Well, I best be on my way. I've got some errands to run. I'll be back next week. You know I care about you, May. I want what's best for you. In the end, the truth will come out. I just hope it's in your favor."

"Oh, I'll be fine, Maude. Thank you for coming by. I depend on you for so much. Why, nobody told me about my house and belongings and that was over a day ago! I do appreciate your visits. Come back next week and let me know what you're hearing. Oh, and bring those Georgian rags with you. It should be amusing to read what they're saying."

"I will, May. You take care now. Good-bye."

I watched as Maude made her way out of the visiting room. I didn't want her to worry. She was getting on up there, although I had no idea how old she was. I had seen her slowing down in just the nearly ten years I'd known her. She was a dear friend and an invaluable resource. I didn't know what I'd do without her. I tried to act unflappable since I didn't want her to worry, but her news was disturbing. I did not like being locked up in here where I didn't know what was going on. I was going to have to do a lot of serious thinking over the next few days.

Next week! Maude said she'd be back next week! Oh Lordy, she must know something I don't if she knows I'll still be in here next week. I'd best be finding out what's going on and figuring out what I was going to do if my story did not stick. Dear God, how much worse could it get? I was back where I started before I came to Atlanta. Not a rag of clothing or a stick of furniture to my name. Why did I just keep getting beaten down? And what did Maude mean with her morose comments about things were just things. Why, things were all I had in this world, except for her.

Yes, all I had in this world was gone, and now nothing but her support and friendship remained. What a sobering thought. Here I was again, swinging from high to low, and who knew, I might even be swinging by the neck in the actual Tower before it was over. And what did I have to show for all my scheming? Not a thing. Not a word or visit from my family. Not even from Wesley Stamper. So much for remaining friends. I could hardly blame him though. I had shooed him away once he had served his purpose.

I thought back over the years I had been in Atlanta. When

John and I were married and out on our own, Maude and I developed our deep fondness for each other, but even Maude had an unnamed sadness about her at times. And here she had mentioned again the truth would come out in the end. I'd told so many lies, made up so many stories, and lost track of events while in tonic-induced stupors, I wasn't even sure I knew the real truth. All my plans and schemes had gotten me nowhere, I had no things, and no one. I needed to do some deep soul searching when, and if, I got out of this predicament. Why wait? Maybe I needed to start now. Although I'd never given much credence to spiritual matters, what could it hurt? Maybe it was my last resort. Although I was not a praying soul, it could not hurt and might even help. I fell to my knees on the cold stone floor. *Oh God, if you'll just see me through, I promise I'll try to make it on the straight and narrow if you'll just give me the chance. I swear it on my own soul!"*

36
MAY

    Another week had passed and I was fit to be tied. Christmas had come and gone, with Bob Jordan, Bessie, Addie, and me still in jail. We had been questioned over and over and our stories stayed the same every time. Where was all this conjecture coming from? And how could they keep us locked up if a different suspect was on the loose? I was expecting Mr. Moore and Mr. Branch this morning. I had sent word I wanted to see my legal representation and I wanted to see them today. I wanted answers, and I wanted them now. Most of all, I wanted to know if the law had a substantial basis to hold me. Enough was enough. I wanted to be released.

    I got the guards to slip me issues of The Georgian and The Constitution on a daily basis, and nearly every day there was conjecture in the papers about John Dodgen's murder. Some said I did it while others said a mysterious stranger fired the shot. Some said he was killed inside and his body drug out on the porch; others said he was shot through the door. Some said there was a fight and others present in the house that night; others said there was only the four of us. Some said Dodgen had been running around all evening to pool halls and bars. Some said he was robbed of a large sum of money before he was shot. One article even said I had named someone else as the murderer! I was ready to get this over with.

"Hello, May! How are we today?" Mr. Moore greeted me as I entered the office where prisoners were allowed to meet with their attorneys.

"I don't know about 'we,' Mr. Moore, but I am mad as a hornet. What's going on? What's the hold-up? I'm ready to get out of here. I've already missed Christmas with my family. If they can't definitely pin this on me, then I demand to be released."

Mr. Moore sat back and put up his hands. "Whoa! Hold on there! I know you've been reading the papers. There is quite a bit going on actually. It's to our advantage to let all these stories get out there. The more confusion about that night, the better for our case. You do want to be cleared of this, don't you?"

"Of course I do. I'd just rather it be sooner than later. I'm tired of sitting in here twiddling my thumbs."

"Well, we're going to ask for a commitment hearing. Dodgen's father is trying to postpone everything so he can dig up more evidence. He's not convinced you killed his son. If he doesn't look out, his goons are going to uncover more information than he's bargained for. There's already speculation John Jr. was mixed up in several illegal schemes. Course, that's no surprise given that most officials in this city and county are working deals one way or another."

"I know that better than anybody. So what happens in this commitment hearing?"

"We go in and ask for things to get moving. Either press charges or let you all go. It'll be up to the judge to decide, based on your stories and other evidence. Naturally, judges read newspapers too. They love seeing their names in print."

"You mean this could all be over tomorrow?"

"Well, not completely. There might be a few details to finish up if they decide to release. But if they go ahead with the charges, that will determine if we go ahead with a hearing or a trial. That remains to be seen. You just sit tight and I'll be by for you before the hearing in the morning." Mr. Moore stood, shook hands, and took his leave. I was left to wonder if this might be my last night in jail, this time anyway.

The next morning the guards came for me, and we were joined by other guards with Bessie, Addie, and Bob. It was the first I had seen of them since that fateful night. They did not look much worse for the wear, so I guessed they'd been well taken care of too. Of course, we were not allowed to speak to each other. They mostly avoided looking my way. That made me a bit uneasy. Had they changed their stories?

We were all marched next door to a hearing room. Mr. Moore and Mr. Branch were both there, as were John Dodgen Sr. and Judge Pendleton. Judge Pendleton started out by asking Mr. Dodgen if he was prepared for the case to proceed.

Dodgen Senior arose and addressed the judge. "Your Honor, I oppose the immediate hearing of the case."

"On what basis, Mr. Dodgen?" asked Judge Pendleton.

"I expect to prove that contrary to Mrs. Stamper's statement, three shots instead of one were fired on the night my son was killed. In addition, the door, which she claimed my son tried to batter in, was not fastened at all. It was found unlocked and unbolted by that colored girl who found my son's body on Sunday morning. I just need a little more time to get the evidence and witnesses together."

"I see," said Judge Pendleton. "I know the loss of your son has been a terrible tragedy, Mr. Dodgen. Let me hear what the applicants' attorney has to say. Mr. Moore?

Mr. Moore rose and addressed the Judge. "Your Honor, we acknowledge that Mr. Dodgen Sr. would certainly want to ascertain the exact circumstances of his son's tragic death, and we offer our condolences and understanding on his behalf. But, Your Honor, we have four persons, one man and three women, whose freedom has been encroached upon. We resist the motion for a further continuance, and insist the State has had ample time to prepare its case and subpoena witnesses."

Judge Pendleton studied some papers on his desk. Then he addressed all the parties. "I must consider the public's rights in this matter. With the death of young Dodgen alleged to have occurred on the porch of the house in which the four defendants were on the night in question, there is clear reason to suspect the defendants may have malevolent intentions and pose a flight risk should they be released. Therefore, I declare that the public's rights in the matter must be protected. I proclaim this hearing will hold over until Monday morning, and Judge Roan will hear arguments before the grand jury of the Fulton County Superior Court. This session is adjourned." The judge rose and strode swiftly out a side door.

I could not believe what I heard. Held over? Monday morning? A different judge? Flight risk? Although I had not gotten my hopes up too much, I was sorely disappointed. It was all I could do to maintain my composure and hold back the tears that were burning my eyes. I had held out a tiny expectation of walking out of jail today. I should have known better. I turned to Mr. Moore.

"What now?" I asked.

"We'll see you in court Monday morning, that's what. Just stick to your story. At least things are moving ahead."

"Well, let's just hope they're moving in the right direction."

"Oh, I wouldn't worry too much, May. You know, there's a lot of unanswered questions surrounding this case; too many, if you ask me. I've seen cases turn on a dime at the last minute, and we've still got a ways to go. Just be patient. It'll all work out just fine."

"I hope you're right, Mr. Moore. I'm finding it very hard to just sit in a cell and do nothing on my own behalf. I just hope you're right."

Bessie, Addie, Bob and I were all escorted back to The Tower and once again had no opportunity to converse. I was deep in my own thoughts anyway. Dear God, did it do me any good at all to utter that desperate prayer? It was a long, cold weekend in that Tower, and I had never felt so despondent and alone.

37
MAY

    The next Monday morning we sat in Judge Roan's Superior Court. The room was full. I looked around and recognized many faces as witnesses who had been at the coroner's inquest that Sunday afternoon after Dodgen was murdered: Frank Lawrence, the colored man who worked at the store downstairs from me; Mr. Peterson, who worked for the railroad; Officers Dunbar, Wagner, and Shaw; the dead man's father, Justice Dodgen; Detective Spradlin, Justice Puckett; and the matron, Miss Sanderson. There were several others present that I did not recognize.
    It did not take long to get down to business. In a few moments, Judge Roan entered and made his announcement:
    "This Court will now engage in a preliminary hearing to determine whether to continue to hold Mrs. Willie Stamper, Mr. Robert Jordan, Mrs. Bessie Gray, and Miss Addie Goss as prisoners. These four have been held in The Tower since December 16 and are suspects in the murder of John Dodgen, Jr. Mr. Dodgen was an officer of the court and bailiff of Judge Puckett. Is the State ready to proceed?"
    "We are, Your Honor." Solicitor General Charles Hill was

representing the State. The courts were undergoing some reorganization, so I hadn't been certain who or what we would be up against. Hopefully, Mr. Moore and Mr. Branch were well informed.

"All right. Solicitor Hill, you may proceed," Judge Roan replied.

Mr. Moore had told me I'd probably be the last to be called, so I had plenty of time to adjust my story according to the other witnesses if needed. The Solicitor started with Addie.

When Addie took the stand, I was expecting the same story as before. I was more than surprised when I realized she said there were two shots fired! I glared at her fiercely, but she steadfastly avoided my gaze, never even glancing in my direction. Our story had always been that one shot was fired. Addie was asked to step down and Bessie was put up next. I was stunned when she also testified there were two shots fired.

"Now, Mrs. Gray, do you recall the testimony you gave at the coroner's on Sunday afternoon, December 16th?" Solicitor Hill was questioning Bessie.

"Yes, sir, I do. Just the same as I've said here," Bessie answered.

"But Mrs. Gray, that is not correct. There is a difference as to the number of shots you said were fired."

Bessie had a panic-stricken look on her face. "Well, I, um, thought I'd said two shots. I'm almost sure I did!"

"Are you quite certain, Mrs. Gray?"

Bessie looked around nervously. But it was clear she was avoiding looking at me, as well, just like Addie. "Well, at that inquest, I may have said just one shot. Mrs. Stamper told me and Addie that if we said two shots were fired it would get us all in serious trouble." There was an audible mumble that spread around the room. Judge Roan peered down at the witness and looked perturbed. Solicitor Hill turned to Addie.

"Miss Goss, do you agree with Mrs. Gray? Did Mrs. Stamper tell you and Mrs. Gray to say only one shot was fired?"

Addie looked scared. She had better be scared! She glanced around at me and then looked up at Bessie. Finally, in a voice barely above a whisper, she said, "Yes, sir. That's what she told us." I was seething!

"Thank you, Miss Goss. And Mrs. Gray, you may step down. Your Honor, I now call Robert Jordan, a bailiff from Justice Jones' court. He was also allegedly at Mrs. Stamper's when this murder occurred."

I watched as Bob Jordan took the stand. "Mr. Jordan, would you please tell us your version of the events early Sunday morning December 16th?"

"Yes, sir. Mrs. Stamper asked me to stay over at her place because she thought there might be trouble. I had gone to bed and was awakened by a ruckus and a shot. When I went out to the parlor Mrs. Stamper told me she had shot through the door to scare away an intruder. We listened and didn't hear anything more, so I went back to bed. It wasn't until the next morning when that colored girl came that I knew anything about poor John Dodgen being found dead."

Bless him! He stuck to our original story. I could have jumped up right there and kissed him. Apparently, the officials did not want to pester one of their own. They let him down without further questioning about the number of shots.

"Thank you, Mr. Jordan. You can step down," was all Solicitor Hill had to say in response to Bob's statement. It seemed clear enough to me they were looking out for their own, and Bob would most likely get out of this untainted.

The Solicitor called other witnesses. The only one I hadn't heard before was a Dr. Hart. They had called him in to talk about blood stains. That did concern me some. How could I explain away blood stains? Well, after all, three women lived in my place. I could claim women's troubles. My mind wandered as the other witnesses droned on, their stories having been oft repeated by now. I had only taken a tiny nip of tonic, but I found my mind wandering off fairly often these days. If I had to, I could put on a performance of the wronged property owner, a single woman just trying to protect herself and her home. I had done enough play-acting before, and if necessary I could lie through my teeth with a face as straight as a razor.

I was joggled out of my designing thoughts. Mr. Moore and Mr. Branch were now standing. Solicitor Hill had taken a seat.

Mr. Moore spoke. "Your Honor, it is our contention that

Mrs. Stamper was completely justified in shooting through her door when she was under the impression that someone was trying to forcibly enter her home after midnight. We believe this is a clear case of a citizen defending their home and request that Mrs. Stamper is released with no further consequence."

"Is that all?" was Judge Roan's reply.

"Yes sir, it is. It is a simple matter of defending one's personal home and property."

That was it! They were not even calling me to the stand. I didn't quite know what to think of this, but I did not think it bode well. I was all prepared to act my part.

"All right, then, Mr. Moore, Mr. Branch, you may be seated. Solicitor Hill, any final statement?"

"Yes, Your Honor. Based on conflicting testimony, the State believes there is insufficient evidence to support the defense council's claims. We request that Mrs. Gray, Miss Goss, and Mr. Jordan be released, and that Mrs. Stamper is committed."

What? Was I hearing this correctly? Let them go, but keep me? I felt a burgeoning heaviness build in my chest and head. Mr. Moore and Mr. Branch, sitting on either side of me, placed a hand on each of my shoulders. Judge Roan was again shuffling papers. My breath became shallow and quick. Was this the tonic talking or my true reaction to what I was hearing? *Come on, May. Get ahold of yourself. Don't act the fool right here in court! Or should I act out? Maybe that would seem more innocent?* Then Judge Roan spoke.

"This is clearly a case for the grand jury. The woman has admitted firing the shots, but the question is whether she knew that the man at the door was Dodgen, or if there was any motive for killing him, or if she is guilty of criminal negligence in shooting before she gave the man time to make known his mission. These questions should be determined by a jury. Therefore, I am ruling Mrs. Stamper be committed without bail. Her case will be considered by the Grand Jury which meets next Monday."

I was jarred out of my stupor and went with my instincts. It was show time! I jumped up from my chair, screaming "No!" I forced myself into gut-wrenching sobs. I wailed, over and over, "I did not murder the poor man!" After a few minutes of this, I sank back into my seat but continued sobbing. I stole glances at others, in between the hankies that were being pressed into my hands. Addie, Bessie, and Bob all got out of there so fast, it was as if they were afraid I would pull out a gun and shoot them next. Mr. Moore and Mr. Branch looked somewhat abashed as they patted and pleaded with me to take control of my senses. Solicitor Hill, Judge Roan, and the other officials looked indifferent and continued packing up their things, making it clear they were anxious to leave. My cell officer, Ed Wagner, fumbled about, looking embarrassed that he didn't quite know how to handle the situation. Of course, I was taking all of this in as I continued presenting the picture of a distraught and wronged innocent victim. I kept up the charade until the courtroom was nearly empty. I wanted to wring every bit of pity and concern out of those present while I had the chance. All of this was flashing through my mind as I plotted what my next steps should be.

    Eventually, I let my sobbing subside into a whimper and let my body slump as though I was completely overcome with anguish. I finally allowed Mr. Moore, Mr. Branch, and Ed Wagner to lead me away. I was sure I appeared quite distressed, but on the inside, I was livid with anger, already plotting my recourse. This was nothing compared to what would come to pass over the next few weeks.

38
MAY

    Sure enough, the grand jury convened the next Monday and I was indicted for murder. I resigned myself that this was going to be a much longer haul. I thought I could count on John Moore and Jack Branch to convince the court and the jurors to see things my way, but a little insurance couldn't hurt. In fact, the kind of insurance I had in mind would be near fool-proof. And these men were fools to think they could get rid of me this easy.

    Once returned to my cell in The Tower, I stewed and paced. You'd think there'd be a trough in the stone floor as I trod the same path back and forth. Knowing that Bob, Bessie, and Addie were free and leaving me to take the blame was eating away at my insides. I was determined that if I was going to be brought down, I would not be alone. Why, more than half the officials in Atlanta were frequent visitors to my place. They would not get away with this. Who did these people think they were dealing with? Hell, they were about to find out.

    I set about a letter-writing campaign Tower officials had never seen the likes of. Nearly every hour I was asking for more paper and ink. I wrote far into the wee hours of the next morning. It was a good thing the guards let me go about my own business and keep my own hours as long as I did not disturb anyone else. I wrote to dozens of my acquaintances, all of whom were prominent Atlantans, and my clientele included law enforcement officials, politicians, several judges, and successful businessmen. I made sure they would know what was at stake. The letter I copied over and over went something like this.

> Dear John,
> I am sure you know by now that I am once again indisposed. My desire to continue to provide much-needed services to the fine gentleman of Atlanta is in jeopardy. I fear that should a jury not find in my favor, I will not see the light of freedom for some time. I implore you to impose whatever influence you have on my behalf. If the worst should happen and the jury does not find in my favor, I will be forced to disclose the names of those who have contributed to my ruin. Thank you for your support, and I look forward to our continued association.
> Sincerely,
> May Stamper

The next day I gave the letters to Maude who posted them. It was early January when some of the finest homes and offices in Atlanta received notice that Mrs. May Stamper would not be found guilty, or else. I was tickled as I imagined there must be quite a buzz in the club rooms and behind closed doors as men from all walks of life debated the seriousness of their predicament. Surely there was anxious speculation from judges' chambers to cooks' quarters. No man could doubt my intention, and certainly, no man wanted to contemplate the consequences of either being revealed or being denied my future "services!" Truth be told, it was hard to know which they dreaded the most, being found out or going without.

Understandably, none of my male friends wanted to be caught visiting me. But I got word of them through Maude, who came often. From what she said my letter writing campaign was having quite an effect. Bessie and Addie had kept Maude informed of what they heard around town, and Maude told me they were downright scared to see me. I let her know I was over being mad at them. They had to look out for themselves, after all. I told her to let them know I would appreciate a visit. As usual, my spirits had swung the other direction back up and I would enjoy some girl talk.

"Oh Lordy!" laughed Maude. "You should have heard them talk. Half the men in Atlanta are buying flowers for their wives and the other half are buying silks and chocolate. May, you're boosting the economy. The men of Atlanta are bending over backward to appear to be virtuous and faithful husbands."

"Well, they better. If I get convicted, I'll name every one of the sorry bastards and they will have hell to pay. I might be in this damn Tower, but they'll be worse off than me."

We had quite a laugh over picturing half the men of Atlanta kowtowing to their wife's every wish. Addie and Bessie began to come nearly every afternoon. You'd think we had a regular afternoon tea party with all the treats they brought. One afternoon as they were approaching my cell, escorted by guard Pat O'Kelly, I could hear their conversation.

"Miss Addie, Miss Bessie," said guard O'Kelly with a wink. "You ladies sure look fine this afternoon, and I think you'll find Mrs. Stamper in fine spirits today!"

Addie giggled. "Whatever gives you that idea?"

"Yes, what makes you think that?" asked Bessie.

"Well now, don't you think Miss May knows what an uproar she's caused? She's tickled to death to hear about all these high falutin' men of Atlanta shivering in their shoes at being found out. Quite a few not so high falutin' ones, too. Amazing how that little twig of a woman can pull strings even while she's locked up. I never seen anything like it – least not in this jail. Beats all I've ever seen."

Addie replied, "Well, you haven't seen anything yet. You just watch what happens if Mrs. Stamper does get convicted. All hell will break loose." Bessie and Addie just kept giggling. I imagined Mr. O'Kelly shaking his head and grinning to himself. He had nothing to fear from me, being a single man and all. He even told me he liked to provide "special treatment" for me since I was a "guest" in his "house" for now.

As they approached my cell I started singing away, so they wouldn't think I'd been eavesdropping on their conversation. "Keep on the sunny side – keep on the sunny side, keep on the sunny side of life…" And that was just what I intended to do. As they arrived at my cell, I greeted them,

"Hello, girls. And Mr. O'Kelly! Is it as fine a day outside as it is in here?"

"It's getting finer by the minute!" was Addie's response.

"Is that so? What's happening in our fair city of Atlanta?"

Guard O'Kelly let Bessie and Addie in and bade us have a good visit. The jailers had long ago given up on escorting me to the visiting room every time I had company come calling. That's all they'd be doing all day long now that I was allowed unlimited visitors. Bessie proceeded to fill me in on recent happenings.

"You are certainly the talk of the town, May. And you should see the men! They all act like they are scared out of their britches. Even Policemen Shaw and Jones wouldn't look us in the eyes. They just pretended like we weren't even walkin' right down the street towards them. Then we happened by Judge Roan's on the way here, and when he saw us a'comin' he turned right around and walked back inside his house. What do you make of that, May?"

"Well, I make of it that he's quakin' in his shoes along with the rest of them. And if he's doing it, then all the other judges are too. Seems like things are going in my favor if you ask me." We shared a few more stories and quite a few laughs at the expense of Atlanta's fine male upper echelon, then Addie and Bessie went on their way.

The next day, the day before the trial was to start, Maude came. She was carrying a large parcel. "Howdy-doo, May!"

"Howdy yourself, Maude. Did you bring them?"

"Oh yes, I even brought a few extra. You are going to be the most respectable looking woman in Atlanta come tomorrow." Maude began to pull out a dress, undergarments, toiletries, hairpins, hairbrushes, and various other items.

"Oh, Maude! I knew you would come through for me."

As Maude unpacked the items, Matron Sanderson rounded the corner. She came over from the police department every few days to check on me and have a little visit.

"Well, what have we here?" she asked with raised brows.

"Just a few things to get May presentable at the trial tomorrow," said Maude.

"I think she could wear a flour sack and no judge or jury in the city of Atlanta would convict her. They all have too much to lose!" The matron declared.

"I do agree with you, Miss Sanderson, I do agree," Maude replied, while I just laughed. I felt like a schoolgirl getting gussied up for a party, or leastways what I thought one would feel like. I'd never been to a schoolgirl party so I wouldn't really know. What I did know was that this was becoming quite a production and downright fun. I refused to let the possibility of a less than positive outcome enter my mind.

"Hey, what else is in that bag?" I said. Miss Sanderson was fingering the fine fabric of the dress.

"It's a little something to top off your outfit. Well, actually, it's not so little, but it will top it off!" With a flourish, Maude withdrew a millinery confection the likes of which I'd never seen.

"It's the latest style!" Maude proclaimed. Apparently, Miss Sanderson had never seen anything like it either. We all gazed at the hat Maude held in her hands. Fan-shaped silk stood up above ruffles and flowers. Ribbons adorned the edges. The black silk and velvet were elegantly detailed with pleats and edged with braided trim. Feathers finished it off in outlandish style. The three of us busted out in squeals of glee.

"Oh Maude, you're such a dear! How can I ever repay you?"

"I'm sure we'll come up with something." Maude winked.

Matron Sanderson went on, "Hmmm. That hat's a hot ticket. And seems to me you might want a little surprise factor when you leave out of here and into court tomorrow. Tell you what, I'll hold onto it for you and we can put it on your head when I come for you tomorrow. How about that? The guards won't mind you having the other things. In fact, they just might enjoy seeing you dolled up!" Her sly grin sent Maude and me back into gales of laughter. We might as well have been in a salon as in a jail.

39
MAY

It was Tuesday morning when Miss Sanderson came to escort me to court. First, we went to a holding room in the jail. True to her word, Miss Sanderson had brought along the hat. She secured it atop the black coils of hair I'd managed to pin up. "We don't want this fancy chapeau blowing off in that January wind," she said. Making sure it was held on tightly with several hat pins, she added, "There, that should do it."

"And I've got one more thing for you. It's mighty cold outside, May. You need a wrap to keep from freezing, even though it's just a short way to the courthouse." As Maude had done with the exquisite hat the day before, Miss Sanderson, with a flourish, drew forth a gorgeous fur collar. Draping it around my neck and shoulders, we could see the black fur wrap complemented the outfit beautifully. I looked like a well-off respectable lady, out for an afternoon of business or shopping. The matron winked and whispered, "It's amazing what one can find in the stolen property room, so let's just keep this little gift between us!"

"Why, thank you, Miss Sanderson. It does set off the dress and hat just right. And it will be our own little secret. Let's just hope no ladies recognize it!"

Guard O'Kelly and Ed Wagner entered the holding room. Both looked astonished at my transformation. "Haven't you ever seen a real lady before? Cat got your tongue?" I said as I sashayed about the room for them.

Ed stammered. "No ma'am, I mean, yes ma'am, I mean, I don't rightly know ma'am …"

Pat O'Kelly let out a low whistle. "I'd say you'd be the belle of the ball, if you was going to a ball, that is!"

Miss Sanderson said, "All right fellas, that's enough gawking. Let's get on our way. Justice waits for no man, or no woman either, except maybe Mrs. May Stamper." She grinned.

We walked the short half block to the court and arrived just in time. John Moore and Jack Branch met me there.

"Just do as we discussed, May. Stick to your same story. We don't think there's any way in hell this jury will find you guilty," Mr. Moore instructed.

Jack Branch had a smile playing on his lips. "Especially after those letters went out. Case you're wondering, my own father got one, and he's the one showed it to me. I just told him all I saw was a piece of paper in his hand."

"Why, Mr. Branch and Mr. Moore, I have every confidence in your defense abilities. I just thought a little insurance couldn't hurt any."

As we stood just outside the defendant's entry door we could see the room was packed. The crowd was murmuring, and Judge Roan had not yet taken the bench. I was prepared to put on the show of my life. I should have been an actress as much as I was being called upon to perform these last few weeks.

Just as we stepped into the room, there were gasps all around. At that moment, the door to Judge Roan's chambers opened. Judge Roan paused, as if he were confused, then, as he realized all eyes were not on him, he followed the stares in our direction. An expression of consternation creased his brow, and he took a step backward.

As we entered, the collective gasp subsided and you could have heard a pin drop. I'm sure most of the spectators were acquaintances, and maybe a few were simply there as gawkers. They clearly did not expect to see May Stamper as the elegant, diminutive woman who stood before them. I knew I did not look capable of murder, prostitution, bootlegging, or any other crime.

Judge Roan entered the room and sat down on his bench. It was as still and quiet as a graveyard at midnight. I gazed directly at him, and then languidly around the courtroom as we made our way to the defendant table. As my eye fell on the men, including the judge, the attorneys, the jury, the witnesses, and the spectators, I tried to appear bemused, as if to say, *"So now, what will it be? Will you go down with me or shall I be set free?"* Most of those upon whom my inquisitive look fell averted their eyes guiltily, even Colonel John Dodgen, the father of the murder victim. The only man in the courtroom who looked me stonily in the eye without flinching was Solicitor General Hill, who was leading the prosecution for the State.

Mr. Charles D. Hill, Solicitor General, had held that post for many years and was known as a fearsome adversary if he believed in your guilt. His problem in this trial was that he was also a man, espousing good virtues while possessing the foibles of many men. He knew from his own experience the weaknesses of men and women. Although he was a respected prosecutor and usually dealt kindly with men who were in trouble, it remained to be seen if he would be as sympathetic to a woman who took advantage of those very shortcomings most men held.

As for the women, my eye never even rested on them. I sniffed and tilted my chin up in disdain as if the women were non-existent. Indeed, they were useless to my case and could not contribute to my cause. Thanks to their prudishness, I had the men in the palm of my hand. Other than Addie, Bessie, Maude, and Annie, of whose testimony I was confident, the women were inconsequential.

I purposefully moved slowly and seated myself gracefully with Mr. Moore and Mr. Branch. The judge called the court to order and the preliminaries were carried out quickly. Within a few minutes, the witness testimonies commenced. The defense was first, and I was called to the stand. I was sworn in and planned to tell my story the same as I had on several occasions by now.

Mr. Moore began the questioning. "Mrs. Stamper, please tell the jury the events that occurred at your home on the late evening of Saturday, December 15 and early morning of Sunday, December 16."

I sat up straight, took a deep breath, raised my head, and stared directly at the jury.

"Yes, sir, I will. I was in my house about one o'clock in the morning, and on hearing someone knock at the door I inquired who it was. No direct answer was given. Then the party kicked on the door and informed me that if I did not open it, the door would be broken in. Then I replied I would shoot if the pounding on the door did not cease. Well, sir, the pounding did not cease. I fired through the door and heard someone run down the steps. The next morning, my cook informed me of a dead man on the porch. I took a look and there he was. I recognized John Dodgen, as we had been friends for some time."

"Thank you, Mrs. Stamper. You may step down."

Mr. Moore proceeded to call Bessie, Addie, and Bob Jordan. Each gave nearly identical versions of the story. So much for their former conflicting testimony! Now that it came right down to it they stuck to our original story like molasses on a kitchen table. Addie and Bessie both stated that they were in rooms of the house and heard the shot, but did not see the shooting. Bob told how I had asked him to come over to my house for protection. He, too, said he was in another room, heard the conversation and shot, one louder than the other, but could not reach the door in time to witness the act.

By this time, it was nearly noon. Judge Roan called for a brief recess for lunch. I was escorted to the prisoner's holding room just off the court. Wagner, O'Kelly, and Miss Sanderson never left my side and we said little as we ate the soup that had been provided for us. In contrast to my grand entrance earlier, the mood was now somber. Our little bit of conversation was mainly just pleasantries. "Pass the salt, please." "Hot soup sure is good on a cold day like this." "Be glad when warmer weather gets here." I could tell from these brief statements that the men were reluctant to discuss anything that had taken place in court. Miss Sanderson, while not saying much, grinned and winked mischievously, a feeble attempt to lighten the serious atmosphere. There was no denying from her behavior that she was in full cahoots with my side. We were all anxious to get on with it. It wasn't long before our lunchtime was over and we were back in the courtroom being called to order.

40
MAY

After the lunch recess, Mr. Moore called several other witnesses. Policeman Shaw testified that he was in the house about ten o'clock Saturday night and that " . . . while seemingly enjoying themselves, none of the persons there appeared to be intoxicated." He added that he also saw young Dodgen there a night or two before, giving me medicine. He said he left his beat around my residence at ten minutes after midnight and up to that time had heard no shots period.

So far so good, I thought. All the stories matched up. Finally, Miss Sanderson was called. I wasn't sure what her testimony would be, but I did know that if Mr. Moore had called her in it had to be in my favor. He proceeded to call her to the stand.

"Miss Sanderson, it is my understanding you were called to the residence of May Stamper on Sunday morning this past December 16th, in the capacity of your duties as police matron. Is that correct?"

"Yes, sir, that is correct."

"Can you please describe Mrs. Stamper's emotional state at the time of your arrival?"

"Yes, sir. Mrs. Stamper was visibly excited. She was pacing, wringing her hands, and was alternately wailing and sniveling that she did not know it was John Dodgen at her door until his body was found that morning. She sobbed that if she had only known, he wouldn't be dead, that she was just trying to protect her home and residents."

"Thank you, Miss Sanderson. Now, I understand you looked around the residence that morning. Is that correct?"

"Yes, sir, that's right."

"Would you please tell the court what you discovered on one of the beds in the house?"

"Yes, sir. I found blood on one of the beds."

"Now, Miss Sanderson, in your experience as a police matron and former nurse, can you speculate on the source or nature of that blood?"

Miss Sanderson sat up proudly. "Yes, sir, I have over 25 years of experience as a trained nurse and jail matron. I believe the blood on the bed could have come from other sources than Dodgen's wound. As you know, there were several women boarders at that house, and the blood could have come from any one of them. That is my professional opinion."

The defense evidence was all in by three o'clock and the judge called a short recess. We retreated back to the same little room where we had lunch. It was silent and tense. None of us spoke a word for several minutes. Finally, Mr. Moore spoke to me quietly.

"May, how are you? Do you need anything? Water? Are you warm enough? Cool enough? I want you in good condition."

"I'll be fine as cotton soon as this is over with. Right about now I'm strung so tight you could play me like a fiddle. I want this done. One way or the other. I'm tired of waiting and pretending like everything's just fine."

"That's my girl!" Mr. Moore chuckled. "Now you are sounding like the spunky May I have heard so much about. Hang on just a while longer and this will all be over with. I've got a good feeling things will go our way."

I looked at Moore soberly. "Interesting choice of words, Mr. Moore. If things don't go our way, I just might be hanging, literally!"

Moore looked taken aback, then I grinned and went on. "Got you there for a minute, didn't I counselor? Oh, I'm not really scared. But I do want this behind me. I've made my peace with God, so whatever happens, I'll be all right. Let's just get it done."

As Moore gave me a reassuring pat on the back, a knock at the door told us it was time to head back into the courtroom. We all stood and smoothed our clothes.

It was Mr. Branch who spoke this time. "Let's go. It's time to hear what our pious Solicitor Hill has up his sleeve." Our subdued little group walked back to the courtroom and took our places. Now it was the prosecution's turn.

The senior John Dodgen, also an attorney, was to assist Solicitor Hill, who opened the argument for the State. He was referred to as "Colonel" in deference to his former military rank. Maybe the prosecution thought it would lend more sympathy his direction. I knew Colonel Dodgen had been the reason for the delays in this case. The newspaper articles said he believed I was covering up for someone else. Was he mad? Hell, there was no way I would take a murder rap for anyone! Being unable to locate the man he believed had actually killed his son, he had decided to let me take the punishment for now. He could still track down the real murderer and get his revenge later. Colonel Dodgen himself was Mr. Hill's main witness for the prosecution.

Mr. Hill stood and greeted Judge Roan. "Good afternoon, Judge." Then he turned and waved his arm around the courtroom. "And a good afternoon to my fine friends and colleagues."

It seemed plain as the back of a picture that from this behavior he felt very at ease and confident. Could it be he didn't know about the letters? That would surely take the wind out of his sails. "Your Honor, I would like to call Colonel John Dodgen as my first and only witness for the prosecution."

"Proceed, Solicitor Hill." Judge Roan did not even look up at the prosecutor.

Colonel Dodgen was sworn in and placed on the stand. I figured Mr. Hill was going to play up to the unfortunate loss of Dodgen's son, and sure enough, he went right to it.

"Colonel Dodgen, please accept my condolences on the loss of your son, John. What a tragedy! A fine, upstanding young man, a come-upper in our justice system, struck down in his youth by a foul murderer."

"Thank you, Solicitor Hill. It is hard enough to lose a son, but losing John in such a senseless and vicious murder is especially difficult. I intend to bring the perpetrator of this horrendous act to justice." At this, he glared directly at me. I returned his searing hot stare with my own, but mine was as cool as ice.

Solicitor Hill continued. "As do I, Colonel, as do I. Let's get straight to the evidence, beginning with the blood evidence that Police Matron Sanderson testified she found on a bed in the house. Would you please relate your findings on this evidence?"

Colonel Dodgen began to speak rather matter-of-factly, I thought, considering he had just described the loss of his son as senseless, vicious, and horrendous.

"As has been previously told, blood was found inside rooms of the house by several witnesses. There were red stains on a bed. What the witness did not mention was that there were also stains on the floor appearing to lead to the door outside of which my son was found dead in the morning. Furthermore, there was some matter resembling a particle of a man's brain found on the wall inside the house."

At this statement, there was a gasping moan from the gallery. However, I did not flinch. How could a man who had lost his son sit up there so dispassionately and imply the son's brains were on the wall of the house where he was murdered? The Colonel, even though he was an accomplished attorney in his own right, seemed to have no inkling of how to gain the sympathy of a jury.

Mr. Hill intervened, "Please continue, Colonel."

The Colonel went on. "There were also charred remains of a rag found in the stove which looked as if it had been saturated with blood. It should also be recalled that the week following the murder when all the residents of the house were in jail, the building was set afire. Two men, both acquaintances of Mrs. Stamper, have been charged with arson in that matter. "

Solicitor Hill intervened. "Yes, we are well aware of the arson at Mrs. Stamper's residence, Colonel. Clearly an attempt to destroy evidence. I understand you have further evidence, though, in your possession. Is that correct?"

"Yes, Solicitor. I do. Could you please hand me that stick

over there by my chair?"

Mr. Hill handed over a slender stick of fresh lumber, several feet in length. "Please explain to the court, Colonel, how this stick could be evidence in this case."

A stick? What in the hell is he going to say a stick had to do with the murder of his son? This I had to hear.

"Certainly, Solicitor. As you can clearly see, there are two marks on this stick. One represents the height of the deceased and the other the distance the bullet hole in the door was from the floor. The hole in the door was 5 feet and 2 ½ inches from the porch. It is too low to correspond with the wound in my son's head."

I was again amazed at the cold, calculated way the Colonel spoke about his son. He continued…

"If my son had been standing on the porch or door sill, the bullet would have gone over his head. I am sure of this because a detective helped me and we stood John's body upright against the door with his back towards it and his heels on the sill, and then thrust a pencil through the bullet hole in the door. It did not match up or strike the wound on his head."

Again the courtroom erupted with moans and gasps of disgust. I could say one thing for sure, the reporters would have a romp with the gory details the prosecution was putting forth. This must be how they were attempting to gain sympathy because the Colonel certainly did not seem grief-stricken. In fact, he seemed hell-bent on portraying as many revolting details as possible. Judge Roan banged his gavel and called for order in the court.

"This Court will come to order! Order, I say!" Barked the Judge, then continued.

"Solicitor Hill, please refrain from such questions that will incite the courtroom. Have you any further questions of a different nature?"

"No, Your Honor. We merely wish to portray the facts of this macabre murder. May the perpetrator of such a crime against a peace officer of our city suffer a commensurate fate!"

Once again the courtroom audience murmured audibly. The judge rapped his gavel again and looked sternly at the solicitor.

"Any other questions, I said? And please do not offer your personal vindictiveness into your response, Mr. Hill."

"In that case, no, sir. The testimony for the prosecution rests."

"Any rebuttal by the Defense?" This by the judge, directed at Mr. Moore.

"No sir, Your Honor, we reserve for concluding arguments." Judge Roan pronounced, "The Court will take a brief recess of ten minutes. At that time, a quarter past four pm, we will reconvene for closing arguments. Gentlemen, please be prepared to make your closing arguments brief and without undue grisly detail." The judge did not leave his bench but asked for water to be brought to him. It was clear he was losing patience. I was sure he wanted this unpleasant and potentially explosive business over. Moore and Branch leaned their heads together and whispered with each other. For one tiny second, as we passed the bench on our way back to the holding room, I caught the judge's eye as he took a drink of water. Placing my hand near my face so no one else could see, I sent him a grin and a wink. Poor man nearly choked.

41
MAY

    Having been dispatched to the holding room once again, we were offered tea and the use of the lavatory. I was finding it difficult to hold my tongue this time. I was astounded at the Colonel's unemotional testimony. It seemed like his intent was to shock the jury, but I noticed they had sat impassively and had not responded as the gallery did. Their faces were blank stones. I thought my frequent accusing glares were more powerful than the repulsive details of blood and brains, not to mention pencils stuck into a dead man's bullet-hole wounds! The ten minutes seemed interminable. Finally, we were called back into the courtroom.

    Judge Roan called the court back to order. "Mr. Moore, sir, have you the closing arguments for the defense?"

    "I defer to my partner, Mr. Branch, Your Honor. He is prepared to present our closing argument."

    "Thank you, Mr. Moore. Mr. Branch, you may take the floor."

    "Certainly, Your Honor." Jack Branch strode to the center of the court. He commanded a full view of the gallery, the defense, the prosecutors, the jury, and the judge. He was sharply dressed and cut a fine figure of a successful young man. Quite handsome, I thought. If I were a little younger... I was quickly brought back to reality as Jack began to speak.

"Your Honor, gentlemen of the jury, and ladies and gentlemen of the court, I ask you to consider the plight of Mrs. May Stamper, a hardworking citizen of our fair city. Not a rich woman, but she manages to get by. Mrs. Stamper takes in boarders to help her meet her obligations, and even at that is forced to live in a less than desirable neighborhood. In fact, her house is in the neighborhood of a Negro restaurant said to be visited by toughs. Mrs. Stamper was prudent in keeping a weapon in her home in order to protect herself and her boarders in case of trouble. On the night in question, she even went further and asked Mr. Robert Jordan to stay over at her house for added protection. We do not dispute that Mrs. Stamper admits firing a pistol, and shot through the door of her residence when she thought someone was trying to force entry. Mr. Jordan and her boarders had by then gone on to bed, and Mrs. Stamper's judgment was to protect them all by scaring away the supposed intruder. She was doing what every citizen in this country has a right to do, and that is, to protect her property and defend herself. We realize and regret that in this case, the result was the death of one John Dodgen. Yet we hold that Mrs. Stamper did not intend to murder anyone. This is clearly a case of involuntary manslaughter with lawful commission, and we implore the jury to find our client, Mrs. May Stamper, not guilty of murder, so that she may continue to be a productive citizen of this community. Your Honor, we rest our case."

There was silence in the court. I tried to look appropriately contrite, but my insides were leaping like a bullfrog. I felt sure the jury would find in my favor so that I could continue, as Mr. Branch so eloquently put it, to be a "productive member of the community." No doubt my services were considered very important to a great many men right here in this courtroom. Judge Roan spoke, "Thank you, Mr. Branch. You may be seated. We will now hear the arguments of prosecution. Solicitor Hill, you may proceed."

After a few brief whispers with the senior Dodgen, Solicitor Hill rose and addressed the court.

"Your Honor, gentlemen of the jury, and ladies and gentlemen of the court. I ask you to consider today the plight of my esteemed colleague, Colonel John Dodgen. The Colonel has lost his only son to a malicious murderer and woman of questionable character. Mrs. Stamper has admitted firing a shot. The theory of the state is that Dodgen was killed inside the house and not externally through the door as the Defense has claimed. The parties in the house then pulled his body to the porch so they could concoct their unlikely stories. This is supported by the fact that a man named Jordan was in the house the night of the killing for the express purpose of protecting Mrs. Stamper. When she heard the noise at the door, she should have called on him to see who it was. But instead, she secured her pistol and shot through the door, regardless of consequences. This was not exercising proper care and resulted in the death of young John Dodgen. We ask you to consider that Mrs. Stamper has a past history of being jailed with threatening murder when she was formerly Mrs. John Collis. She has also in the past harbored young girls at her house for questionable purposes. In addition, she has been admitted to the Grady Hospital due to morphine overdose, and we question her ability to think clearly as a result of such imbibing. We suggest that she does not represent the image of an upright citizen and, in fact, contributes to illegal activities that are inherent in any city. While we know that no man is perfect, and we are all susceptible to temptation from time to time, we put forward that in the case of Mrs. Stamper, she represents a danger to our community. We respectfully request that the jury find Mrs. Stamper guilty of murder, so that she may be incarcerated and executed by hanging, and therefore not pose a threat to any more innocent persons. Thank you, Your Honor."

 I was seething. How dare him! He was certainly no paragon of virtue, yet he called me disreputable? I knew he frequented the town's most expensive brothel, and it was certainly not as clean and discreet as my own. There were thieves and thugs, scam men and scalawags that posed more of a threat to anyone than I did. Of course, I was fuming, but I still did not think the jury would go along with the Prosecution. When it came down to it, most men looked out for themselves. They were more afraid of being exposed than they were concerned for any future victims. Most of them also knew of the widespread corruption in law enforcement in Atlanta and did not want to tread on any toes in that camp. I was so incensed, I didn't realize it when the jury had been charged and sent away to debate the verdict. I was startled back to the present by Mr. Moore speaking to me.

"Well, May, it's five o'clock in the afternoon, and I can understand Judge Roan saying that if they reached a verdict this evening it'll be sealed until the morning." He chuckled, mostly to himself, and continued.

"If you were found guilty, which you won't be, he would have at least one more evening of calm on the homefront. He's scared that if you are found guilty, all hell will break loose if you follow through with those threats of exposing your clients. There would be innumerable cases forthcoming, and some fellow might just have to try his own wife for his own attempted murder! 'Course, there may not be any judges left on the bench to try anything by that time."

"Mr. Moore, Mr. Branch," I began, "I can't thank you enough. I do feel confident about the outcome. How long do you think it will take the jury to decide?"

Mr. Branch responded this time. "I don't expect it'll take too long, given the circumstances. I know most of those men are anxious to get this over with and probably have already made up their minds. It's mostly just a formality at this point. You just try to relax, and we will send word if a verdict's been reached. Even we won't get to hear it until morning, but we'll all be right back here at nine o'clock tomorrow."

"All right, I'll try to get some rest, but naturally I'm on pins and needles. So it's back to The Tower for me, for one more night at least. I sincerely hope and believe it will be my last night behind bars."

42
MAY

On Wednesday morning the court reassembled. Once again, I was led into court by Miss Sanderson, O'Kelly, and Wagner. I was dressed to the hilt, just as I was the day before. As I looked around, I noticed many of the same spectators were present. My defense attorneys Moore and Branch looked relaxed and confident, as well they should. The evening before, scarcely an hour after I had been returned to The Tower, I had received a note from Mr. Moore saying the jury had reached its verdict. He said this was a good sign, as a quick verdict was usually in favor of the defendant.

The jury appeared relaxed, and maybe just a tad bit smug, even celebratory. I'm sure they were glad to be relieved of the threat of exposure if indeed their verdict was not guilty. I couldn't imagine they would look so relaxed and pleased had they not found in my favor. They would have been shaking in their shoes, fearing the outcome should their private social lives be splashed about if I named them as frequent visitors to my abode.

As for Solicitor General Hill, his face suggested defeat and resignation. Haggard and drooping, apparently he could read the proverbial writing on the wall. He was no fool. I'm sure he was interpreting the demeanor of the jury, just as I, and expected to hear a not guilty verdict. The very fact that he looked so contrite gave me even more confidence. I perceived all of this in a matter of seconds and relaxed in my seat. I was certain the atmosphere was in my favor.

Judge Roan entered and called the court to order. "Good morning, everyone. The court is now in session. We have before us the defendant, Mrs. May Stamper, who has been accused of murder. Testimony for both the Prosecution and Defense was heard yesterday. Closing arguments were presented and the case was sent to the jury at five o'clock yesterday afternoon. In less than an hour's time, word was sent to me that the jury had reached a verdict. As I had instructed in my charge to the jury, the verdict was sealed until such time as it could be read this morning. This court will now proceed to disclose that verdict."

I wanted to sit forward in my chair, just as everyone else in the courtroom was doing, but I did not want to seem over-anxious. I had steadfastly maintained my innocence and did not want to compromise that appearance now. I did sit up straight and look directly at the jury foreman when Judge Roan addressed him.

"Will the foreman of the jury please stand?" the Judge asked. A man I recognized stood up quickly as if he wanted to get this over with as soon as possible. Judge Roan continued, "Now, will the defendant please stand and face the jury?"

I rose and drew myself up, trying to make my slight stature seem as powerful and large as possible. I always felt my slight build did not suit my personality, although at times it could be an advantage. My adversaries were often surprised at the vehemence that came forth from such a diminutive woman. I faced the jury with my head held high and my back straight.

The Judge continued, "Will the foreman of the jury please read the verdict? Please read in a clear and audible voice so that we all may understand and hear sufficiently."

The foreman did not look at me, the gallery, or the attorneys in the court. He looked only at the judge. He proceeded to unfold a single sheet of paper. I looked at the paper that held my destiny, at least in the near future anyway.

"Your Honor, we the jury find the defendant, Mrs. May

Stamper, not guilty of the charge of murder. Further…"

The court erupted as if someone had opened a door on a bawdy stage show full of sailors. The hooting and hollering, shouts and applause, obscured whatever else the foreman was trying to say. I didn't hear anything else myself beyond "not guilty." Mr. Moore and Mr. Branch were embracing me. I felt hands from behind the bar clapping my shoulders and back, and even trying to pat my head, but the fancy hat got in the way of that! After a few moments of jubilation, the judge began banging the gavel.

"Order! Order! I will have order in this court! Sit down! Sit down! All of you!"

The court officers began moving about and raising their billies. The crowd noise slowly subsided and folks were taking their seats. Although I had been extremely confident, I was now speechless. The simple release of tension upon hearing those words, "not guilty," had overwhelmed my senses and left me in stunned silence. I sank into my seat in a near state of shock. The judge was once again addressing the foreman.

"Please continue, Mr. Foreman."

"Yes, sir." The bewildered man looked doubtful that this would be possible but he resumed where he had left off. "Further, your honor, we the jury find the defendant not guilty of involuntary manslaughter with lawful commission. Indeed, we find the defendant not guilty of any crime and therefore recommend her immediate release." The man sat down just as quickly as he'd stood up. He looked down and did not engage anyone's glance. The judge responded.

"Sir, is this the true and unadulterated verdict of this jury?"

"Yes, Your Honor."

"And was this verdict reached without undue influence of any party?"

There was a titter throughout the courtroom. Glances were exchanged among many men present, including the attorneys. The foreman looked up quickly and looked directly at the judge once again.

"Yes, Your Honor, yes it was."

"Please bring me the verdict, Deputy."

A deputy stepped forward and took the paper from the foreman and delivered it to Judge Roan who read it to himself over the spectacles that rested on the end of his nose. He looked up, surveyed the room with a look that seemed to say *"Is there not one man here brave enough to stand up to this woman?"* Only silence greeted his gaze.

What now? I thought. What happens next? I could sense a rising level of hesitancy. Had I misinterpreted something? Then the judge gave a long sigh and began to speak.

"This Court, under the condition of the verdict of the jury herewith, releases Mrs. May Stamper from imprisonment and from all consequences suffered as a result of the unfortunate death of Bailiff John Dodgen. Court adjourned." He rose quickly and retreated back through the door behind the bench and into his chambers.

I didn't realize I had been holding my breath, and it suddenly went out of me in an audible whoosh. Thank God this was over! A crowd began to gather round. Maude was the first to reach me.

"Oh Lordy, Lordy, I swan'! This trial 'bout did me in, May. Let's get you out of here!"

Before I knew it, I was hustled out by Maude, Mr. Moore, and Mr. Branch. Bessie, Addie, and Bob Jordan were not far behind. We emerged into the bright sun. The kind of piercing light that only shines on a clear, cold as ice winter day in Atlanta, with a sky so blue it hurt to look at it. I was beginning to regain my senses. I shouted, "Let's celebrate! To the Kimball House!"

Our noisy entourage made our way to the grand hotel. Reporters and hawkers followed and shouted. Men we encountered moved aside quickly, fearing their relief would be seen as a sign of guilt. Women pulled their children aside as if we had the pox, but I didn't care – I was free!

43
MAY

We headed straight for the dining room of the grand Kimball House Hotel. Mr. Moore, Mr. Branch, and Mr. Jordan parted with us girls, and I couldn't much blame them. I'm sure there were many men in this city who wanted to put as much distance between me and them as possible. The wait staff looked down their noses at us, but we were seated. It was early and not much of a lunch crowd had gathered yet, so I supposed they were willing to take our money.

"How was that for justice?" I laughed to my friends as we enjoyed a celebratory drink.

"That was some show!" Maude avowed.

"I was so tickled by the squirming men in that courtroom I could barely contain myself!" declared Addie, while Bessie just guffawed and agreed with the rest of us.

I lifted a glass to my collaborators. "I think we all deserve a reprieve from all of this commotion, don't you think so, girls? Each nodded and waited expectantly for me to proceed. "We should probably keep a low profile for a bit. I'm going to move back over to my Bush Street house and maybe visit family in the country for a while. My folks back home are usually fairly resourceful at drumming up resources. You all can pursue your own interests for a while. You'll know when I'm back in business. I'm afraid our gentlemen friends had such a scare, they may be giving their wives a little more attention these next few weeks." I winked. "Now, Bessie and Addie, I don't want any of you to suffer over this setback. If you need anything at all, you just get in touch with me. Maudie here will know where to reach me."

 We had a few more drinks and delicacies. I spared no expense. Finally, in high spirits, Bessie and Addie took their leave. Only Maude stayed behind, and together we sat quietly. I was contemplating my future, and I suspect Maude was too. I was in no rush, but I would be back in business. I was well provisioned and could take my time. Besides, if I ran low on funds or "resources," I could always send word to any number of men around the city and they would be sure to grease my palm to keep me quiet.

 Presently, Maude spoke up. "May, I declare you're as slick as butter. Nothing sticks on you! But this was a close call and it might not be so easy next time. I think you've got the right notion to lay low for a bit. Here's your money I've been keeping for you. You've got plenty to get by on for now." She pressed a small pouch in my hand. "Got any idea what your future plans are?"

 I knew she was fishing. I had some ideas, but I didn't really want to jump back into running a toffer house too soon. I wanted to give it some thought. I just might come up with a better idea. Things would be getting tougher in Atlanta. The city was so corrupt some were calling for an all-out turnover of officials. There was more talk of prohibition. Cocaine had already been taken out of Coca-Cola, and what tonics there were to be found were getting more dangerous. And I hadn't forgotten that low place where I'd fallen to my knees.

 I sighed. "Thank you so much for keeping this safe for me, Maude. I'm going to need every penny of it. I don't rightly know just yet exactly what I'm going to do. I want to take some time away to think about things. The atmosphere here in Atlanta is getting pretty strained. I'll go see my mama and daddy, visit with my sisters. Maybe I'll even go up to the mountains for a bit. I've got plenty of money, thanks to your bookkeeping. I think for now I'll just enjoy being a free woman."

MADAM MAY

"Dearie, I think that's good for now. You just take your time. Old Maudie will be right here in Atlanta on Gilmer Street when you're ready to come back to town." She sighed heavily. "I'd best be getting on. This whole ordeal has been pretty tiring for an old lady like me. I'm ready for a nap!"

I looked at Maude. She did look tired. Maybe it would be just as good for her if I was gone for a while. She was a true friend, and I didn't want to be the cause of an extra burden on her. After all, she had to be getting on up there in years. I didn't know just how old she was, but I figured she had to be at least 60.

"And I think that's a good plan for you, Maude – you get on home and rest. I can't tell you how much I've appreciated your friendship and help through all my troubles. I can't thank you enough. But I do have one small favor to ask."

Maude turned her kind but tired eyes on me. "Anything, dear, what is it?"

"Well, I certainly don't want to impose or put you in a questionable position, but it seems I don't have anywhere to go! From what I understand, that fire ruined everything I own. I'm not worried about replacing things, but I do need somewhere to rest my head tonight!"

"Of course, May. You're welcome at my house anytime. You remind me so much of myself at your age. I just want you to make something of yourself. Maybe get married one day and have some little ones. Someone to take of you when you do get old like me. You don't want to be alone in this world."

"Oh, you shush up about that, Maudie. I've got plenty of time for that. And besides, you're not all alone, you've got me. I'm going to stroll and shop a bit, and I'll bring home some supper for later. By then, I'll have decided what I'm going to do. You just rest up and I'll see you in a few hours. Now get on home and take your nap!"

Maude wearily got to her feet, bid goodbye and made her way out of the dining room. After a few minutes of quiet solitude, soaking up the luxurious surroundings and especially enjoying just being out in the world, I took care of the bill and made my own way out to the streets of Atlanta.

I strolled, glad to be a free woman. It was a cold but clear day. Not too unpleasant if one was wrapped up good. Oh my, how the city had changed in just the eight years I'd been here. Automobiles everywhere. More buildings, each one taller than the last. People everywhere. Work had started on viaducts over the tracks, streets were being paved. Many ladies avoided me, stepping far to the side so as not to be in close contact with someone of such ill repute. Others gawked and taunted. Still, others seemed congratulatory and winked or gave knowing grins to the infamous May Stamper.

   Before I made any stops, I wanted to see my house on Marietta Street. I walked that way and was saddened at what came into view. The fire had blackened the brick. The windows were boarded up. There was debris in the side yard and on the sidewalk. I assumed it was the remains of furnishings and such that were destroyed in the fire. There was no one in sight. There was definitely nothing salvageable. I would be starting all over. I let out a long breath. Oh, well. I had started with nothing and did all right on my own. I could do it again. But first things first; I needed a new wardrobe!

   I walked back toward the shopping district. There were several shops selling ready-made clothes, even underthings, and they would have to do for now. Styles had changed. I purchased a few things here and there, enough to get me through the rest of winter. Some did not fit perfectly, but that was the trade-off when buying ready-made. I could get them tailored later. I also needed some toiletries. Another stop and I had those, too. I took my time in the shops, passing the afternoon to give Maude plenty of time to rest. I stopped in at the telegraph office and the train depot. My final stop was the market where I bought a few things for supper. I smiled to myself. It would take some getting used to not being waited on hand and foot, having meals delivered right to me, clean linens every other day, and all the frivolities I wanted – even if it was in jail!
I thoroughly enjoyed the afternoon, breathing fresh air and strolling the streets of the city I had come to love.

   After a few hours, the cold began to sink in and I started back to Maude's.

   "Hello, madam! I figured you'd be here round about now." was Maude's greeting. She looked much more rested and sounded like her old jovial self. We enjoyed the supper and visited a bit. I shared some of the jail stories, and she laughed with me about how I was not going to have anyone waiting on me all the time. You'd have thought I'd been in a hotel! I had given some thought to what I needed to do in the coming months.

"Now, Maudie, I don't want to involve you in my business affairs. This last debacle was a bit too close for comfort. I'm getting a little old for some of this nonsense. If you could help me out finding a residence though, when I get back from Covington, I would surely appreciate it."

"That won't be any problem. I'm sure I can find just the place, May. And I too think it would be good for us to keep our distance, at least for a while."

We turned in early. It seemed strangely quiet at first, not hearing the soft muffled sounds of other women settling down to sleep. I suppose I was more tired than I thought. I did not remember falling asleep.

The next morning I was awakened by the smell of strong coffee. I was a bit disoriented at first, but it came to me in a flash. I was free! I actually caught myself thinking, praise the Lord! Of course, I quickly amended my thinking - the Lord had nothing to do with it, or did He? I had once again managed to get out of trouble, but was it really all on my own? I allowed myself a bit of self-congratulation, but in the deepest corners, I knew this had been a very close situation. It could easily have gone another way, but it was s a new day, I was free, and I was ready to move on.

I greeted Maude in the kitchen. "Good morning! Isn't it a beautiful morning?"

Maude looked up from her newspaper. "Oh yes, dearie, a fine day indeed. Help yourself to biscuits and coffee." She turned back to the paper as I helped myself to coffee and hot biscuits with butter and syrup.

I prattled on about my shopping the previous afternoon and my immediate plans.

"Maude, I had to buy brand new ready-made every stitch of clothing a woman needs! Then I had to get toiletries and other what-nots. And, I've decided what I'm going to do."

Maude had uh-hummed and continued reading her paper as I continued to chatter.

"I arranged for everything to be packed and it will be waiting for me at the station. I've got a ticket on the 11 o'clock train to Covington. I even sent a telegram ahead and Ollie will meet me there. You won't have to put up with me, but I do so appreciate you letting me stay the night."

Maude looked up from her paper. "That sounds like a fine plan May. I really do think it best you're going to leave town for a while. It seems like Solicitor Hill is not holding much respect for that verdict. He's making his opinion plain in this morning's paper!"

Maude handed over the paper, turned out to page five. The first thing I saw astounded me.

There I was, staring off languorously as if I didn't have a care in the world. The artist had captured an amazing likeness and every detail was there, right down to the ribbons on the hat and the fur collar! I couldn't help but grin as I read the headline accompanying the illustration:

Mrs. Stamper Freed After Murder Trial

I quickly scanned through the article. The trial was reported truthfully. The witnesses' testimony, my own statement, the closing arguments, and the brief time it took the jury to come to a decision. At the conclusion of the article, in a statement he must have given outside the courtroom after the trial was over, Solicitor General Hill was quoted as stating, "The price of meats and other foods and commodities is rising each day, but the price of human life is rapidly going down And it is because juries so frequently turn men loose who destroy human life." He was correct that prices were certainly rising. But there was one error. This time, a jury had turned loose not a man, but a woman!

44
MAY

    I took the train that morning and headed back to the country. My sisters were all married now and scattered among Newton County's little communities: Covington, Porterdale, Mansfield, and Social Circle. The county was growing and Stansells and Gaithers had been swallowed up by Covington. Mama and Daddy lived with my brother Ollie. My plan was to stay with one sister then another for a few days until I felt my welcome was worn out, then go to Ollie's and spend time with them. This worked out fine for a few months.

    Come early summer, it began to get hot as blazes, reminding me of the time almost ten years ago when I met up with John Collis. It seemed like a lifetime had passed since then, but it did make me itch to get back to the city. I'd pretty much given up my tonics, but staying out in the country was enough to drive anyone mad, just like it did that time after I nearly killed myself with the tonic. I needed more than red dirt, squalling young'uns, and beans for supper. I had not forgotten the promise I'd made back in the cold winter on that stone floor in my Tower cell. Could I make a go of it on the straight and narrow? I was going to try harder than I had ever tried my entire life. I was concerned for Maude and wanted to take care of her after all she'd done for me. Maybe I was alone in the world, no husband or babies, but I could be a good friend, a good daughter, a good sister, and maybe even a good person.

I sent word to Maude I was planning to return to town soon and that I wanted to try and lead a quiet, normal life. Maybe even get a job. More women, especially single ladies, were beginning to work. Maude assured me she would work on finding me a place to live and even see what she could do about rustling up some legitimate employment. I did not know at the time, but she had some other plans in mind for me as well. Although my life would never be what one could call mundane, I was about to set off on an adventure that would lead me to experiences I never dreamed of. Life would not be easy, and I would be known by several additional monikers, but I vowed to never again be the infamous Madam May.

THE END

ABOUT THE AUTHOR

Janet Hogan Chapman, Ed.D. aka GeorgiaJanet
The Bohemian Southern Belle

Dr. Chapman was born, raised, and lived all her life in Georgia. Growing up in Atlanta in the 1960s could be wonderful, traumatic, exhilarating, and frightening. It was all of those things at some point or another. Those rich experiences provided stories just waiting to flow from the heart to the printed page. Her mission as The Bohemian Southern Belle is to empower strong women through prose and poetry. Just what is a Bohemian Southern Belle? Check out the blog post at http://www.georgiajanet.com/?p=2225 to find out!

A life-long writer, Dr. Chapman has published professionally on historical topics, infant education, preschool ministry, elementary education, and teacher education. You can read her essays, poetry, blog posts, and other information on her website, www.georgiajanet.com. She has published three novels, all based on true events. *Madam May, a Tale of Madams, Morphine, Moonshine, and Murder. After Madam May* (novella) tells what became of Madam May after being on trial for murder and how she came to be Dr. Chapman's grandmother. *Dorothy May*, tells the tragic but enduring story of Madam May's informally adopted daughter, Dorothy. She also has published one memoir, *This Teacher Talks, What Really Goes on in America's Schools*. It describes the events that take place over a school year among the faculty and staff of an elementary school.

Dr. Chapman has worn many hats throughout her life, ranging from children's party costume character, to caterer, to Pediatric Physician's Assistant, to Preschool Minister, to Elementary Teacher, to University Professor. Now semi-retired, she is officially an "author." She enjoys spending time with family and friends, travel, reading, and genealogy research.

BOOK CLUB DISCUSSION GUIDE

1. Madam May is based on true events in the life of the author's paternal grandmother. How do you feel about someone airing their family secrets? What kinds of problems do you think this could cause in some families? What about your own family?

2. May wanted to become an independent woman of means in a time period when that was nearly unheard of, especially for a poor, uneducated, rural woman. How would her circumstances have been different if, instead, she were an educated young lady who lived in the city?

3. Do you think there are parallels in present day where women find themselves in situations where they must do something illegal to survive, or in circumstances in which they have little control over their lives?

4. Were you surprised and how did you feel about the morphine usage, questionable business practices, and corrupt law enforcement officers portrayed in this novel?

5. If you lived in Madam May's era, what advice would you give her? How would it differ from advice you might give a young woman today?

Janet Hogan Chapman Ed.D.

List of Actual Newspaper Articles

The timing of actual events was modified in the storyline. Most events are factual and many details were taken directly from old newspaper articles.

July 3, 1904. The Atlanta Constitution, p. 9. May Collis admitted to Grady Hospital with morphine overdose.

March 23, 1906. The Atlanta Constitution, p. 6. Headline: HIS TWO WIVES FIGHT OVER HIM. John Collis' Present Wife Prosecutes his Divorced Wife

June 6, 1906. The Atlanta Constitution, p. 2. Mortuary notice of John Collis' death.

December 17, 1906. The Atlanta Constitution Morning Edition, p.1. John Dodgen murder.

December 17, 1906. The Atlanta Georgian: Strange Man Who Fled Wanted by Police as Suspect in Tragedy

December 20, 1906. The Atlanta Georgian: Missing Companion of Slain Bailiff is Found by Georgian

December 21, 1906. The Atlanta Georgian: New Evidence May Identify Man Wanted

December 28, 1906. The Atlanta Georgian: Mrs. Stamper Names Slayer of Dodgen

December 29, 1906. The Atlanta Georgian: New Light is to be Shed on Dodgen Case, Warrant is Sworn Out for Another Man

Sunday Dec. 30, 1906. The Atlanta Constitution. Mrs. Stamper Asks for Trial; Commitment Trial Wanted by Four Persons in Tower

December 31, 1906. The Atlanta Georgian: Mrs. Stamper Held, Others Released

January 1, 1907. The Atlanta Constitution. Woman is Held in Dodgen Case

January 2, 1907. The Atlanta Constitution: Grand Jury Meets Monday

January 2, 1907. The Atlanta Georgian: Mrs. Willie Stamper goes Before Grand Jury on Next Monday

January 7, 1907. The Atlanta Constitution: In The Courts:

January 7, 1907. The Atlanta Georgian: Two Noted Cases Go To Grand Jury for Indictments

Jan 8, 1907. The Atlanta Georgian: Woman indicted by grand jury on charge of murder.

January 8, 1907. The Atlanta Constitution: Murder Charge Against Woman

Jan 12, 1907. The Atlanta Georgian: Odd Fellows Aid in running Down Dodge's Slayer

January 21, 1907. The Atlanta Constitution. In The Courts:

January 22. 1907. The Atlanta Georgian: Mrs. Stamper is on Trial for Murder

January 23, 1907. The Atlanta Constitution, p. 5. Mrs. Stamper Freed After Murder Trial

January 23, 1907. The Atlanta Georgian: Mrs. Stamper is Free; Her House was Castle and She Defended It

January 24, 1907. The Atlanta Georgian: Accused of Arson, Johns is acquitted

August 28, 1907. The Atlanta Constitution, p. 10. Police Court ...Mrs. Willie Stamper was fined $10.75 for allowing Mary Hutchins, a 13 year old girl, to visit her house . . .

April 10, 1910. The Atlanta Constitution, p 4c. Was Holland Slain Because of Woman?

May 8, 1910. The Atlanta Constitution, p. 1 & 2 c. Night Watchman Holland the Victim of Man Who Fell in Love With Wife

May 15, 1910. The Atlanta Constitution, p.1c. David Phillips Held by Court Without Bond

March 28, 1911. The Atlanta Georgian: Women Bound over for harboring girl.

March 29, 1911. The Atlanta Constitution, p. 9. Led young girls to lives of vice

April 24, 1911. The Atlanta Georgian: Stamper Woman fined for harboring girl

Made in the USA
Columbia, SC
18 August 2024

40601373R00145